AF575697

SHAWN STEWART RUFF

Published by DOPAMINE
301 N. Kenwood St, Glendale, CA 91206
www.dopaminepress.org

Special thanks to Katie Fricas

Covert Art: Polly Adams
Layout & Design: Brooke Palmieri

ISBN: 978-1-63590-223-5
Distributed by the MIT Press, Cambridge, Mass., and London, England.
Printed in the United States of America

10 9 8 7 6 5 4 3 2 1

To my done and gone beloveds.
You know who you are.

Last things I remember? Mom's face floating above me. The ambulance screaming through traffic.

That happened last night or the night before. Hard to know which.

Now I toggle between sleep and waking, unsure of what's going on or where I am. I know Mom is near, though she seems to be looking away when I come and go.

A tube in my arm sucks from a saline sack. I see letters and numbers scrolling across monitors to my left. A window, tall, wide and with many panes to my right. The glass looks between the cold, snowy morning outside and the fluorescent warmth inside the room. In a trick of light, I can also see two reflections of me. One is outside the room and the other inside, and they seem to be watching each other shyly. Outside me has a swollen face and bandaged head that makes inside me wince with pain. My skin tingles when his finger touches the area around his eyes. Now it tickles along my neck and then stops where swallowing hurts. A shadow passes over him before darkening over me, too. Outside me and inside me cry out for Mom.

I knew I wasn't alone but now I feel the presence of others. The professionals in the room promise me she's nearby. Soon her presence and her smell of baby powder calm me down. "Cliffy, sweetheart, we've been waiting for you," she says.

She is a blur to my eyes. I need reassurance and want her to climb into bed beside me. I want to feel the bulge of her pregnant belly between us. But Dad is here, too. He passes like a combat shadow that blocks the window light and the mysteries within the glass. "Boy, glad you're back," he says.

Another professional arrives. This woman's voice is familiar to me but like in a dream. My parents—or LACK as we teen offspring call them, short for the first initial of Mom and Dad's first and middle names, Lacey Ann and Clifford Kelsey—want real answers from her. So do I. But the story she's telling confuses me, and probably confuses them, too, as if she's talking about somebody else's son named Cliffy. That Cliffy suffered injuries from a recent encounter: a concussion, hematoma, head and face lacerations, a bruised rib, bruising throughout the body, ligature marks on the neck. She says, "Your son appeared to be under the influence when he was admitted last night, which isn't uncommon in this area, we see a lot of cocaine and angel dust overdoses."

My understanding is smudged and won't wipe clear. What she is saying doesn't jibe with me at all. I am not a party boy, I'm a stellar student. OK, the occasional joint, screwdriver or equivalent, a hit or two of speed during finals. Nothing else. I want to explain but my voice is a smudge, too. But then this same doctor recommends a few days in the hospital for observation. "Keep him as long as you need to. Just take care of our boy," Dad says.

I don't need to see clearly to know that my parents are leaving. I feel angry before realizing their going is a good thing. I want to speak with the professional alone. I want to stand up for myself in this flattened state. I need to resolve the Cliffy I am with the Cliffy in the glass and the Cliffy she's talking about. I try to cough up the smudge voice and now feel something major is wrong. My body hurts with throbs, burning sensations, and tightness, but only now do my legs act up. They seem unable to move—and me, a runner with legs that won't move! Words scrape out through my pained throat, trying to ask if I'm paralyzed.

This professional says, "No, you're sedated. Try not to speak. Your vocal cords have been bruised from the strangulation. Your voice will return in a few days. Don't worry."

Strangulation? The word, the meaning, chokes me.

Now I do remember being overcome, with my neck in a grip. And I remember an awareness of fighting that grip, of being reeled in like a fish and then clobbered—out cold.

I see that it connects to the reason I lie here now, glazed by sedation.

It's more important, though, to assert myself. I want this professional to know I am the Cliffy going to UCLA. I want her to know I remember today is the first day after the end of Christmas break. I want her to know I don't have time to laze for days in the hospital. Failure is like a hematoma that clots the future—that is something the Cliffy I am might say, if I could speak now.

I am fading again. I point to the window and gesture for her to close the curtains against the view, against the iterations of me and the fights between light and shadow.

She is close enough that I can make out her name tag.

Dr. Fang Fang.

She knows more about me from last night.

»»»

It's morning. My thinking is less fogged by hospital drugs. In view are two white cops entering my room. I remember overhearing them last night instructing the nurses to contact them when I came to. Though I can't say this pair is that pair. The taller one introduces himself and his partner as detectives. Their names don't catch. The taller one says, "We're here to find the person that did this to you. Anything you can tell us will be helpful, no detail is too small."

No details here, big or small. Which isn't to say there aren't details of all sizes, only that I'm not sharing. More talk slips by me. The TV is on, it's like the room itself is chattering, laughing, crying. If gray could be a sherbet, that's the color of this room. In their dirty blue jackets, Cincinnati's Finest toss phrases around meant for my memory to catch—how many were there? Did you recognize any of them? Tall, short, black, white?—and I shrug my sore shoulders. This game stops when Dad wanders into the room.

He is Vaselined to a glossy sheen, which means *Don't fuck with me.* He looks between the white cops and me and says, "I'm his father. Who are you?"

The lead detective makes introductions again. This time I catch their names: he is Tass Moneymaker and his partner's Billy Teachout. Dad has my backpack and a bag of goodies, which he swaps me for the TV remote.. My joy is White Castle onion rings. Down the onion rings go, past the ache in my throat. I watch their handshakes, the smooth way of Moneymaker. Dad *haha*'s over his surname, and Moneymaker assures him the *do-re-me*, as he calls it, is in name only.

Laughter. A sussing among brutes.

They are almost flirty, or is it just me? The Detective mentions he's met my dad before, adding nothing of where or when or why. Maybe to spare Dad embarrassment in front of his offspring. As if I didn't have the dirt on my shameless father. As if anything could embarrass him.

"Green Beret," Dad says, and Detective Moneymaker seems to blush. Dad draws the curtains, ignoring my Dracula face recoiling at the light. I suck the life out of the last onion rings as the brutes talk about training at Fort Dix. Though Dad's Army, I have noticed Marines, Air Force, and National Guard all give each other the same respect, the same consideration and understanding. In the brief history of our two-parent household, Mom has brought Dad home from jail twice, no explanation offered for his bloodied knuckles and odd scars. One time we saw stitches from a knife wound; I remember a wide bandage encircled his waist just below the ribs. I also remember answering the phone and finding one of these ex-military cops checking on him.

It's like gaydar, the almost fairy dust-like ability to spot your kind.

»»»

Gaydar led me to my boyfriend, Chip. Out of scores of people on a rollercoaster queue at Kings Island, on a scorching day last summer. The zigzagging in the queue of a dozen lanes brought us face to face, smile to smile. Blush to blush. All around us, the towering hills of the rollercoaster tracks and the faint screams of joy. Our connection refused to break, drawing us together each time we came close. I had seen him before in the employee's locker room, and, I would soon learn, he'd seen me too. When my turn came to board the rollercoaster and the ride attendant shouted for a single to ride with me, up went Chip's hand. Somehow, I knew it would. The day was rendered technicolor like in *The Wizard of Oz*, fairy dust twinkling in the air. "Hi," I said; "Hi," he said. It was love. We thrilled together as the ride scaled its first peak, our hands touching and legs colliding in the headrush dive. Speeding, we turned to each other and our bobbing heads somehow met in a kiss.

That's how it started.

»»»

But I'm the magnet between Dad and the detectives, not the warring history of some enlisted men. I'm actually glad Dad's around, a reversal that confuses my feelings. I'm used to being the object of his frustration; now, I'm the subject of his protection, a new role for me and a new role for him. Perhaps roles that will suit us well.

Just now he seems to notice how Moneymaker's eyes play games. One minute I don't exist and the next minute, I'm the everything of his unblinking focus. Moneymaker looks at me, though he's speaking to Dad, and Dad is nodding at him, though looking at me. We learn that Mom flagged the detectives down in the ER just after midnight. That was thirty-six hours ago, I think, but I'm not sure. We also learn that I screamed when I came to.

I want to ask if it was a rollercoaster scream, or a scream of real terror.

Then Moneymaker goes cryptic. He says teen boys are reluctant to speak out when they are crime's victim. Fear of retaliation, fear of lacking masculinity. Shame. Humiliation. Embarrassment. Juvenile crime is complicated, especially when sexual assault is involved.

"Wait, you're saying my boy was sexually assaulted?" Dad says.

"No, but we've encountered a few boys like him recently, only they were raped."

I am shocked again. He insists that the Cincinnati Police Department is on the side of justice for victims, they'll do everything in their power to find the perpetrators. "I was saying to your son when you walked in that holding back only helps the criminals."

"Cliffy's a good boy," Dad says.

"I don't doubt that."

"He's gonna be a lawyer so he won't be holding anything back, knowing those punks would get away. We'll be in touch."

Dad knows so little about me. That will change as the facts break like freak waves. Watching their handshaking I think how Dad doesn't need to grease his skin to shine. His studly looks are those of a glowing and knowing sun god. Even buttoned and zipped up in a white factory uniform, he radiates. Heavenly to ladies and soldiers and gay boys alike. None would believe he is a death star. That's what he is, though.

The cops leave, and Dad says, "Boy, in case you don't know it, a Green Beret is straight out of a comic book, a goddamn Captain America. That dude'll be bagging up suspects and closing this case fast, watch."

"Good, I can't wait to catch the punks."

"Good."

“Thanks for bringing my backpack. I appreciate the White Castle onion rings.”

“Yep.”

I decide not to complain about the burger, if you could call that greasy swipe of gross chewiness a burger. I know that we, his children, are five in number with a sixth on the way, but I shouldn’t have to remind him that I only like the fish filet. A good dad would know this. A good dad would deduce that I don’t want the curtains open.

I should say something about what’s happening to me. About my being hospitalized. Or about my alleged drug problem, which is a damn smear, a smudge on my character. Dare I bring up the fourth dimension in the windowpanes? And what about missing school?

But anything I say could backfire.

It’s easier to yawn like I mean it. In my listless, sarcastic way, I do mean it. He leaves, and I close the fucking curtains myself.

»»»

It’s 4:30 a.m. I’ve been off Valium since yesterday. I feel shaky outside the drug’s calm, though I appreciate the crystal clarity of even ugly things. Even ugly truths. A nurse or orderly has opened the window curtains. I pad across the cold floor to close them. Contrary to my nightmare, I do get that a certain monster—no, a certain motherfucker—isn’t in the windowpanes. Still, he is somewhere in this universe, waiting to obliterate me.

On my way back to bed I realize my sexuality is awake. My hand strays under the hospital gown, my fingers only stiffen the evidence, and the murkiness of what happened to me that night lifts somewhat. That sexuality could easily cause me embarrassment here in the hospital, and maybe it had set me up to be attacked that night. I’ve worried that I think about sex too much. I can’t say I wasn't thinking about fucking Chip just now, though I don't think I was. But, stupidly, I had been thinking about Chip when I was outmaneuvered and beaten up by a certain motherfucker. And I can't say I wasn't high, either, because I had been earlier. A joint, a few Screwdrivers, and a motel stay of about twelve hours with Chip. The overnighter was our Christmas present to each other, the best gift I've ever given or received. Corny to say, but if anything, I was high on love and, of course, a fuckful overnight. Which is why I also can't say we *weren't* lip-locked in the car in front of the gas station. I remember Chip had just dropped me off when the attendant I've always known suddenly appeared at the door. But little did I know, he had shape-shifted into a certain motherfucker, jacking me up before trying to force-fuck me.

»»»

Now it's 5:15 a.m. I will myself out of the warm bed to call Mom. I learned of the payphone's existence from a nurse, the same one who alerted me to my room phone debacle. It seems LACK refused to pay the additional $1.50 per day for a private phone, proof they don't listen to me or care about me. So like LACK to fuck me over when I need them most. The payphone is down a long cold hall with a floor like black ice that feeds into the elevator lobby. I feel strong enough for the journey there and back. Several times I've walked outside the room to orient myself in the maze of halls. The bruised rib has turned me into a creaking centenarian. I also notice weakness in my legs and a wobble I didn't expect. But I feel better, stronger, more sure-footed with each step.

5:19 now. I know Mom's mornings to a T, plus or minus a minute or two. She should be finishing Wheat Puffs or Rice Krispies, or just washing her bowl before collecting her things for work. I know she doesn't want to answer the phone, but she will because she is drawn to bad news and worries she might miss something devastating. I count the five rings before she picks up. "Cliffy!" she says. She seems surprised and wants to know why I'm up at this hour. She also seems irritated when I say, Chip. Far as she knows, he hasn't called—though she says she remembers the phone ringing last night, maybe Corey took the call.

"Mom, I would appreciate it if you didn't say anything to anyone about me, including and especially Chip. Just tell everybody I'm not home. Maybe you could tell Corey and Dudley to do the same. And to always get a number, obviously."

I have communicated versions of this before, and I'm met with a familiar telephone shrug. She maintains that it's asking too much of my brothers to jot down a phone number. She tells me she can't be late, she'll call when she gets to work if she has a few minutes. She hangs up before I can remind her I don't have a phone in this hospital room, that I'm standing in a cold hall on a freezing floor right now, thanks to her.

I scurry down the hall with my pains, cold feet, hot-bloodedness. In bed I search for meaning in sleep but find neither. At home I crave being alone; here I can't stand being alone. What I wouldn't give for the baby talk of the Twins, my toddler sister and brother. Emotion breaks over me like a squall. Missing Chip, oh how I miss him! My face clenches and the cry muscles hurt. A squirt of tears burns, then squeamishly turns off. I notice a strange gurgling sound in the body of the building. Plumbing tucked in the walls or the splish-splash of a radiator a floor or two away. It's the kind of sound that could stop a person from sleeping. The kind of sound that could drive a person—me—nuts.

At 7:00 a.m. I'm clear-minded enough to lug open my United States Government textbook where I left off. We learn Congress makes law, and the execution of those laws is the role of criminal justice. My TV-based knowledge about the law doesn't include the simple job chart of who does what in the criminal justice system.

I have paid attention to commercials advertising the services of a stentorian black lawyer—"I am Lester Gains, Attorney at Law." His giant black self is buttoned in a dark, serious suit. If wearing a coat, it is always black and trimmed in mink. A fedora is coordinated with all these effects, to complete his image of a pimp for the law. His sign-off: "I'll put the law on your side."

I've been taken in by glamorous sedans before. We Douglasses are poor people with automotive aspirations. My relatives probably imagine a Lincoln Continental Mark V coupe in my future. There are no law degrees in our family, and only a few college-educated, far flung on the family tree. Their degrees are in accounting or nursing or pharmacy. There's a dentist called Cousin Tibbs, but he's a non-blood relation on Dad's side of the family. I could be the first lawyer if I wanted.

To be a lawyer sounds like something important. Very important.

Dad walks in like he's a big deal. It's hard to read concern for me on a face so high-glossed. He offers a bored *How ya doing?* and a bag he warns contains a baloney sandwich and potato chips. He drops into the Naugahyde chair like dead weight.

He knew he would be coming, so why didn't he ask me yesterday what I wanted for lunch today? Or why didn't Mom step up? She should've told him I prefer my baloney fried with mayonnaise and cheese and pickles. She knows I hate mustard to the point of gagging. Does LACK ever share their knowledge about us, their offspring?

I should be grateful that he brought anything at all.

"Sorry, boy, money is tight," he says. I say, "That's baloney." He says, "Hahaha, you're funny. You get your sense of humor from me."

I've got nothing from him that I can see. I loathe everything about him except his looks and pendulous dick. That—the one thing I wanted—I didn't inherit from him, getting instead a cork-sized version.

But for a few, all the potato chips are tainted by mustard. I'm salvaging them when he says, "Ain't nothing worse than not having money. Think about that before you ever think about quitting school or giving up on your dreams."

The chair is near the foot of the bed. He tilts his head away from me toward the wall-mounted television. Onscreen is journalist Max Robinson offering an update on the swine flu's bronchial rampage through the U.S. That it started in Mexico City has convinced Dad that the killer flu is a retaliation against the United States for its theft of California, New Mexico, Texas, and Arizona. If my Anatomy & Physiology teacher were here, she would say, *Flus don't plot revenge!*

Dad talks over the TV—Max Robinson's pandemic reporting means nothing compared to what he has to say. I would ignore him completely, except now he's talking about me.

Dad says, "Boy, you said you been thinking about the law, but I could see you doing the TV news. Seems to me you got what it takes. TV's nothing like it was even ten years ago, in 1967. Max there got a nice voice, but he ain't got nothing going on in the looks department. Except for that new, big-ass knot on your head, boy, you're a good-looking kid, if I may say so myself, and I'm gonna say, since I got something to do with it —but not as much as your momma got to do with it, you look more like her than me. But you still good-looking, and she was fine, mmm, mmm, mmm, back in the day."

I thank him. I mean it, except I don't like the way I look. Never have. But I'll say anything to help the hour pass. Plus, TV journalism does sound more interesting than Lester Gains, Attorney at Law. Probably being on TV news pays a lot more money than the law. Probably includes flying all over the world, covering pandemics and bombings and coups and queens and Michael Jackson. Sounds fun.

He says, "You should check it out. I think old Max there has got a book out. Or somebody Black in that world has got a book out, because they all got a book out now. And I wouldn't be surprised if one of the SoCali schools you applied to has got a program to get a job like Max got, because LA is about TV and entertainment, everybody you meet wanna be an actor or make sitcoms or movies. I lived in LA, so I should know."

Here come the highlights of his year in SoCali—what he calls Southern California. His beach fantasies make it easy to forget he couldn't have cared less about us, his destitute family back in Cincinnati. My brothers can't stand to hear about his good times. Mom can't either. Me? I applied to three colleges in SoCali, maybe to succeed with a West Coast life where he failed. Not that I remember him from when I was five, my age when he was running, roller skating, and whoring around on the Santa Monica boardwalk, because I don't. But I do remember wondering about the dad in the photo on Mom's dresser. The dad me and my brothers didn't have because there was something wrong with us.

Those deadbeat years to us were wander years to him. And never has he apologized for overlooking us. So why should I care about his two fucked up tours in Vietnam? That he takes pills because of what happened to him, and because he suffers manic depression. That's the crazy part of Dad. The scary part.

I glance at the clock and see it's finally time for him to leave. I say, "Dad, if any of my school friends or friends from Kings Island call, please just say I'm not available and take a message."

"Boy," he says, "I damn forgot. That King Island friend of yours did call this morning. I was getting the Twins out the door and I told him to call back. He said he would."

"Great. I'll tell him and everybody else when I'm out of here.

There's no phone in this room, so I have to use the payphone down the hall and can't leave a number. You know that, right?"

"Yeah, but you ain't gonna be here but a few days."

I watch him leave, glad to see the back of him. I'm even OK with the curtains open, braving reflections and shadows in the panes. I'm too worked up to be depressed, and crying still hurts. I fantasize toppling the bed, hurling the chair through the window.

All better now.

»»»

Boredom won't turn me loose. I'm climbing stairs as far as I can now. Sometimes two at a time. Then I hear someone a floor or two above me. Someone probably equally bored. But this person isn't climbing up or down. I hear a click followed by another click. I slow down and wonder if I've been noticed. Then I see a boa of black hair and a camera pointing at me. I put up my hands to block the picture-taking. A dude's voice says, "It's cool. I'm not one of the goon squad or the pigs, I'm legit, I'm an artist."

An artist in the stairwell of Cincinnati General Hospital?

I see the outline of this skinny guy in the stairwell. Then the waist-skimming boa of black hair and a hospital get-up like mine. He peeks out from behind the camera, and I can see he's browner than me. He says, "Sorry, I didn't mean to scare you. I'm Punch, as in punch drunk or sucker punch. Like I said, I'm an artist, I take pictures. Which ain't allowed in this fucking place. Privacy shit."

I introduce myself. Strands of his restless hair tangle in our handshake. I see beaded leather bands at his wrists and a feather that looks stabbed into both earlobes. Some exaggerated Native American dude.

He says, "Can I get a few pictures of you?"

"Why you wanna a picture of me looking like this?"

"Because you look like this. The body wears violence like

clothes. You ever heard of the British painter Francis Bacon? He paints that violence. I was fagbashed once and I took a lot of pictures of myself. I put them in an art show of my work."

"Fagbashed? Are you?"

"Yeah, and proud of it. Ain't you?"

"Yeah, I guess I am. I mean, I'm not out about it. Though I do have a boyfriend."

"Hello!"

"Maybe I was fagbashed, too. I didn't think that's what it was though, until you said the word."

"What did you think it was then?"

"I don't know. I mean, I know the guy, he works at a car garage and had just fixed my bike for me. It was late and that blizzard last Sunday had started. I needed my bike, so a friend, actually my boyfriend, dropped me off, and I was gonna ride the bike home, it's not far. The place was closing. Nobody was there but me and him. I knew him back in junior high. I remember asking him about his Christmas holiday, that's when he grabbed me. And I was like, *Hey, what are you doing?* He called me his baby, *baby bitch boy*. He tried to make me suck him off and more, and then he beat me up. He had me on the floor. My pants were off. Somebody came and was banging on the door. Somehow, I got away."

"I'd say that's fagbashing, maybe with a pinch of tainted love."

"Tainted love?"

I'm a guy who doesn't blab about himself, normally, but nothing is normal about how I ended up in the hospital. So, I tell him I've known the twisted fagbashing motherfucker since I was thirteen. He had stopped some bullies in junior high from beating me up. He was probably eighteen then and in the eighth grade because he was kept out of school. I hadn't seen him for a couple of years before he started working at the gas station.

I'm blabbing so much, I don't even see the tears coming.

"Let it out, you're still alive," Punch says, touching my shoulder.

"I don't even know you."

"What's there to know? I've been there. Shit happens. You're not weak or stupid."

"That's how I feel."

"Fake it till you make it then. Remember: we're an endangered species, and that's on top of being fags. I'm Sioux, or Suzzie if you like. White guys love telling me how iconic I look before fucking me over. Your people's history and my people's ain't the same, but you get what I mean, right?"

"You saying white guys fagbashed you?"

"Well, it ain't racial like that. First time, some Sioux boys done it, and mind you, I knew 'em. One of 'em, Randy,he flirted with me, he tricked me into going out. He told me to meet him, and I did, I had the hots for him. His friends Petey and Ward were there. They called me a bunch of names and beat me up and then took turns making me suck them off."

"Did you go to the police?"

"Hellnaw, I didn't. I would've been the one in jail."

"Whatcha do?"

"Like I said, I really liked Randy. He weren't the one that fucked me—that was Ward. Ward called my house and said he was sorry, and I let him dick me again. He said he wanted to be friends."

"That's crazy."

"It was. But I fixed his ass, permanently."

"Whatcha mean?"

"Got revenge. That's all I'mma say. Mind you, nobody gave a shit about us. We were nothing but runts on the reservation. See, where I was, about ninety miles north of Cheyenne fucking Wyoming, was depressing as shit. I ran away as fast as I could, and you know what—I didn't even know how to read a map. I was thirteen and living roadside, hitchhiking from A to B, sleeping in the armpits of bridges, and a whole bunch else that makes me surprised I survived when I think back on it. I found out how strong I am."

"Wow, you've been through a lot. How old are you?"

"Twenty-six and just as iconic as I wanna be. And you?"

"Sixteen. I'm going away for college in the fall and never coming back."

"Good you got a plan. But make sure you stick a knife in the heart of your twisted fagbasher before you leave. That's the therapy you need! Even better than going to art school."

The door above us swings open. A professional insists Punch come inside, that patients aren't allowed in the stairwells. We wave as he passes through the door, PSYCHIATRY spelled out on the wall. I worry for him, and for me, now. Going crazy is second only to being homeless on my list of fears. I've read about gay homelessness, and I'm terrified because it creates craziness. Right now, I feel I'm close to being both.

The door has a No Reentry sign. On the way to my room, I encounter Dr. Fang Fang. She says exercise is good but I shouldn't overdo it. Some hours later, I wake from a nap with her looking over my chart. She announces that a hospital bed seems wasted on me and promises to get me released, hopefully by morning.

I know she will instruct LACK. But I park myself at the phones anyway. I'm counting the rings on my fourth attempt to get through. I can't understand why we don't have an answering service or a phone with multiple lines. When I complain Mom always says, *You can get whatever you want when you get a job to pay for it.*

I give up but try again one hour later. Then, after what must be twenty rings, Mom answers. She complains of being rundown, on top of the Twins not sleeping well. Everything's always about her, but this is about me. I say, "I'm fine, in case you're wondering about your kid in the hospital who is, by the way, getting out tomorrow."

She says, "Yeah, that Fang doctor called us. I can't wait for you to come home, I miss you, the Twins miss you, they ask about you all the time, wondering where you are."

I can picture the long list of chores with my name on it. It's like nothing has happened to me. As if catching up on schoolwork won't be hard enough when I've got a twisted fagbashing motherfucker to worry about. I keep my cool though because I want out of here. Even if it means more chores I resent, and the people I love and hate. Home is home.

"Mom, please, please, please, don't forget."

"Your father knows. He will pick you up in the morning."

I wait.

»»»

5:20 a.m. is a lonely hour. Blinking lights remind me I'm not alone. Passing staff engage in tasks. I arrive at the payphones eager to annoy Mom. There's no answer after five rings. Her not answering sometimes makes me think the worst. I no longer fear Dad will murder her. That was back in the days when he was out of control. Raging, high, delusional, confused about where he was, unsure about who we were. Accusing her of whoring behind his back. Never mind he's the one whoring behind her back. This was before we learned he is manic on top of being traumatized by war—on a rollercoaster of moods. She is alive thanks to his antipsychotic prescription refills plus weekly counseling. All of us are alive thanks to the same reasons. I no longer sleep with a knife under my pillow. We rang in the New Year together, none of us scared shitless.

I now fear her falling, though. Or something related to being seven months pregnant and preposterously huge.

Knowing Mom, she's not answering because she left early to work an extra hour of overtime. I have faith because Dr. Fang Fang assures me they spoke. And Mom has said she spoke to Dr. Fang Fang. I have less faith that Mom relayed the message to Dad. I have even less faith that Dad will turn up sometime in the morning. I'm ready by eight, which gives him twenty extra minutes for the morning rush hour and dropping the Twins off at the Lilliputian Daycare.

I'm alive. I have faith. I wait for him to free me.

Nine, ten, then eleven o'clock. No sign, no word, no LACK.

My discharge would be botched. My terrible, imaginary reasons for it expand to Dad and the Twins. Best to stop these runaway thoughts of gore and death and plot my escape. I have no change left to call Blair, my best friend, or Chip. It's a suicidal five-story plunge from the window. But I'd land on a mattress of snow. If I survived, the walk home would be close to six miles. Easier to just make a run out the door. My restlessness alerts the nurses to strike first. I'm told that I, as a minor, can't discharge myself. That action can only be performed by a parent or legal guardian. So, I should calm down and be patient.

Dad's laughter rings in the hall just before noon. Nurses always fawn over him, especially the white ones. He says, "Cliffy-boy, sorry to keep you waiting. Your Mom didn't tell me until five this morning and I had a dentist appointment, and you know they charge if you don't cancel within twenty-four hours and you ain't got a phone in this room." And I say, "Because who needs a phone in their room, right?"

I giggle that everything's OK, though it isn't. My family lies all the time. I learned to play kitten from Mom, her little lies purring to appease him, and the boldfaced ones he tells her. Those lies we boys tell, if caught, usually get the strap, our skin flayed raw. Here, though, I pretend to have enjoyed my hospital stay. I thank the flirty nurses because I have manners. In their batting eyes, Dad must look dashing as he wheelchairs me off the ward. I note the exit signs along the labyrinth of halls I've walked many times by now. We elevator down several floors to double doors that swing open to the patient lobby. Large glass windows look out upon a spearmint green courtyard. I note that, innately, Dad's presence must be a scarecrow against certain motherfuckers lurking in the glass. I feel free of fear as we pass through the doors. I bask in this first chance to feel the bright bitter cold on my face. The first chance since having the shit beaten out of me.

Into the parking garage we go. Dad asks if I can walk to the second floor. I strap on my backpack and follow him through the shadowy maze. There are no corners to look around, just the wide pillars holding up the four-story structure. I'm behind him, and now these concrete columns hide him from me. He vanishes for seconds, just long enough that I feel scared I'll get lost. I rush forward to keep him in sight, wondering if I'm retrograding to childhood—but he wasn't even part of my childhood! I've never been so happy to be inside his Marquis. The safety of his spongy coupe, though I've never felt that safe with him, especially in this car.

"Cliffy-boy, I got some bad news. So, the doc says you should stay home another week or two."

"But I'm ready to go back to school tomorrow."

"That's what I told her. She said you ain't gonna be back to normal for at least two months, and I told her ain't no way you gonna sit around for no two damn months, and she said you need to stay put for at least two weeks because of the dizziness and the headaches, and I told her ain't no sixteen-year-old boy gonna sit around like that? I wanted to say to her, *OK, you gave us the white people's advice, but we need the Black people's version*, taking into account that nobody can afford to be sitting out recovering that damn long."

"That damn long is right, Dad. She doesn't understand, I've gotta go back tomorrow."

"Boy, here's what I think. You definitely can't go back tomorrow, but soon as the headaches go away, hell yeah. Me and the doc gonna talk about it in a week. Not to scare you, but it ain't just that. The doc explained how you might suffer from PTSD, that's post-traumatic stress disorder."

I don't say that I know what PTSD and mania are, thanks to him and the crash course he continues to provide. I instead say, "We covered that topic in school, and Dr. Fang Fang is wrong, because I'm fine, I have no problems. I mean, you could drop me off at school right now and I'd do just fine. The worst that could happen is that the way I look might freak out a few people."

"You're not OK, boy. I know cuz I got the same problem, and it's a motherfucker. The war loops in my mind and I can never turn that shit off because sometimes I don't even know it ain't for real. All the vets have the same problems. The doctors give me drugs, and that helps. I know you ain't had experiences like mine, but your mind might be in a different battle, according to the doctor, and I think she's right. Anything you wanna ask me about my PTSD, I can tell you what I know from personal experience. Maybe I can help you get a grip, talk you down when you're feeling crazy or you don't know what's going on, because sometimes that might happen to you. A lot of shit happens, and you'll be like, *what the hell*? The therapist that runs our support group showed us a couple coping tricks. I can show you if you want."

"And then you'll let me go to school Monday?"

"No, I ain't saying that. I'm saying I can help you cope, that's all."

"Ok, help me cope."

"Well, without getting too particular about the shit, I can say you feel like you're caught. A buddy of mine said it's like a washing machine that's stuck on the spin cycle. But the spin cycle might be cutting somebody's throat or watching your buddies blown up after a landmine. Even if you like being in the war, like I did, everything gets turnt around. I slept through the bombs and felt like the world was ending, but it wasn't till I came home that the reckoning happened, when it hit me, when it took over. And now, when I actually think about what the fuck it all meant and what it was I went through, what we all went through, I just get sick to my stomach, and the PTSD is kinda worse in a vomity way. Boy, I can't tell you how many hours I've spent over the toilet throwing up all that shit. The pills help, but I still feel like I can never stop seeing what I've seen, or like I can't leave the spin cycle to get to the finish. Like I said, your experience ain't nothing like mine, but the sooner you face what happened, the better off you'll be, or that's what they tell me."

"You don't believe them?"

"Don't misunderstand me, I do believe them. I'm better than I have been the last five, six years. But boy, you know, I used to count the days thinking that after X, Y, Z I'd go back to feeling normal, and I guess at some point I lost track, and it was like one day at a time, one foot in front of the other. That's what normal was for me, and it still is. So yeah, I think it's good to believe in something, especially when you're trying to find your way in the middle of the shit. I mean, it's nice to think God's holding a flashlight showing you the path, but then you got to forget that God turned the flashlight off and let all this horrible shit happen in the first place. So, I just can't ask questions like that because nothing makes sense. What I've learned is to remind myself that I got me a life I care about. Sometimes it don't feel like I got anything, or that what I got ain't real, but I do got a life I care about, I have a family. It's the same for guys that have been through what I've been through. At our support group, we talk about the shit, the deep shit. We don't put

God on the witness stand to testify. We just don't. That's why me and Detective Moneymaker are friendly. We know. We recognize it when we see the war in each other. It's something."

We finally leave the parking garage in time for him to list his symptoms: blackouts, rage, disorientation—and the drinking and narcotics and pot that he thought would make him feel better. He says, "Shit, I bet you remember seeing me some of those times, the things I said and the things I did. But you know what, Cliffy-boy, you didn't see the worst. Whatever you think, you didn't, trust me. I was in SoCali for that, so I spared y'all.. Tell the truth, it's a wonder I'm still alive or that I ain't locked up for some of the shit I've done."

I'm unsure if I should thank him for sparing us the worst. Nothing short of killing somebody could be worse than New Year's Day a year ago. We were driving to see my Mom's sister and her family for dinner. I was wedged between my brothers Dudley and Corey in the back seat. Mom had one twin in her lap and the other in a blanket between her feet on the floor. I remember her asking Dad to slow down because we were speeding 100 mph, thirty miles over the limit. And then I watched as he lifted a gun from his lap as if handing Mom a tissue. I remember not believing what I was seeing and then believing it but being paralyzed, muzzled. Suddenly the gun aimed at her, and he shouted, *Nothing better goddamn happen*. Dudley was behind Dad and couldn't see clearly. But we all heard the gun click and this crying sound from Mom. I remember the music suddenly blasting and the sun burning my lap. I closed my eyes and heard the gun clicking again. I remember thinking I just wanted it to be over. But then I felt the deceleration. I saw the weapon retreat into his lap. It was like we time-traveled back ten minutes and then went forward to arrive at our cousins' house for good luck black-eyed peas, chitlins, collard greens, and cornbread. Mom still claims he remembers nothing about the drive. The way she kittens to him, it's hard to imagine her even asking what he remembers. I don't care about his memory. But I want to know now which symptoms are PTSD and which are manic depression. None of us kids are supposed to know about his mental problems or the Lithium among the pills he takes. I know, because I overheard Mom say it to one of her sisters, and I looked up the drug on one of his pill bottles.

Dad says, "Cliffy-boy, at some point, you'll remember the one thing that bugs you the most, and you'll realize it's a turkey vulture gnawing on your bones. Think about that, Cliffy, some boys put you in the hospital five days ago. And I can guarantee you that shit won't sit right with you."

Dad makes up for the baloney snafu by pulling into the McDonald's Drive Thru. I'm allowed anything I want, and he orders, too, making this outing feel special, like a planned father and son day. I picture him shaking the money tree for our outing. I picture Detective Moneymaker surveilling us from behind bushes from an anonymous Ford.

Big Macs, fries, and shakes pass through the take-out window. We park to gorge. I'm surprised because he's a dad fussy enough to ban eating in his car. He's a talkative dad that chews and spits words and food. What I hear, though, is the earthquake in my stomach and an aftershock in my bowels. Plus, severe pain. The constipation of the last five days is now rushing for the exit. The sensation only intensifies as I clench to hold the dam. I push the Marquis door open and catapult outside. The McDonald's entrance is steps away, and I'm hopeful. But the bathroom is occupied, apparently by someone only just getting started. I wait until the ooze and the gush break free. The bathroom occupant, an old man, finally emerges. I rush into the lemony-colored bathroom as the last of the sludge landslides out of me, but not before it breaks free of the underwear's elastic. The cleanup is the final humiliation, captured in the mirror over the sink. My tears boil.

"Boy, I was just coming to check on you. You alright?"

"Yeah, I was kinda backed up."

I stew in foulness and fear he will joke about me. But Dad lets music fill the car, canceling criticism and conversation. We are driving, and a surge of exhaustion sedates me. I realize I've dozed off because now Dad's lifting the garage door open. Near the basement entrance, he tells me to call my school about my bike.

I snap awake to tiptoe around several lies about my bike. We are climbing the stairs to the kitchen when he says, "The other day you said you left it at school, and it might still be there. Claim it before they cut the chain off and get rid of it."

"Oh, OK, but Dad, I'm sorry, it's not at school. It was stolen from me that night, too."

Then I recall telling him yet another story at the start of Christmas break , the original story, the simple truth. I had dropped the bike off to get fixed because of a problem with the gears that caused the chain to slip. I told him this because he had asked me why the bike wasn't in the garage. He always notices the bike. He cares about it, it's the only thing he's ever given me, other than his lousy name, and he comments if the tires seem low, he asks about tire treads in the snow.

"Cliffy-boy, first you told me it was getting fixed. Then you said you left it at school. Now you're saying it was stolen when you got jumped. Sounds like you're still confused, boy."

I agree that I am still confused. I blame a headache coming on, on top of being sick from lunch. The thought worries me that more purging from my body is coming. I'm afraid I can't think straight and need to lie down. But just now I don't care what he thinks. And anyway, I don't think much about dads who don't think much about sons.

Nothing to question about that.

»»»

My thinking is sharper in my top bunk bed, even when Dudley's in the bottom bunk. I stenciled the Milky Way on the ceiling above me, claiming it as my corner of the universe. Back when we first moved here, none of us figured out how to escape our rampaging dad, but I learned to dodge his rage at Dudley. His twisted face would bulge at eye level to mine, and I'd launch my focus toward the parental gas giants Jupiter and Saturn. Dudley would pace the room afterward, plotting the takedown of our live-in monster. Now, Lithium and Valium have tamed the beast, and Dudley no longer plots. Now, I calmly stargaze at the glittery dots meant to be galaxies in the Milky Way. Dudley mostly stays with his girlfriend, dropping in once or twice weekly. Always ready in case the rampaging Dad returns.

It's possible Dudley doesn't know what happened to me.

Hunger is my only reason to leave my room. No one has to tell me to say hi to the Twins. I love them to pieces. The list of people I don't want to see includes everyone living in this house above age four. I drop by the den to kiss the babies. Each at first winces and seems scared of me. I ease myself to the floor to play with them. The girl twin says, "You got a boo-boo," and I say, "Yeah, I got a boo-boo." The boy twin shows me his elbow, he says, "I got boo-boo, too. Ouch!"

I nearly collide with Corey as I'm leaving the den. He says, "What's happening, Cliffy, I heard you got beat?"

I hear the boast and the glee. His teeth are sharpened with hostility. Beneath his landscape afro and fifteen-year-old mustache and goatee, he's enjoying the knocked-down sight of me. Me, the model brother he'll never be. His idea of sport is running with a bad-boy pack, looking as if they'd just left a felony scene. Visiting me in the hospital was asking Corey too much. But then, I wouldn't visit him either. Unless ordered by LACK.

"If the dudes that beat you live in Evanston, Walnut Hills, or Avondale, I'll hear about it. Niggas love to brag. You got robbed too, right?"

"Just my bike and five bucks."

"That's a good detail. Stealing bikes is what little boys do. Honestly, I figured you were fagbashed."

"You didn't tell LACK that, did you?"

"No, I wouldn't do that to you, but I mean, you ain't so good at hiding it, you got to tone it down, you got to talk like you live here with the niggas, not like a bank teller. I been telling you that from the jump."

"Fuck you, Corey, the only reason you know anything about me is because you went through my things."

"In a blindfold test, nine out of ten local dudes hearing your voice would say, *faggot*. You know it, Cliffy. You're a target."

"I'll remember that when you're doing time in Sing Sing."

"Sing Sing is in the Bay Area, stupid!"

"No, that's Alcatraz, stupid. And Sing Sing is in upstate New York."

We snarl then separate. I have one good thing to say about him. To his credit, he thought up the LACK nickname for our parents. Corey can be sharp like that.

I would lock my door if Mom didn't freak out over locked doors. I'm settling in my bed when Dudley turns up.

"Oh man. Mom said you were jacked up, but at least your nose ain't broke and teeth ain't missing."

"I don't feel so lucky, but I guess you're right."

"I am right. Ain't you watching the news? Somebody is always shot or stabbed in robberies around here. Now that you've been targeted, you got to be ready to protect yourself."

"Whatcha mean by that?"

"These nigs in Evanston don't play. . .They're gonna keep coming after you."

I know the advice I don't want is coming: my older brother is suggesting the best choice of weapon to defend myself. Unlike me, he has always taken self-defense seriously. He points out that I'm not a fighter like him, and that anything he might recommend is wasted. I don't ignore him, though; I actually admire my big brother. Deep down I never believed any of us could end up dead in our own home. Maybe dead by unforeseen forces, like fire, carbon monoxide, a tornado, or a break-in robbery. Then came the New Year's 100-mph drive to Dayton and the gun pointed at Mom. Dudley had the cigarette burns to prove Dad was a psychopath. He'd also been the only one of us to put himself between Mom and Dad. The only one of us to take the blows meant for her, Though he was at least four inches shorter than Dad. The last time they battled, it ended when a neighbor called the cops. Dad went to jail. Dudley doesn't believe a few pills a day change a monster like Dad. Deep down, I don't either, sometimes.

And yet, no rampaging monster since the anti-mania cocktail.

Dudley says, "A knife probably won't do you any good, but a gun will help, even if it's just to wave it around so you can get away. If you gotta use it, because you're about to get the shit beat outta you, you aim for the chest. Personally, because I know what I'm doing, I'd aim for the shoulder."

"Knife or gun, those are my only choices?"

"Well, you can look the other way and be a fraidy cat for the rest of your life."

I don't fall for his goading. Still, I know what he means. I don't think of myself as an angry person. I admit the anger is fired up in me now. I could pull the trigger or stab the motherfucker, that's how roused I feel. I also don't see myself caring about revenge more than leaving home for Los Angeles. I want to be somebody, not a prison statistic, or a dead one at that. I need to stay focused on my long-term plan. I don't need to fall into a Black Evanston fate. I think about Punch, the guy I met at the hospital, hitchhiking his way out of his Sioux horror show and sleeping in bridge armpits, and probably turning tricks at truck stops, like the queer boys chucked from their families in George Baxt crime novels. The life of a runaway isn't for me either. For me, the way forward is not out but through my problems, and biding time. Yes. *Time is on your side if you let it*, Grandpa always says.

The day I leave for college, I'll have a tell-all with LACK and the cops about me and Chip, and about me and the motherfucker. Or, we can never speak of my senior year of high school again, ever.

"Cool, Dudley, I'll think about it," I say.

»»»

I'm lifeless, a slug. The Detective calls again. Chip's the only person I want to talk to, but he didn't leave a number in New Orleans. Crying over him won't make him call. Plus, calling him costs long-distance charges. I'm in no rush to phone the Detective or Mrs. Johnson, my Anatomy & Physiology teacher. A Jehovah's Witness, she told Dad she keeps me in her prayers. She left her telephone number, probably wanting us to pray together. I always feel silly down on my knees, knowing there are more exciting things to do in a crouch. I'm uncomfortable lying to her, though. I'll just pretend I never got the message.

I'm not excited to call school friends. Though I do need to be caught up on classwork. Fellow AP students Mathias, Tasha, Neicy, and BellaI tell I was biking home when I was ambushed, robbed, and knocked unconscious by at least three guys. That it was nighttime and the streetlights were busted out. And that my clearest memory is waking up in the hospital. My tale produces the right horrified gasps. They want to know street names and landmarks. It's laughable because only my Black friends know Black Evanston. My White friends live in White Evanston or adjacent White neighborhoods and fear the color line. That's fine by me. Nothing would embarrass me more than my friends visiting our cuckoo house. We live across the street from the jewel of Evanston: Xavier University. That should be a good thing except our house is among twenty on the crappy side of the street. The street is like a moat separating Black Evanston from the school's Catholicism, money, and white people. And our little bacon strip of land is all that's left of this side of Black Evanston. From day one, I have felt like we're a little Galapagos Island with Xavier scientists studying us to observe how we evolve while their faculty homes, student services, dorms and frat houses encroach on us. So far, two doors up from us, Mr. Lewis, with a master's degree in accounting, made the TV news with an embezzlement scheme that got him a fifteen-year prison sentence.

»»»

Mom thinks visitors will cheer me up. What she means is she's the one needing cheering up. Luckily, Blair's the only school friend that wants to drop by—he's also the friend that never has time. Rehearsals. Auditions. Always some obligations related to his portfolio of talents. We're best friends, but I'm jealous and in awe of him. He's religious, too, but a safe Methodist, not a fanatic Baptist or toxic Jehovah's Witness or zombie Born-Again. I can tell him I was fagbashed without being made to feel I deserve it for my church-free deviant life.

"Oh, man, that really sucks. I've heard of that. How do you know it was that?"

"I got called a bitch boy, which is the same as faggot. I don't like being called names, period, but faggot, which is kind of generic, is better than bitch boy, which is like saying I've got a pussy."

"Sticks and stones, sticks and stones."

"I know."

"It's weird how you remember name-calling but not the dudes that beat you up."

"Yeah, I hear it in my sleep now."

"Hey, maybe it's good you don't remember the rest. You probably wouldn't be able to sleep or go out at night without being afraid."

"Maybe."

"Well, you know you call me anytime. You need a ride, call me and I'll come if I can."

"I know."

"And you can tell me anything. If you need to talk, I'm always all ears for you, twenty-four-seven."

Blair and I once held hands. We were hiding in a closet from the junior high bullies. Facing what we feared was near death, we kissed. But nothing about it was romantic. It was like a sad, final goodbye. That we survived made us closer, though not in a kissy way. Between us is a brotherliness that I don't have with my own flesh and blood. Blair would say he's gay, but in a theatrical, emotional sense. We joke that I'm more straight-acting than him. Which isn't true, I'm the one called faggoty names, and now, fagbashed. He's the right shade of brown and I'm the wrong shade of light. That makes me a target in mostly dark-skinned Black Evanston. He's flattering me when he says he believes handsome boys like me are more likely to be harassed than big-boned ones like him. He says he likes to make people laugh—though he doesn't want to be laughed at or made fun of—and is grateful for his thick skin. I always feel he's on my side. I have always thought we could share anything, even blowjobs. I have to be especially careful though. Just by mentioning the motherfucker, Blair would know what happened to me. Of course, he remembers the motherfucker from our junior high school days. He's the one that told me the dude was working at the gas station. Back in junior high, he even warned me, saying the motherfucker was a crazy doofus and to stay away.

»»»

"Cliffy, are you sure you don't want me to come over? It's no big deal to cancel the rehearsal. I mean, I really want the part, but you come first."

Blair is being serious but hopes I don't need him.

"No, go to your rehearsal. I hope you get cast. You know how much I want to ride your coattails."

"I'm betting on your coattails, too. LA. Or New York or wherever you want."

"I hope you're right."

"Well, you will get there. Even if I have to get there first, we're gonna be best friends. Always."

We hang up, promising to see each other in school in the next few days.

»»»

It's zero days until Chip's return. That's according to the dates he told me. There's probably a simple reason he hasn't phoned. I gnaw on awful thoughts anyway. Plane crash. A drive-by shooting in the French Quarter. Maybe he's found a new love better than me. On and on I go. Round and round I go.

Even Chip has called out my negativity, that I'm always thinking the worst. He loves to say I need to work on the chronic gloom of my otherwise bright character. He doesn't know the extent of it. I was one hundred percent convinced our relationship wouldn't last past our Kings Island summer. Not just because of the obstacles of driving, scheduling, and hiding our relationship. We are both high school seniors, and college will put me on the West Coast and him on the East Coast, or keep him in the Midwest. And then there's our age difference, he is eighteen and I'm sixteen, jailbait according to the law. And there's the anti-sodomy laws. I think about these things; he doesn't.

Still, we agreed not to break up, that a lot could happen in the year before college. And wow, a lot has happened! Frustrated that he hasn't called again, I realize I was never convinced we should stay together. Maybe that's why I sometimes apologize for no reason. I know I'll be responsible when we break up.

I wouldn't be negative now if he called, though.

I wait until Dad and the Twins leave before dialing Chip. On the eighth ring a woman answers. I don't recognize the voice, though it reminds me of his dead mother. It can't be one of Chip's sisters either, with their high, giggly, girly voices. Now a voice I do recognize speaks from another extension. Chip's dad tells me Chip missed his flight last night and should be home sometime this morning. I leave my name, and he says, "Yeah, I recognize your voice. And how do you know Chip, again?"

I knew calling was a mistake. I tell him we know each other from Kings Island, and then I make up that Chip worked with my girlfriend and that a bunch of us all got to be friends.

"Girlfriend, huh? You're the only one that calls and calls and calls."

"He's tutoring me. Calculus."

"He didn't mention that."

I pretend Mom is calling for me. Chip warned me his dad is a musclehead, a former jock and Marine, a man's man, a complete jerk. The kind of dad who probably won't take well to learning his only boy is into boys.. The same is true of my dad. Poor Chip doesn't have a mom fallback. Not that my mom would save me.

I flip on the TV and land on a show about plastic surgery gone wrong. Now I wonder if my battered appearance will turn Chip off. I wouldn't make out with me, swollen and bruised. I don't feel turn-on-able, I feel nuts. I can pinpoint the source of my headaches as somewhere between the hematoma and the laceration at the back of my head. I've gotten used to a continuous low-grade throb. It hurts only when it butts against my skull.

Chip is a no-call no-show. At noon Dad finally turns up to drive me to the outpatient wing of the hospital for the removal of my stitches. I'm too preoccupied with the pain this procedure will bring to care why Dad's late. He doesn't explain where he's been all morning, but the wisp of perfume, and what I guess is pussy, gives him away. We look at each other with a sense of a chore to be gotten over with. "Boy, this better not take all damned afternoon," he says, and then lets the radio talk.

Time either moves too fast or too slow, never just right. We are at the outpatient clinic in supersonic time. A professional immediately leads me into a torture chamber to take out the four stitches in my scalp. She isn't into small talk or advanced warnings and gets down to business. I'm on the tip of my seat, each stinging snip of her scissors worse than the one before. Her advice is to not focus on the hurt but on the healing. Done, she offers a mirror to show off the little troublemaker—a bloody, sickle-shaped wound that she says will shrink as the new hair grows over it. She says I'll never know it was there. As if not seeing it could erase all that came with it.

"That was quick," Dad says. I nod and we're soon zipping homeward along I-71 with the radio blasting. We're exiting the highway when he says, "Boy, I need you to help me get the Twins to daycare. Not tomorrow, we can start on Monday." I don't immediately answer, and he says, "I'm asking if that's OK with you?" I tell him it is, though we both know I don't have a choice.

"Good, you know what to do," he says. He doesn't pull into the driveway, he lets me out in front of our house and drives away before I'm inside. I watch until the car tops the hill, excited to be alone.

I park the hall phone on the toilet seat by the tub in my bathroom. I lift my shirt and pull down my pants for a probing look. I try to imagine what Chip sees in the sexual me. What about my body turns him on, and where's the lust with me looking like this? My hickey-prone neck, my skinny chest with nipples like stickers, and further south, an always-hungry dick. If these are the parts of me that do it for him, then I'm unchanged. I throb just thinking about being together again. Then something weird happens. Like my mind switches to a different channel. Instead of me in the mirror I see myself lying face down with my cheek against the icy gas station floor. I can feel the bold burn on my skin. I'm wet and there's blood, and there are other deep, dizzying hurts. From where I lay, I see the blurry hulk of that motherfucker coming for me. I'm desperate to get up and get away, only I can hardly move through the pain. I'm in his grip now, his hands snatch at my sweatpants, dragging them to my knees. He dead-weights himself, flattening me on the floor, rubbing himself on me. I can hardly breathe and scream when I hear banging and shouting from outside that grows louder.

The channel changes again. Now I'm looking at my mirror reflection as the bathtub fills. I realize I have been afraid to fully examine myself, and now I'm not. The channel switching is the reason I have to look. I go to get the hand mirror from LACK's bedroom. Then I get down on my knees in front of the full-length mirror and lower onto my forearm. My free hand tries to get a lock on my butthole with the hand mirror. Your own butthole is hard for you to see, and I have only ever glimpsed mine before. Not that I haven't been curious, I just never tried after a neck strain from a self-suck failure. Capturing it in the twisting hand mirror isn't easy and makes me queasy. I try without the hand mirror now, sloping downward to angle my head and rest it lightly on the bathroom rug. Because of the motherfucker, I have hurt in so many parts of my body, and maybe here, too. I remember feeling ripped open and this terrible burning sensation. Now a sudden spiraling up of nausea catches my throat. I spring up to perch at the toilet just in time. I'm determined and go on now. I pull my cheeks apart at the right moment. Peeking out is a shy if swollen little blob like a wad of bubblegum stuck between fleshy butt cheeks. Its cinnamon color, and the pleats, surprise me. I smile. It smiles back. It says I'm OK.

I do and don't remember what happened, which means it did and didn't happen, whatever it is.

I soak in the bath. The phone rings once but it's not Chip. I nearly drop the handset into the suds. Wouldn't it be something to accidentally, intentionally electrocute myself?

I climb out of the tub feeling feverish, shivery, and drained. Maybe the swine flu has claimed me.

I make it to my bunk, and hours pass before I wake up. I know something's wrong with me and wonder if I should call the hospital for Dr. Fang Fang's opinion. Then I hear Mom downstairs. I instantly feel better.

She pushes into my room and wants to know why I'm in bed. She doesn't trust me or the hematoma. She has confidence in the thermometer that she sticks into my mouth. "Your temperature is normal," she says and lures me down to the den.

I don't want to be with her. I also don't want to be alone. She's anxious but not about me. She empties her purse on the couch, she says, "Oh Lord, please" and explains she's missing fifty dollars, wonders if I know anything about it. It's not an accusatory wondering, but the panicky kind over a costly loss that can't be made up easily. She questions me about Corey, she says, "He's been acting funny, I know you would tell me if you knew he was on drugs or doing something he shouldn't be doing, wouldn't you, Cliffy?"

Both her fears are true, but I don't tell her that. I also don't know that I would tell her anything, though I do know I would never tell her that. She says, "Why couldn't he be like you, you're the only one of my children I never worry about. Not until this recent business. Should I be worried about you?"

"No."

That's my cue to go back upstairs. I nap again, and the same reel plays from the motherfucker dreams again. This time, though, the reel is so loud it even wakes me. This time I am so fucked . . . I'm being pried open. I realize that I'm all loose lips and a night's sleep away from blabbing about everything that happened. I grab the Scotch tape on my desk, and I apply a small strip across my bunched-together lips. It's not uncomfortable, but lately everything about my being me is uncomfortable.

»»»

The headache butts against my skull for an all-out blitz. I hear Dad calling my name as I wretch over the toilet. Through the barrage of pain, I've been stranded for some minutes before he pushes into the room. "See, this is what that doctor was talking about," he says. Reeking of aftershave, he tows me to Dudley's bunk with a wastebasket in case I vomit. His schedule is busy, he's got the dentist again, but he promises to check on me after dropping the Twins off at daycare. I nod yes to everything and am asleep when they leave. It's near noon when I surface again. There's no sign of Dad anywhere. If he returned to check on me, I slept through it, dreaming about running. Running fast. Not competitively or for training. And not to something or from anything. Purely running.

»»»

I barricade myself in my room until I figure out what to do. The last person I want to see is Dad but there he is standing at the kitchen sink, rinsing his mouth out. All year-round it's summer for him. He is always Vaselined, shirtless, barefoot, and in briefs, not the bikinis of the past. A layer of gut is beginning to muffin over the elastic.

Spitting out what looks like water, he says, "Cliffy... boy, whatever you do, take care of your teeth. I just had to go back to have a molar pulled. Damn that hurt! Your granddaddy got all his teeth, but that don't guarantee shit because you grandma ain't got none of hers."

He then asks if I could see the missing tooth when he speaks. I tell him I can't. He makes it sound like he's talking, only no words come out. "What about that time? You see a hole?"

"No, looks like you got all your teeth."

"Not good for my image to be running around snaggle-toothed. Shit, five kids, plus one on the way, two of them almost grown ain't good either, but cain't do nothing about that, now can I?"

I figure this unanswered question had probably escaped a thought bubble of complaints. Still, it carries him down into the basement to forage for a work shirt and me back to my room for more of the same cycle of boredom, sleep, and screaming. That must be why my throat hurts.

»»»

I may have slept through calls, too. Even the one I want most. I feel weird but better enough to worry about Chip. This phone tag is cruelly drawn out, like we are meant to stay separated for now. Did he miss his rebooked flight, too? Or maybe I misunderstood his asshole dad? Maybe his "this morning" meant *this* morning, and Chip is landing in Cincinnati right now? Or maybe he's at school and thinking I'm at school, too? Or maybe he's forgotten about me? I don't dare to call his house again.

The last thing Chip needs is to be grilled by his dad about me.

But Blair could call for me. He could pull one out from his gag bag of hilarious voices. Maybe his Dudley Do-Right, Bill Cosby, dumb baseball jock, or disapproving Mom. He loves a prank but probably won't appreciate me summoning him to the principal's office. He'll think I'm nuts, and maybe I am nuts. Going from 100 to zero activity—on top of PTSD, on top of being all but aspirin-free, on top of strange rumblings and tectonic shifting in my body, on top of twinkling headaches and sonic bursts of distress, on top of idle feet meant to run—any one of these things could make a person nutty.

Running is how I beat back the nutty. It's hard not to circle the suckhole of dark thoughts, but running usually drains the poisons, sheds light and leads to a place of calm. I haven't run since before the holiday break, which seems like forever ago. Right now, I miss running so badly I could scream. Why sit around when I can be moving, so what if it's in slow motion?

I wedge my snow boots on and head outside. Like the backyards of our neighbors on either side of us, ours is snow crusted, narrow but long like a domino, and ends in a sixty-foot-high brick wall. Me and my brothers used to use it as a prop. Dudley would bolt up its face before flipping back to earth, and me and Corey would throw our bodies into handstands with the wall's backing. Now it's just an eyesore locking us in from the west and casting a long shadow over the yard most of the day.

I imagine a course that cuts a baseball diamond, the corners touching the yards on either side of us. I don't want to anger our neighbors, who seemed cool and welcoming until we got a dog two years ago, and he was poisoned while we were out shopping. We think the cat lady next door did it, perhaps provoked by her horny tabby and his litter mamas and their endless output, which kept our dog constantly barking, so much even we couldn't stand him. The neighborly tension persists, and I wave my hand in a friendly greeting should anyone be watching.

The cold air prickles my skin. The ground sloshes and sponges underfoot. The boots feel heavier with each slippery step. I manage to get up to ten walk laps before my ribs complain. I've probably been at it twenty-five minutes when I'm hit by knee-buckling fatigue. I imagine Mom finding me frozen in the yard. I barely manage the energy to make it back inside. I have to concentrate to wedge my feet free of the boots. I cling to the banister to hoist myself upstairs to my room. I don't remember locking the door or falling asleep. All I know is Mom's panting and shouting and banging on the door.

Facing me, she says, "You scared me to death. I come home and all I hear is you screaming, Lord have mercy! You were fighting Brock or something. And Chip. Was he there? You were calling for him. And for me. My poor baby."

I tell her I'm OK, I don't know what the screaming's about, I don't even know I'm screaming, just that my throat hurts a little. And suddenly the screaming fills my memory, but the volume is turned way down so that I hear Mom's voice saying something generic about nightmares, and then: "And Chip called at the same time I was coming in, just before all your screaming. I invited him for chili."

"What? No, I don't want him here. I wanna talk on the phone, not in person. Why didn't you ask me first?"

"Every morning it's Chip, Chip, Chip, and now you don't want to see him?"

"Not looking like this. Not for a few weeks."

"Cliffy, why would he care how you look, he's your friend?"

"Mom, please call him back and uninvite him."

"Sorry, he called from a payphone. He's on UC's campus, he should be here in about twenty minutes."

“I told you I don’t want to see anybody. What’s wrong with you?”

“OK, just stop it and pull yourself together. Go shower that funk off you and hide the bandage under a cap. And don’t slam that door!”

I slam the door anyway, and she bitches that I’m on her last nerve, and I want to scream louder than I did in my sleep. I mean, what’s so fucking hard to understand why I don’t want to be seen? Unlike her, I can’t tuck a black eye behind pancake makeup and sunglasses and go about my business. At Kroger’s I’ve noticed black eyes screaming behind the sunglasses of other women going about their business. How do you tuck a hematoma? What makeup color gives the illusion of shrinking the barnacled swelling?

I don’t even have a brave face to put on.

Our doorbell chimes and Mom shouts he’s here. I freeze. I could scream. I push myself out of the room anyway. Down I go, one squeaky, carpeted step at a time. I follow their voices like breadcrumbs leading the way. They’ve spoken on the phone many times but have never met. I know Mom is thinking how handsome he is, and he is handsome in that way jocks are handsome, with their wide necks and superhero silhouettes. He’s sitting at an angle that shows off the deep bronze of a New Orleans suntan. I physically feel it when he notices I’m present. As if his eyes were fingers on my skin, his eyes themselves a dark brown that suddenly brightens with light. He springs from the table, and I feel like I’m falling, and we don’t so much as hug as save each other.

“Cliff! Oh shit, you’re really hurt, I didn’t know. Your mom told me on the phone, what happened?”

“I’m fine, I was jumped, wrong place, wrong time, no big deal. Mom exaggerates.”

“Chip, don’t listen to him. It’s a big deal, you coulda died, Cliffy. That knot on your forehead is a blood clot and could cause you to have a stroke. At sixteen!”

I cringe as she describes details I still only vaguely recall. Like Dudley finding me naked and unconscious on the bathroom floor. Like her terrifying ambulance ride with me to the hospital, not knowing if I'd live or die. It's obvious she's basted this turkey of a story to serve it now. Every time I try to stop her, she raises her hand in warning. Just when I think she's scored all her points, she changes tactics: "Chip, how are you and your family doing?" I'm shocked when she tearfully cups his face saying, "I know you miss your mother something terrible. She's the only one you'll ever have."

"Yes Ma'am," he says.

"God bless her," she says and then leaves us both scraped raw. I apologize for her annoyingness—nearly calling it *overkill*, a gruesome word given all that's gone on. His pooling eyes say he's thinking about her words, not mine. I want to warn him about Mom's manipulating play: cupping his cheeks while looking into his eyes. It bends my will to hers without fail. I know from him that his mom was a kissy, huggy type, and that he misses that quality most of all. I want to warn that my Mom isn't the Madonna his mom was. But Chip would think badly of me.

"Sorry to be a crybaby," he says in a low voice. "But it just kills me that you're hurt like this." I say, "I'm OK." More tears splash out before he wipes them away. I see that he isn't OK and worry what's next. We gobble chili and whisper about leaving. When he's done eating a second bowl we pass through the front door onto the porch. I switch the lights on and anyone watching can see our arms around each other as we climb down steps to the street. "I got you, you're not gonna fall," he says.

So much to say, so much to share. We are mile-a-minute talkers, yet we don't speak. The car radio is off, the tape player, too. The sounds are our breathing and the engine's breathing when the gears shift, grinding noises. The ride is short to our favorite make out spot, a grassy stretch between the road and woody hillside. By now I would have squeezed his hand, kissed his lips, palmed his nuts, or even kissed his thickening crotch. I hunger for him, but I feel repulsive and self-conscious. The quiet is repulsive, too, exaggerating the self-consciousness. I feel the pressure to say things I'm not ready to say.

Instead: "I thought you'd never come back. I know it's only been ten days, but it feels like you've been away a long time. A lot of shit's happened." He says, "I want to hear all of it."

Mom's version of events have tripped me up. I start off describing our goodbye that night. Chip and I were parked in front of the gas station garage for me to pick up my bike. I remember talking and kissing in the car and then he drove off. He says he remembers we were talking and kissing goodbye, too. Neither of us saw the motherfucker, neither of us noticed if anybody was even there. We both remember the garage lights were off, the store lights were on, the gas station was still open.

I say, "I noticed him right after you drove off. I knocked on the store door, and I had this feeling like he'd been there watching us kissing goodbye. It was like he came out from the shadows or from behind a door or something."

"An ambush," Chips says. I say, "I was startled, but I don't remember feeling awkward or anything. I mean, I know him from junior high. He said he was glad to see me, he was just closing. I asked about his Christmas, he told me he spent it with his grandma. But then he just got weird. He was showing me the repair he made to my bike, and then he came and pushed me against the wall, but in a playful way, Chip. You know, locker-room kind of playful, nothing more. He smiled when he did it, so I smiled back and that felt weird. Then he grabbed me by the head and pushed my face into his crotch. I guess he thought I was cool with blowing him, because he wasn't prepared for me to fight back. We fought, but he's a big guy . . . he put me in a chokehold. I couldn't breathe. I thought I was gonna die."

"The fucking motherfucker, the fucking motherfucker, the fucking psycho motherfucker. He beat you up? Why? Why? Why?"

"Probably because I wouldn't do it. It was fagbashing."

"The police have him?"

"I don't know."

"You didn't report him? Why? . . . Because? . . . What? . . . He needs to be in jail. The psycho motherfucker, he needs to be locked up."

"I didn't want to tell the police . . ."

I try to explain but he's heaving anger, and I'm blubbering, crying in my frustration to explain and justify what now seems pretty stupid.

"So, Cliff, what you're saying to me is this brute goes fucking psycho on you, and you didn't tell the cops because you were afraid they would find out about me and you?"

"Yeah. Remember, we told our folks we were checking out Ohio State and we would be in Columbus all weekend. But that's not where we were, we were in a motel in Loveland. You could be arrested for sex with a minor since I'm only sixteen. Remember, sodomy is against the law in Ohio anyway, so you could end up in the newspapers and all this could ruin everything."

"I don't give a fuck who knows."

"Yes, you do. And I do, too."

"Jesus, this is insane."

"It is insane, until you think about it. Everybody knowing about us. Especially our dads. We could end up homeless. It happens to guys like us all the time. I met a gay guy in the hospital who said he had been homeless for years. He turned tricks to survive and slept under bridges. And George Baxt novels are about boys that end on the street."

"Please don't tell me about your fucking novels, Cliff."

The park is onyx dark, yet everything becomes clear in my mind. The headlights of passing cars are a sideways meteor shower on the southbound parkway. Chip is now outside the car, leaning against the door. I want him to see that I'm tough and believe what I did was right, so I go outside to lean with him. He wants to know how I escaped. I tell him I was on the floor after being hit on the head by some kind of club. I tell him I heard banging on the garage door and shouting from a man outside, and that I screamed as loud as I could.

I also tell him I remember that the man was threatening to call the cops.

While they argued, I got away through the fire door at the back of the garage.

"I shouldn't have left you there," he says, crying a little, fighting it, crying a little more.

"No, I told you to. If anything, I should've let you drop me off at home like you wanted. But I didn't, Chip. Shoulda, woulda changes nothing."

Now there's only our nostrils spewing fighter jet contrails in the cold. Inside the car we hold hands then let go. We drive, and I don't question why we pass my street, or when we steer along the route we drove that night, because I'm clear where we are going. With the crime scene before us we stop, and Chip switches the lights off. The L.L. gas station is brightly lit, with a pair of customers in the store. Someone at the pumps, too. Chip wants to know if that guy is the motherfucker. I tell him that guy is one of several employees. Chip says, "It's just as well, I don't have my bats in the car. I took them out before I drove down to UC."

"Bats? What do you mean?"

"We're gonna bash his fucking skull in. We need to find out which nights that psycho motherfucker works. You can handle that."

I realize I'm not being asked, I'm being told what to do. But I go along because I don't want to argue. Fatigue steals my energy.

We usually stop for a goodbye kiss at the top of the hill. This time he U-turns in front of my house. He says, "I'll let you know when I can come back. Maybe Wednesday or the weekend. It's a little crazy right now. Missing my flight, plus a lot of shit I don't want to get into. You know, I missed the first day of school and my first day back at work. It's a lot."

"You haven't told me about New Orleans. Did you have a good time?"

"It was fine. I hung out with my sisters. Not much to say, really. Call you later then."

"Right, I understand. I love you."

"Yeah," he says. Then, "Me too."

»»»

I am more focused and charged than I felt yesterday. Now that Chip is home, I feel strong, reassured, braver. I try searching for the calm at my core. It's a meditative trick I do before a race. The dive inward. Though I've probably never found it, it's the journey that counts.

I promised Dad to help him.

I hear the Twins' baby babble and find them plotting an escape from their cribs. The girl is the brains, the boy the action figure. He has already figured out how to scale the crib rail, just not how to not crash-land. Seeing me, they giggle with happiness and raise their arms to be set free. I pluck the girl first, for she's eager to show off the potty skills that her other half has yet to master. He follows her lead to his potty,too excited to hold the flow, though the poop part lands just fine. Underwear gets changed, hands get washed, teeth get brushed. They climb into outfits Mom picked out. The boy takes the stairs first to show off his fearlessness, hands-free and bouncing all the way. She isn't so confident, scooting on her butt step by step.

By the time Dad appears, the Twins are fed and ready to go. He says, "Cliffy-boy, I sure appreciate you getting them ready. How's the headache?"

"It's okay. By Monday I should be completely ready for school."

"Maybe. We'll see."

The basement stairs are steep planks of wood. Dad carries the girl twin down while the boy balances against the wall. From the solarium windows, I watch them progress to the car and launch from the driveway into the day. Suddenly I'm riled. The big houses of White Evanston agitate me. How does their snow stay tidy even a week after the last storm? Our side of the street is sloppy with scraped driveways and snow piled at the curb like burial mounds. The sky is a tie-dye of warm colors that give the finger to yet another frigid day.

I pace between the TV in the kitchen and the solarium. I'm confident I can do laps in the backyard. Or walk to the University's track. I probably could even make it to school, just not for the full day. I'm looking out the solarium window debating what to do. I notice a bike riding the median. The rider looks like Punch, the long braids give him away. He's tipped forward, bowed over the handlebars, speeding down the street. I flail and flap my arms and shout into the glass—*I'm here, I'm here*—as if he were looking for me. Then I notice the low-riding sports car gaining on him. I shout, "Look behind you!" As though he hears me, he glances to the side and angles toward the curb. The car tacks left into the oncoming traffic. Horns shriek and tires scream in what could become a pile-up. But then the car swerves back across the median, and suddenly Punch is so close that he kicks the car door. The impact sends him careening sideways and skidding onto the sidewalk. Somehow, he doesn't crash. Somehow, the car barely avoids a smash up. I realize it's a dogfight when Punch charges down the street in pursuit. Or a death wish.

I snatch my jacket, jam my boots on, and follow in their direction. The disaster I'm sure is at the bottom of the hill isn't there, but I keep walking anyway. I finally see him, and miraculously he isn't bleeding out on the curb, he's walking his bike on the other side of the parkway. I'm trailing him by about fifty yards. The road twists as it climbs up from the valley, then turns to hide him in places. He crosses at the top of the hill, twice looking in my direction but not noticing me. A red car U-turns and glides to the curb near him. He and the driver, a black dude, seem to know each other by the way Punch leans into the window. The car takes off again, this time turning at the next intersection. Punch follows. When I reach the corner, I see him enter a mostly empty parking lot where the car is parked. I watch from a bus shelter as he leans his bike against the car door and joins the guy. The two share what I guess is either a cigarette or a joint before Punch disappears into his lap. With Chip, I've given more than a blowjob while jackknifed over the stick shift console, just never so brazenly as what I'm seeing now. Punch surfaces some minutes later, wiping his mouth. A station wagon pulls into the lot. He hops on his bike and escapes another near miss. All this seems reckless and wacko to me but in a way brave and fearless.

I head toward home, but I end up walking on the University track. Even jogging some in my heavy, awkward boots. My muscles are stiff, but I can feel that the running isn't far off. Something to be happy about.

»»»

A Kool cigarette scolds from Dad's lips. The smoke churns up a thickening cloud that billows over my brother Corey in the backseat. The child-proof features lock the doors and windows of the front seat, where I am. Cruel history has taught us that Dad intends us to beg while he pretends to read what looks like a bill or money statement. Neither of us gives in, though Corey is a carburetor of wheezing, and I have coughed twice. Cursing under his breath, Dad finally cracks the windows and puts the car in reverse. The smoke sucks out as we speed up our street toward the next torture he's planned.

I'm first. We're on our way to a police lineup that Detective Moneymaker has arranged. Dad makes it clear I'm the star of this show—and the reason it may backfire. He says, "Cliffy-boy, you know what they say in church, the truth's gonna set you free. Now, the Detective thinks you're either protecting somebody or hiding something here. If you got yourself in a jam, you need to say it so we can get the sumbitches that did this to you. Otherwise, you're wasting a lot of people's time. Including mine. You need to stop the I-can't-remember shit. You tell the Detective the goddamn truth."

I don't acknowledge the Detective's suspicions. But I do listen anxiously to Dad's wish list of outcomes. He wants arrests and criminal charges before lunchtime. I'm not the only one to hear Corey sneer over the screws being put to me. Dad shouts—"What you laughing at Corey, ain't shit funny here!"

It's hard not to see that Dad enjoys berating my younger brother about his dead-end path. And that Corey enjoys that the berating comes with togetherness and attention. It's like standing in the path of a tornado touchdown. The roaring air churns with refrigerators and fence posts and rooftops that mean to kill, though Corey will only end up with little bruises and curfews. Everyone says Corey isn't just Dad's look-alike, he's a behavioral copy of Dad's younger self. Maybe jerk-genetics have wired them to respond to each other in this twisted way. There was a time when Corey was even angry at me for being Dad's namesake, not him. I may yet become an Everett, Mitchel, Lionel, Dale, or Xavier when I can legally control my name.

»»»

The police downtown headquarters are a brute among friendly houses. Dad orders me to get out and then ratchets up the intimidation of Corey. He wants to parade him inside the precinct for all the cops to see. He says, "And maybe they won't shoot your silly ass the next time you get caught busting out some damn windows."

We three file in, me first and Dad bringing up the rear. I feel like we're on a perp walk into a hive of cops. The tall, buzzcut Detective Moneymaker is coming toward us. He paves onto his lips some Chapstick. He and Dad shake hands and wrap shoulders. Dad introduces Corey, and it's obvious the Detective endorses the tough love approach. He points to chairs in the sightline of a clunky ceiling camera that he says is recording the scene and everybody in it. Dad says, "Boy, you see that. Smile, cuz you're on every cop's radar in this city now."

We split off, with the Detective and me heading toward the lineup. Moneymaker palms my shoulder in a not-so-gentle way. He says, "You're looking better than the last time I saw you. Maybe your memory's cleared up some, too."

I nod. My mind always runs from the rhetorical questions of threatening adults. We walk along a long gray hall, down one flight of stairs, and a short distance to a darkened room. It feels oppressive, live-wire dangerous, like a wrong step could bring on the firepower. He switches the lights on and announces to invisible people that he's ready to start. I can see into the window of a connecting room. The Detective says, "This lineup is just like you see on TV. You're looking through one-way glass. A few guys will come out, one at a time. Relax, they can't see you. Let's see if we can find your guy."

I find his *your guy* funny. Like I'm a contestant on the crime edition of *The Dating Game*, here to make a love connection.

The first man, in jeans and a white T-shirt, sets the pace for the others. Each man is handcuffed and necklaced with a number placard that shows his place on the line. Each is taller, shorter, heavier, thinner, browner, darker, or lighter than the one before him. So far, they have in common that nobody looks familiar. I'm relieved this has been easy and am ready to say my guy isn't here. Then dude #8 appears. It's the psycho motherfucker, and the delay stands him out.

My gameface cracks. The Detective is watching me more than the lineup. I'm suddenly afraid and wonder if the motherfucker knows I'm on the other side of the one-way glass. Or does he think I'm too cowardly to sic the cops on his motherfucking ass?

The black and white yardstick on the wall shows him to be six feet six inches tall. I calculate the other advantage he has over me to be about forty or fifty pounds. He is an apex predator, and I am lightweight prey, comparatively speaking—five ten and 145 pounds.

I have no good enough reason not to finger him right now, yet I have every reason not to explain to Detective Moneymaker why I can't do it. Still, I take a long, centering breath and calmly insist I don't recognize anybody. Moneymaker insists I look closer at the three men who most resemble the motherfucker.

#3 approaches the glass and poses left then right. His profile lasts long enough to show moles, scars, wounds, ear piercings, and the tattooed fangs of ferocious mammals or deadly reptiles. Just long enough to unnerve me. #5 makes the same moves, and I'm stony this time. Then the psycho mothefucker's dead center again. His shoulders swing heavy and low with a few swaggering steps. But then I see my reflection in the glass, too, as I had in my hospital room's windows. In the trick of light, I'm standing side by side with him. And Detective Moneymaker is there, too, next to me. I am between them, unclear which reflection throws me off more—mine, the cop's, or the psycho motherfucker's.

I turn to the detective and say, "I do, or did, know him, #8. I knew him back in junior high school. Buster is his name, or what we called him back then."

"Just so you know, he's a felon with a long rap sheet that includes assault and battery. His victims are male and female, but mostly queers . . . sorry, I mean homosexual males. And there has been an accusation of rape. The accuser was a teenage boy like you, but smaller."

I try not to let this new information throw me off even more. "I don't remember him like that."

"How do you remember him?"

"He seemed to be nice. If somebody was being bullied, he'd jump in."

"Did he jump in for you?"

"Yeah, he stopped some guys from picking on me and another guy. I was new at the school. We had just moved to Evanston."

"Were you friendly with him?"

"No, I didn't know him. I mean, I knew him the same as everybody else knew him. He should have been in high school, but I guess he missed some years."

"He's not a minor, so I can say his rap sheet started when he was eleven. He was a bully then and now. Maybe he just liked you?"

I can only answer with a shrug.

Any runner knows when he's failed to perform as expected. Detective Moneymaker seems unsatisfied that I have held it together, outrunning him in a way. I try to throw him off with small talk—asking why he became a cop, how many kids does he have, any my age—but feel like I'll crack. His answers are stingy and uninterested, making me feel even more obvious.

Before handing me off the Detective says, "I didn't want your Dad with you so you wouldn't feel pressured. You can tell me anything. I'm not here to judge you. OK?"

"Thanks. When my memory comes back, and hopefully it will, I'll let you know. Promise."

"Just remember, there'll be no arrests without you. And your attackers will be on the loose to hurt other people."

We join the others, but he wants a word with Dad. While they talk, Corey is excited to know if I recognized anybody from the hood in the lineup. I tell him no. "Too bad," he says. "Nobody knows shit about you getting jumped. The dudes that did it must be from OTR or Price Hill."

Dad joins us and rolls his eyes at me, not even pretending to hide his disappointment. He keys the ignition, and we're backing up. He says, "Cliffy, Detective Moneymaker figured you might recognize somebody in the lineup. He said they had a couple of sex offenders—one of them is accused of assaulting two black boys, one eighteen, the other fifteen who was also raped. Punks. I told the detective my boy wouldn't be caught up in no shit like that. So, I'm glad you didn't point him out, whoever he is. But the somebody that did this needs to be caught."

"Dad, I'm sorry it didn't work out as you and the Detective wanted, really. But I couldn't just randomly pick somebody. Detective Moneymaker told me an investigation is a process. And so is getting my memory back, that's what Dr. Fang Fang said. I guess we all have to be patient until I remember everything."

"Guess it do," he says, angrily, letting the rest of his thoughts fly away. He leans on the steering wheel. We zip onto an overpass that climbs high above the new canyon of I-71. The expressway is a thing of beauty. Bright concrete and blacktop with white dashes dividing lanes that vanish over the next hill heading south, banking into the valley heading north. The acceleration is an adrenaline rush; it feels like we could leave the earth for the moon and stars. In a grounding voice, Dad says, "I'm taking you home so your mom can get her groceries done."

As we swing across six lanes into eastbound traffic, the deep expanse of expressway shows I-71's brutal surgery that sliced and diced Black Evanston. As quickly as we enter, we exit and loop toward home. The windshield curve bends the view of trees low along Black Evanston streets. The mix of shadow and light blends naked limbs and snowflakes whipping over me. At our house, Dad U-turns toward the curb. There's no traffic around when I escape into flurries and instantly regret not thanking him. I know my mistake will ricochet as ingratitude. Dad can be petty like that.

»»»

I can sometimes sense that Chip is about to call. Seconds before the phone rings, I feel I'm in the air and treading for ground. Sometimes I pick up just before the ringing, and our voices overlap—*It's you; Hi there; Hey*.

I tingle that we even found each other in this big spinning world.

That tiny miracle happens now. High. Grounded. Tingling.

But Chip is frustrated, not into the mysteries but the miseries. I assume the psycho motherfucker's the reason, but I'm wrong. His workday was abruptly canceled; now he's wallowing at home. If only he'd known, we could have planned this day with our Fuck Sunday in mind. I'm glad a bat's beatdown isn't on the agenda. I picture us romping and slurping in the backseat of his car. My stomach sloshes with biliousness, but I'm tingly-high knowing he still lusts for me.

I tell him my family is visiting my dad's dad. That my poor eighty-two-year-old grandpa got banged up sweeping snow in his driveway yesterday. I list the injuries—a contusion, a broken arm, and a cracked rib sent him to the hospital, but now he's home to recover. Mom thinks he's home to die. I joke that my mom has a morbid side. Then I realize how insensitive I sound.

Chip says, "Your Mom is sweet. You're lucky to have her," and then he tells me he's been alone since yesterday. He says, "While I was away, my dad got a girlfriend, and she's obviously been here like every night since I left! Fucking in my mom's bed—if that isn't giving her memory the finger, I don't know what is. It's disrespectful. And disgusting. I mean, fuck him."

I get that Chip doesn't want to be reasonable or understanding, just like I don't want to be gloomy or mom-trashing. I tell him that his dad is being a jerk and that I'm sorry he's so upset. He says, "My Dad is a selfish alcoholic asshole, in other words, a big loser." Then I say, "You won't believe what my asshole Dad did to me."

I recount the police lineup starring the psycho motherfucker. Chip calls the motherfucker a fucking psycho motherfucking *nigger*. I'm shocked because Chip has never said nigger before with me. I refuse to accept this radioactive denigration of us, and he says, "Sorry, but that's what the dude is. As you know I'm biracial, and it might've sounded like the white half of me talking but it's the black half. If it makes you feel any better, my black mom would totally freak out over me saying the N-word at home, or at all for that matter." I say, "Because it's abusive to us as black people." He says, "You are my first boyfriend, black or white, but that doesn't mean I don't know black people. My mom's brother laid it all out for me, so I know the difference between nigger and nigga. Nigga means what you make it. So, to me, when I just used the word, I meant loser. My whoring Dad is a nigga, and he's white, as you know." I say, "What?" And he says, "So, if I call you my nigga, it means we're boyfriends. My nigga. Baby." I say, "Don't you ever call me that! And you're totally missing the point." He says, "My only point is he's fucking psycho motherfucking black ass nigga loser. Is that clear enough?" I say, "Whatever!"

We breathe at each other in place of words. This infuriating, thoughtless side of him is why I know we will break up. I am not my weak mother, I will quit him if he doesn't quit me first.

Not now though, I'm in love.

"So, getting back to what's important," he says, "the dude's probably still in police custody. Maybe you should see if your bike's at the gas station." I say, "Wow, you're so right, he might be, why didn't I think of that?" He says, "That's why you need me. Plus, my good looks and X-rated charm mojo." We both try to laugh to lighten up. He says, "Just call the gas station. If the psycho motherfucker answers, well . . . but if somebody else answers, you can go Columbo on him—you know, you ask a bunch of questions that seem stupid but get him to tell you what you want to know."

I know Columbo. Everybody knows Columbo-ing. Ack.

Then he says, "If it's too weird for you to call, I'll do it. It'll make me feel good to do something against him. It'll only take a minute, too, so what if it's long distance, it's cheaper on Sundays. I don't have a Cincinnati phone book. Can you look the number up for me?"

I know he's thinking I'm chickenshit. I insist on making the call myself, because I want to do something against the psycho motherfucker too, obviously. We hang up, and I lug out the ponderous Yellow Pages to finger my way to L.L. Gas & Garage, which everybody calls the L.L. In search of my calm center, I take anxious breaths—in 1-2-3, out 1-2-3. The rotary's winding dial irritates me. That the line rings many times could mean many things, including the gas station is closed. I let it ring a few more times, and finally someone answers. I recognize the voice of the white attendant; he doesn't seem to remember mine. I do a Columbo and learn the psycho motherfucker isn't there and my bike was there two days ago. I say, "Buster was supposed to leave it for me. I really need it." Then he says, "Maybe he took it home. You should try there." I say, "Oh, but didn't he move?" And then he says, "You know the Doris Day House, I'm pretty sure he's still there." I thank him, hang up, then crack up. Doris Day or, as Black Evanston calls her, the *Que Sera, Sera white lady* who sings that damn song the radio plays a thousand times a day.

»»»

It's because of me that Black Evanston knows the *Que Sera, Sera white lady* lived here. I know because I saw *The Tonight Show with Johnny Carson* the night she was on, when she told viewers where she grew up. She wasn't specific about where and when she lived in Evanston, and there are no plaques or streets in her honor. Then I learned that our school librarian, Mrs. Krautheimer, knew the movie star in 1946. She warned me that those few blocks weren't what they used to be. Like I didn't know Black Evanston. I biked to the address and saw it was next to one of the streets I avoided in junior high. The only person I saw was a guy walking down the sidewalk. He looked like he'd just gotten off the bus after a long day at work. He seemed friendly enough, even asked if I was lost or looking for something. So, I told him about the movie star. "What!!! The Doris Day House," he said, laughing and guessing she's the reason a lot of white people must be coming through. Then he said, "Man, the moment them whities see me or my boys they burn rubber outta here." I learned from Corey it was a drug house now, and that it belonged to King, the man I was talking to—coiner of the term *Que sera, sera white lady*. Now, it's the home of the psycho motherfucker, *Que sera, sera*.

»»»

When I tell all this to Chip, he says, "My mom used to love Doris Day. Not me, though. I did like the Hitchcock movies she was in." He mentions a couple that I've never seen either. And he says, "So, back to what I was saying, that psycho motherfucker could still be in custody or maybe he's on his way to prison, wouldn't that be something"? I say, "Or maybe he's been let out of jail but is laying low because somebody's after him?" And he says, "Let's call the police station." I say, "I don't want to talk to that detective, he's onto me and anything I do will only make him more suspicious." And Chip says, "OK, I'll do it. Give me the number."

He knows and I know I'm not going to let him make a long-distance call about my problems. We go back and forth until I insist I'll call myself. He says, "Cliff, I love how offbeat and sarcastic and nerdy you are, but don't get all elaborate, keep it simple. Just ask if the psycho motherfucker's still in custody. It's a yes or no question. If they want to know who you are, say you're the gas station manager and you're worried about him."

I hang up and resentfully wonder why Chip's pushing me like this. I've memorized the police headquarters' number and the Detective's too. The turning rotary dial ratchets up my nerves. I take more 1-2-3 breaths in and out, hoping I'm right and Chip is wrong (not that I'm keeping score). I ask the Cincinnati Police Department about the psycho motherfucker, and they confirm Chip is right, that the motherfucker's still in custody.

"That's good," Chip says. "Maybe they've got him on something else. I was looking forward to batting practice with his head, but if they've still got him that's enough revenge for now." I say, "It is good news, and you were right as usual, Chip."

I ignore the batting practice comment. My true love can spiral into contests and disagreements when he's emotional. I learned that when his mother was dying. One minute he'd be crying his eyes out, and the next minute was all hard-ons and blowjobs.

The minute after that, he'd get hung up over a term like h*abeas corpus*—which I decide not to bring up concerning the psycho motherfucker.

He says, "I got Fuck Sunday blues bad. I wish I could come over and ravage you."

"Eighty miles roundtrip for a quickie isn't worth it, no matter how bad you need it."

"Boy, did I need to work today? I'm broke after New Orleans. My grandfolks paid for the ticket and everything we did together, but I paid for the things I did on my own. Plus, I'm working out with my baseball teammates at a private gym. It's not free."

"Fuck Fuck Sunday."

"Hahah, I know I'm a horny freak. I hope I'm not freaking you out . . . I mean, after all you've been through."

"No, I'm the same as you, and only for you. And it's Sunday."

"Fuck Sunday."

I imagine we both have hard-ons. He wants to know about my lingering aches and pain. I single out the headaches and the delicate rib that flares up only when I try to lift the babies from the crib.

"Poor baby. At least it doesn't hurt to fantasize."

»»»

Chip's fantasies worry me. Neither of us is the other's first time. My story includes lots of simple sex with a first-love boyfriend in eighth grade. Chip's story includes dangerous stuff that scares me when I think about it. He had his first experience a month before we met. He was on his way home from a regional baseball tournament. He turned off the highway for a piss at a rest stop. The guy at the next urinal was jerking off. The guy looked only a little older than himself. A little smaller, too, and military clean-cut. Big porn lips that whispered what was coming next—a hand reaching across the void between urinals. Chip told me he was shocked, but he could not *not* be turned on. He told me he closed his eyes and felt the guy's mouth taking him in. He told me he then fled to his car. But he lingered in the lot, wanting to go back inside. Another car turned up with another military-looking guy; this guy went inside. About ten minutes passed before state troopers showed up and took both buzz-cuts away in handcuffs.

That urinal scene stays with him. I can only imagine the raunchiness and germs and the troopers. Imagining my boyfriend as the object of other guys' lust bugs me. Chip said I'm just jealous. He would like us to do highway rest stop sex together. "Are you crazy?" I always say. Meaning, no.

»»»

He's now describing our overheated overnight at that Loveland motel. Memory is a live current crackling with static throughout my body. My fingers ping and spark as I push my jeans down to my knees, dick in hand. Our breathing and whispering overlap. Now there are only the breaths of a peak about to be reached. Then I hear jangling keys and the creak of the front door. I yank my pants up saying, "Goddammit, Chip, somebody's home." The phone slips from the cradle of my shoulder and slaps the floor. I grab the receiver and wave as my brother Dudley rounds the living room into the dining room. I say, "Chip, you were saying," and he says, "Aww," and I smile at Dudley as he enters the kitchen and fusses over the apples in the wicker basket on the table, then heads upstairs. I say, "Chip, I've gotta go." And Chip says, "No, baby, just a second. Open wide and stick your tongue out, I wanna cum in your mouth." I say, "Chip, I've really gotta go." Then he says, "Wait, give me a second, just a second, just listen, I want you to hear me when it shoots out."

I know Dudley would never eavesdrop, so I wait for the slapping sound of a jerking dick, the being on the verge and then the *aww, aww, aww*. I say "Chip, Chip, I really have to go."

He says, "OK, OK. I'll be home by ten. I'll buzz you if I can. Love you."

I hang up feeling giddy and guilty but hot-wired to do something daring.

»»»

I jump into my running gear. It's ice-cube cold but I'm sweating and horny and all jangly nerves in a steady jog. The morning's sunshine has been overtaken by afternoon haze like skimmed milk. My glasses steam up, making it impossible to see. Not just in front of me, but who might be seeing me. But I know the route so well I can run there blindfolded. Turning onto the psycho motherfucker's street is like being halfway through a race. I feel as brave and determined as I've felt since all this shit started.

Sound waves hit me first, like a quickening heartbeat. The twang of guitar and vocals join; it's the Ohio Players's "Runnin' from the Devil." I swipe my glasses with my sleeve. Twenty or so people come into focus, they're grooving to the devil beats. All stand around a tall drum of burning wood. Drinks in gloveless hands, cigarettes too. Maybe it's a house party. Or a block party. I can also see an upside-down pig on a spit, a blistered, greasy, disgusting sight. The scent of scorched pig fat sashays past me like a Montgomery Street hooker, to the lyrics: *Yes I'm livin' at a pace that kills*. Howling dogs in the distance, the smell of pork fat to them a bitch in heat.

I'll have no better luck than the yowling dogs. The party is growing and seems to spread between the Doris Day House's yard and the one next to it. That makes me wonder if King the drug dealer has both properties. They are rundown and haunted, mirror images of each other. The psycho motherfucker could be in either. So could my bike, which this mission is about. I can't get any closer without giving myself away, but I'm not close enough to see what's on either porch. I can see faces in the crowd. I don't see the psycho motherfucker. I do see Corey.

He stands out only because I thought he was with LACK, visiting Dad's dad.

What if Corey finds my bike? Would he make the connection to the psycho motherfucker? Would he say something? He'd probably bring it home if he could. More to boast than out of concern for me. I hang onto this hope all the way home and all evening.

When he finally comes home, he tiptoes upstairs to his room. One thing about Corey is, he's a blabbermouth. If there's something worth telling, he would have popped into my room already. Not knocking, just to annoy me.

My fruitless run was as much about Chip, but an action that doesn't get the goods isn't worth talking about. I probably did it only to impress him—not that I don't want my bike, because I do. But I'll say nothing, because he'll pile on the ten things I did wrong. That's not what I want to hear.

»»»

I'm going to school after we drop the babies off, no matter what Dad says. If he refuses to take me and insists I stay home, I'll sneak out anyway.

My backpack is ready to go; now for the Twins. They do their usual slapstick morning ritual, little clowns in cribs. We go down a checklist: peepees, doodoos, washing faces, hands, butts. Both love dressing themselves, though Mom picks out their clothes. I watch for the sweater or pants put on backward or wrong-side-out, the neck-opening mistaken for a sleeve. We gaggle downstairs to the kitchen, where I hoist them into highchairs for Sugar Bears. I laugh when they make faces between spooning up and slurping their kiddie bowls empty. I sponge little lips and sticky fingers and set each on the ground with a big juicy kiss. *I love you*, we each say, and they run amok. I hear Dad shouting from upstairs, insisting he'll be down in a minute. Even the babies know five minutes is usually ten. That means I'll be late for first class. And that's on top of the two weeks I've already missed.

The Twins dawdle into little coats. The wait isn't minutes but seconds. Dad rounds the dining room brined in Pierre Cardin. Who wears cologne for a daycare run but a man with pussy plans on the sly? LACK is LACK. Mostly I feel bad for Mom's never-ending struggles with Dad's zipper problem. Fuck, I hope I don't turn into her with man problems.

"Cliffy-boy, you sure you're up for this? It's good having you back, but you shouldn't do more than you're up for."

"Yeah, I'm definitely up for this, and for school. Don't worry about me."

"Good, cuz your Daddy can't wait for you to get a driver's license. Then you can do all this baby shuttle shit yourself."

Me completely taking over his morning baby route is his long running joke. I won't be of driving age until July when I turn seventeen. There'll be no daycare because there's no school session, it's summer break for kids everywhere. Best of all, I'll have graduated and be ticking off the days before I leave for college. I don't understand why he finds this joke amusing enough to drag it out. "Oh, but you'll be in SoCali getting a la-di-da white-man education—excuse me, getting your TV-star education, move over Max Robinson! Leaving us all behind to say we remember you from way back."

I giggle at him insulting the ABC TV journalist.

Sometimes he sounds like a dad that loves me. At times I feel I love him more than I hate him. My extreme ambivalence is useful, I think; a trick that might come in handy someday.

Lilliputian Daycare is an easy five minutes away. The sun beams bright and what's left of the big snow looks plasticized. The wet and dirty street is stalled with little people being dropped off. We double-park and I run the Twins into their miniature, happy world. They love to sprint across the crunchy snow. We kiss goodbye and I say hello to big-cheeked Ms. Bringle. She's one of the staff, she *oohs* and *awws* and *ouches* over my knots and bruises. She offers all kinds of makeup tips, thinking nothing of a boy in makeup. I wonder if she's a black-eye-behind-sunglasses lady.

Dad seems impatient waiting for me, like he's been simmering on thoughts that are now ready to plate. I'm barely in the car when he starts. "Listen up, Cliffy-boy, this is important. I was thinking about what the Doc said about your PTSD. Now, you being back at school is a good thing, especially knowing how bad you want it, but you might have moments when it ain't so good and you feel like you're losing it. Now, for me, the hardest part of losing it is when things get all twisted and I don't know where I am or what I'm doing, so I carry something to remind me. It ain't a good luck charm, I think it's called a talisman or a touchstone or some shit like that. Sounds stupid but a vet friend of mine with similar 'Nam issues suggested it, and it works. Whatever your thing is, make sure it's invested with all kinds of meaning, so that when you look at it, you snap out of whatever's happening. Maybe it don't work for everybody, but I swear it works for me. Sometimes it stabs me like a damn switchblade, and hurts like one, too."

His hand opens and cups a pink diaper pin. He says, "I don't want to fuck up anything that's got to do with the babies, and when I see the pin it pricks my brain, telling me I got to deal with them. The pink color reminds me of our only babygirl. You see how practical it is?"

Already I know this is BS. I can cite instances where his diaper pin failed the Twins. But I guess other factors matter, too. Like the degree of craziness, what extra drugs are sloshing in the bloodstream. Also, a diaper pin that deems some of his kids worthy, while ignoring the rest as unworthy, sucks.

"Cool, Dad." I thank him for showing me his secret superpower, which I dub the PRICK.

We're at the mouth of my school's driveway. My hand is on the door handle. Dad reaches across and squeezes my shoulder. He says, "You're gonna be fine. You call home if there's a problem, and your Daddy will come get you."

I'm touched by his *your Daddy* promise—his strange way of referring to himself that used to make me think he wasn't my real father. I'm also touched that his diaper pin seems to have pricked him about me. I won't put him to the test. He'll probably be too busy between some woman's thighs to care. It's the thought that counts.

»»»

I run, feeling the push of the late January wind like a small hand at my back. On the field the snow crunches and breaks like Saltines. I leave the field to run along the shoulder of the slick driveway. I'm just five minutes late. I press upstairs and follow shiny floors and creamy halls, going straight to Anatomy & Physiology. I acknowledge the teacher but keep my head down. I take the same seat I occupied last semester. I guess she saved it for me.

Thanks to my friends, I'm up to speed on the reading. At times my brain flickers, like lights before a power failure. I feel fine, physically, until I realize I can't keep up. Plus, I don't know what we're talking about. Seconds pass when I can't even understand speech. The hour drains my patience and confidence. I think about diaper pin Dad rolling up in the Marquis to rescue me, though I know better than to depend on him.

Mrs. Johnson signals me to stay after class. She carries the Lord with her everywhere and prays for everybody. I meet her at her desk. I watch a noodle of oily hair sneak out from behind her ear. It swings over her glasses before being speared by a glinting bobby pin in a fast hand. She says, "Good to have you back, Mr. Douglas. You've been through it, I see, but you're on the mend. Your father mentioned that the police are involved in your case. Any progress?"

"Nothing that I know of. And maybe there won't be, since I've got amnesia. I learned a lesson, isn't that the most important part?"

"Whatever lesson you learned, Mr. Douglas, remember justice is also important, in this life or the next. It's the only answer to crime and the reason we have the law. From what your father told me, you are blameless."

Lying to a Jehovah's Witness is so hard. "Oh yes Ma'am, that's true. I mean, if I had waited until morning to get my bike maybe from that gas station, I wouldn't have this ectoplasm lump in the middle of my forehead . . . maybe I was tempting fate or something, I don't know."

"Mr. Douglas, please do not succumb to guilt, doubt, and thinking you deserve to be attacked. I remind you your injury isn't an ectoplasmic port in your head for the supernatural, or the mark of a sinner, or a scarlet letter. Rather, it is a hematoma, a medical issue to be fixed by nature or by medical intervention."

A sudden snarling voice in my head: *Fuck You! I can call my hematoma whatever the fuck I want*! She asks if I got my college materials in, and I nod yes but the snarling voice speaks again: *No, bible bitch, I didn't apply to your alma mater, and I ain't going to a historically black college, fuck that*!

She says, "Take care, Mr. Douglas, and don't overdo it. Give yourself time to get in the flow again. If you need a ride home, let me know."

I thank her and take off for the bathroom. Even now, I refuse to think Dr. Fang Fang was right. I splash cold water on my face and hide in a stall, breaking for lit. class just as the bell rings.

Same diminished listening and understanding as before. This time exhaustion makes my confusion even worse. I'm thinking about leaving school during the next bell between class, then I see friends at the lockers. Not just APer's, but friends waiting to see *me*. I put on my I'm Okay face and answer their questions. I enjoy the haiku catch-ups the most, especially Black Bruce's family funeral in Detroit, Black Tasha's used Ford Pinto Christmas present, White Annie's Christmas in Paris, and White Gary's weekend camping in Red River Gorge in Kentucky. Best of all is seeing Blair. He's got a surprise souvenir to show and tell of his holiday in Las Vegas: a photo of a showgirl striking a high kick pose in sparkly feathers. He doesn't lie, but I find it hard to believe he fucked her.

Now I have faith I can last the day. I stick around for another period with the same aggravating outcome. This time I bargain with myself; I'm three classes down with two classes to go. It works. By fourth period I have three offers for a ride home. This is great, but now I'm determined to manage on my own. I rush from the main building after fifth bell. I take my usual route, passing the long bike rack I would normally lock my Schwinn to. Just thinking about the psycho motherfucker having it sets me off. A rush of anger, despair, and confusion follows me to the bus stop. I wait long minutes in the damp cold before climbing aboard a crowded bus. I sort through the scarecrow faces of the grizzled and the hyena laughter of the young. I cling to a pole to stay upright through the jostling stops and starts. Exhaustion orders my body around. I rush to the first available seat. The last thing I remember before nodding off is thinking that I should walk by the gas station. I wake up from a deep, slobbering snooze. I've overshot home by a couple of miles.

I'm tired enough that I should wait for the next bus back. Daylight savings is months from giving us more light. The cold makes a miserable walk home.

»»»

I feel I am more like my old self again. I wake up confident I can breeze through the day. The mirror shows that the old me is just below the crusty healing. The hematoma has flattened into a watermark shaped like Cuba. My eyebrows line up and act like twins. The bruised cheek now shows the depth of my dimple, and the head laceration nestles in the down of new hair. It may be my imagination, but since the choke marks faded there's no catch in my breath. I can even hoist both Twins to their highchairs at the same time.

I'm serving them a bowl of the usual when the phone rings. I assume it's Mom, but it's Chip. The line is full of clicking sounds that scissor his words into pieces. Then I hear, "Sorry, our party line connection sucks. I'm trying to say that I'm coming to Clifton so you can check the bats before I unload them on PMF, who's back in town; I Columboed."

Flatfooted me would know this if I had gone by L.L. gas station last night!

I decode that Chip's revenge plan is underway and tell him I'll be home by 5:30. He'll confirm by then. I hear more clicks before we hang up, then Dad's descent down the groaning stairs. He swaggers into the kitchen saying, "Boy, you ready, I got an appointment to make. Was that your friend Chip on the line?"

I say "Yeah," and then he asks why Chip's coming from Wilmington, a full hour away. I realize Dad's probably responsible for the clicking on the line. I also realize he's interrogating me, probably at the urging of Detective Moneymaker. I spin out an answer, "Chip's checking out a course he wants to take at UC." Dad says, "First you said he's going to Cornell, and then you two visited Ohio State for the weekend, and now you say he's going to UC." I say, "Dad, sorry to confuse you. UC is for summer school. He's waiting to hear from Cornell and U of M/Ann Arbor, just like I'm waiting to hear from UCLA. Ohio State is his fallback. And it's mine, too." Then he says, "Unloading bats?" I say, "Chip is selling his baseball bats and getting new ones."

Dad says, "Cliffy-boy, I like that you surround yourself with smart friends. You know what they say, you're only as smart as the company you keep. Right?"

»»»

Before the diagnosis, before the therapy, before the Lithium, before the diaper pin, I recall him once shouting at me, *Boy, you ain't shit and you ain't ever gonna be shit.*

"Right, I want to be somebody," I say. I show off my good boy smile. I show off for a dad that works in a bakery. Keebler's Cookies. That's what he does. Five days a week or more. Eight hours a day or more. Dusted in flour. A hot cookie.

Now I'm freeing the Twins from their highchairs. The boy twin freaks out over pooping his pants. Dad wants me to let the Lilliputian Daycare ladies clean up the mess. He carries the girl down to the car. I carry the boy to the den bathroom for a quick diaper tidy-up.

Behind the wheel and ready, Dad's babbling about Cincinnati Tech. He wants to know what I know about it, which is basically nothing.

He says, "I got an appointment there this morning. I'm hoping to get a Machine Maintenance Certificate. The bossman at work personally encouraged me. With the certificate, I can get promoted and make a lot more than the chump change they pay me now."

He tells me he's nervous, that it's been so long since he set foot in a classroom. He tells me he skipped classes all the time in high school and still got a diploma and passing grades. I listen because I'm a good listener—everyone says so. He goes on about what he calls shop math: hydraulics, pneumatics, the stuff of industrial bakery infrastructure.

Without it, Keebler's Cookies wouldn't need him.

I don't know what he's talking about. I pass in and out of listening. I'm thinking about the psycho motherfucker on the loose and Chip's scheme. I feel free running the Twins into Lilliputian Daycare. I think I should keep running. Instead, I return to the car. Dad picks up where he left off. I'm lost in a rush of thoughts about bats and beatdowns when I see the L.L. The Marquis wobbles onto the lot. Dad says, "Run in and get me a pack of Kools. No Lites or 100s, just regular damn Kools."

I stare at the dollar in his hand and the callous fingers pinching it. This is the ask I can't refuse, though I think up a handful of excuses anyway. It feels like slow motion when I climb from the car. The odor of gas wafts over from the pumps. The multi-paned garage door is fully open. Two cars levitate with their grimy privates exposed. I see the fringe of an afro. It's the psycho motherfucker's mane squeezed into a skullcap.

I rush inside the gas station store. The white attendant is the same one that told me the psycho motherfucker was living at the Doris Day House. He greets me in a way that shows he doesn't recognize me or my voice. I ask for regular Kools. We stare at each other. I say the Kools are for my dad, and point to the Marquis idling outside, engulfed in exhaust. His arms fly upward as if for a chin-up bar. They return empty-handed. He looks me over again and says the Kools are in the stockroom. I have to wait, it'll be a couple of minutes. I don't want to wait even a second, but returning to the car empty-handed will mean a second trip for another brand. I nod that I can wait, and the attendant lifts the keys from the cash register. He disappears into the storage room. I could fill my pockets with gum and candies. Somehow, he knows I wouldn't.

My eyes are drawn to the door into the garage—and into memory. I can almost hear the psycho motherfucker, he's explaining to me the problem with the gears job and pointing to my bicycle's chain. I remember everything. The lights of the garage are off, he's holding a portable utility light. We are standing close in the dark, so close I feel somehow touched by his words, but like tiny shockwaves. He clips the light onto a rolling toolbox, I think he wants to show something else. Then he pulls me into a bear hug, he laughs like we are bear-hugging friends. I pull away from him, though not angrily; I'm more confused—what's going on? All is clear when he pulls my hand onto his crotch. He says, "You like a real man?" and then rests his other hand on my shoulder. I try to step back, but the arm spring loads into a chokehold. "Hey, man, let me go . . . I need to get my bike and go home." I feel myself shifting from standing side to side to his hold tightening from behind me, his dick stiffening against me. We are moving. I notice the wrench on top of the toolbox cabinet, a fire exit just behind the elevated cars. "Buster, man, you're hurting me," I'm shouting into my own compressed throat, my feet treading just above the ground. Screaming produces the same muffled effect. I kick backward, hitting him several times; he shuffles his legs side to side. Then he lets me go and I drop to floor, gasping for breath, desperate for something to grab—how can I get to the door? Then comes a sharp, bright, dazzling pain. I think I've been struck by lightning. From the floor, I see him staring down at me like Zeus.

"Punk ass bitch."

»»»

The gas station attendant says, "Lucky you, there's a promotion, it's two packs for a dollar. Well, we always have a promotion. A different brand every time."

Lucky's not the word, but I agree I am lucky, as in lucky to be alive—and not to be sleeping under bridges, turning tricks. Lucky to have a hot, smart, and funny boyfriend, nevermind aggravating tendencies. Right now, I'm lucky to be here with Dad, Dad sitting in a two-door burgundy Marquis brougham just outside the door. The psycho motherfucker is lucky, too. I could end his future in an instant. Tell Dad the justice he wants for me is fifty feet away, pumping gas while I'm buying his Kools.

I focus on fishing my pockets for the sales tax. I grab the cigarettes and rush to the car. Dad says, "Boy, what the hell took so long? You sweating like a pig, and it's cold out. Don't you be coming down with no swine flu. That's the last thing we need."

We pull away in a wide arc that puts us where the psycho motherfucker is gassing up a car. I grip the door handle; I slump into the seat. Dad lets the window down and waves, "My man, good to see you," he says. I poke my head up and catch the motherfucker waving back. Dad says to me, "That nigga just got out. He's been locked up downtown since last week, and he ain't even been out of prison for about five or six months."

But all I hear is Dad's *My man*. His man? I didn't even know they knew each other. We come here to gas up sometimes, in the rare emergency, once or twice. Dad knowing him makes me feel sick. I think about Punch, Punch running away because everybody on his poor reservation knew everything about him. No escape. Dad drops me off, but I don't feel better. Cincinnati is closing in on me.

I sit through five classes and claim laryngitis when called upon. The only questions I want to address are the ones that bumper car in my head. Why would the motherfucker do what he did to me? I've been a bullied kid since I could talk, since I could walk. Talking and walking marked me as a sissy target. Everything about junior high was war. Kids threw books at teachers. Beat each other with locks and chains. Burned the principal's car in the school parking lot. Turned a VW Beetle on its side. Every day, a new horror. I dreamed of injuries beyond black eyes and bruises. I dreamed of a broken arm, a broken leg, my teeth knocked out.

I wanted to be ugly enough to be left alone.

I survive the school day angrier with each class bell. Chip's right, taking up bats is our right. I know I can't wield a bat while shaking in my bones. I tell myself not to be a coward. I want bruises as big as plums on the psycho motherfucker's face. I want him maimed and lame with fear. I want him to see the swinging bat that cracks his skull.

Soon as I'm home, I make an obliged pass to the den. Mom is on the phone. With a smile and a wave, I detour upstairs. I bring the phone into my room and wait until the line is free, imagining Chip's bat swinging like a samurai sword. Finally, I call the gas station. I go mute at the sound of the motherfucker's voice. He gives the L.L. Garage spiel. I don't hang up, I breathe into the receiver. Then I hear, "Bitch-ass punk, I know who this fucking is. Stop fucking calling here, or I'll finish your ass off next time."

I'm afraid, until I'm not. How could he know it's me calling? What if he thinks he's talking to some other boy? Maybe one of the boys Detective Moneymaker mentioned. A boy like me with fantasies of maiming and torturing and taunting him with phone calls. I imagine each of us wrecked boys dreaming his own revenge plot. It would be something if we teamed up to take down the psycho motherfucker.

At 10:00 p.m. the weekday long distance call rates drop. Chip rings with the news his car broke down. It happened near Kenwood, and the transmission's shot. He's sorry things couldn't work out. We're both aware of the crackling party line. We save up the details we cannot share. We are silent.

Fingers crossed for Sunday, hopefully—we both say it in our own way. Though I guess we both know it's not happening.

»»»

I don't want Mom to know I'm home. I sneak in through the garage. In the basement I swap out my school get-up for sweats and sneakers. I leave the way I came, and she's none the wiser. I'm not in the mood to run in circles on the track. Though the parkway is best when traffic's light, I take my chances and go there for the long straightaways. It's six-point-five miles to the downtown public library and back, and there are sidewalks the whole way. Plus, the parkway is flat from beginning to end, tracing the buttcrack of two of Cincinnati's many large hills.

I ease my way into a slow jog. One foot at a time, the kinks and squeaks in my knees and ankles go quiet. I run with the traffic flowing at this hour. The sky brightens and the clouds drift in an easterly direction. The tree lawn between the sidewalk and road grows and shrinks the farther I go. I speed up as the shrinking brings the vehicles closer, at one point so close there's only thin air between me and metal. It's like riding the curb, and I realize I could be punched or clipped by a suddenly swinging door. I reach a turn that climbs uphill to the University of Cincinnati campus. An ambulance shouts from that direction, a warning sign. I see the traffic clog ahead and decide to turn back. Out of habit I cross at the intersection to run with the traffic. I notice a car filled with Evanston junior high-age assholes. I can't make anyone out, but it doesn't matter. I'm already stirred up, they might as well be anybody who has ever looked at me the wrong way. I duck into the nearest shrubs and wait until they've passed. I tighten my hoodie for better cover and pick up my pace. Near the I-71 underpass, I hear an engine gunning. I look over my shoulder just as the car grinds past me, down the parkway out of sight. Now I run against the traffic. I don't stop until I'm at my front door.

I dream I am somewhere I shouldn't be, though I've been to this place before. I recall tall steps and a peeling, wizened house perched on a steep hill. The steps are concrete and wooden and seem mossy in places; cracked and broken, shoddily installed. At the foot of the stairs is a small gate like a turnstile. In my dream, I'm about to go through. Then I hear Dad's nasal, phlegmy morning voice shouting.

"Boy, get up, it's almost eight and the Twins ain't even dressed."

His urgency defibrillates me into the right now. I skip the me part of the morning routine to focus on them. In less than ten minutes, the Twins are cleaned and dressed. I'm coaxing them into coats with Dad looming over us. He isn't angry but amused I'm sockless and shoeless. He is convinced I was hostage to PTSD sleep. He says PTSD sleep is like a fever dream—meaning I was delirious. I haven't said a word about my dream. He insists those boys that beat me up will star in my sleep every night; doing the right thing by putting them behind bars is the only way to stop them. "They still might mind-fuck you up, but at least you'll have justice."

I don't understand him. I don't care. I'm just glad my Scotch-lip-tape came off before he woke me up.

Right now, justice is permission to grab socks, shoes, and my backpack. Breakfast is a glob of toothpaste before we rush out the door. We are fifteen minutes late for Lilliputians and nearing twenty minutes for my school. Once there I'm embarrassed and overdo the model student act. That's when I act like I know more than everybody else and sound like I'm high on speed, which I'm not.

It takes three periods before I slow down to normal speech. I still don't have an attention span. My mind drifts back to my dream. There's now a small yard standing between me and the wrinkled house on the steep hill. The gate is now a nappy hedge low enough to hop over. I look up, and from the sky comes a pair of feet climbing downstairs. They are like puppet feet but without strings or a master. Brown ankles, shins, and calves; long, lean legs.

Bright red shorts and brown arms dangle from a grimy T-shirt. The head topping the thick neck isn't the motherfucker exactly, but an earlier version I know as Buster. Buster who plucked me from junior high bullies. He seems happy to see me. He lowers himself into a crouch, then sits on the step licking his lips. He says, "Hey, long time. Cliffy, right? See, I ain't forget, I remember those cute dimples you got." His hand reaches out from between his legs to shake mine. He says, "You live around here?" and I pull my hand away and tell him I live near the Coca-Cola Company. He says, "You on your way home from school?" and I say I am. And he says, "So you wanna come in, we can play cards or play Monopoly, we can have a little drink, I got a Rum & Coke, I even got some smoke if you want, just me and you, ain't nobody home? Come on, it'll be fun."

I tell him my mom is waiting, but he says I should come on. His legs open wider like swinging doors. The space between the thin fabric of his shorts and his leg begins to expand. His dick turtles its way out, thickening and lengthening into a python, until it's cut off by his legs squeezing together. He smiles, opens his legs again and says, "See what you did! You wanna touch it," and I say nothing, and then he laughs, he says "It won't hurt. It's just excited to see you cuz I got a lotta love for you, babyboy." I say, "Really?" and I want to tell him that nobody loves me. And he says, "Really, baby, I always got love for you. You 'member what I did for you? Well, you owe me some love back, don't you?" I say, "Yeah, I do owe you, you saved my life, but I have to go home, my mom's expecting me." He says "Come on"—and he holds my arm and pulls me into the hedge, and I'm between his tall knees. "Come on, it'll be fun," he says, bunching his lips and kissing my cheek. Nobody kisses me but Mom, and I like to be kissed, I have been kissed before, I have even French kissed before. I've sucked a dick. Been fucked by one. Fucked a butt, too. Nothing virginal about me; still, I feel out of bounds in a flirty game that confuses and scares me. "Come on," he says, now standing up, as tall as the steps are high, his shorts tented out and pointing east. He pulls me by the hand, up up up. I'm excited that he likes me because no boy likes me that way anymore. Except he isn't a boy, he's a grown man. A grown man still in junior high school. Like he is reading my mind, he says, "You wanna be my babyboy?" I want to say *Yes, I want to be your babyboy*, but now I see a woman at the top of the steps. She stares down at us, shouting at him: "Boy, get your sorry black ass in this house right now! How many times you got to be told to stay away from these wicked boys . . . And you, you nasty thing, take your yella ass outta here and don't you ever come back!"

He looks up at her, then back at me, and says, "I'mma kill that bitch."

I hear Mom's voice telling me to run. I break from his hold and the mean eyes of the woman cursing us. I leap to the ground and run fast. But not fast or far enough to forget. Nobody has ever fought for me. And nobody wants me like he does. For days, weeks, and months, as scared as I was, I looked for him on every street corner to tell him that. The wait would be seasons and years.

The dream that isn't a dream. The truth that the dream tells must mean I'm the reason he chose me. It happened long ago. That day he, a bully, saved me from the bullies. That day he, a grown man of nineteen, claimed me as his babyboy. Now, the young guy that I am knows better, yet still that motherfucker trapped me in his spider web.

»»»

A note peeks from the bottom of my locker. I pull the strip of paper out to learn Blair wants us to meet up. He says it's super important, otherwise he'll call me later tonight. It's probably about the Las Vegas showgirl. He isn't the kind of guy to knock a girl up. Definitely not the kind to elope. But I realize, anything's possible.

A Las Vegas showgirl being with him in the first place is proof. That's assuming he hasn't made the whole thing up. but that's not like him either.

On my way to him, a worried excitement replaces the feeling that I'm circling the suckhole. I reach him in the parking lot as he's getting into his car. Sweaty, he says, "Sorry, I'm in a rush as usual, but I had to talk to you. Fuck, Cliffy, I saw your bike at the L.L., you know, that gas station at the corner of Montgomery and Dauner. I know you remember Buster from Sawyer, he's that eighteen-year-old doofus stuck in seventh grade everybody was terrified of, remember, I told you he was out of prison, that guy. So, I was there this morning picking up my mom's car. I'm standing just outside the garage, and as he's rolling the car out, I see this bright yellow Schwinn in the back corner of the garage. And I'm like, wow, that's Cliffy's bike. So, I tell him it belongs to you and yours was stolen. So, then this doofus had the nerve to claim he doesn't remember you. And he said that some *faggot* dropped it off and never came back, and he'd know the *faggot* if he saw him again."

"That lying psycho motherfucker. I left it with him before Christmas break . . . and, and I went to get it back, but . . ."

I realize I have tripped myself up. Blair is sharp, sharper than I am.

"Okay, Cliffy, my head's spinning. I don't know what's going on here but let's talk later. I know you want your bike. Just please, call the cops and let them deal with him. That guy will hurt you. Seriously, even back when we were at Sawyer, the sicko way he looked at you, it creeped me out."

"What do you mean, the sicko way he looked at me?"

I want to say it wasn't sicko, it was a crush. He had a crush on me. He wanted to protect me.

Blair says, "He looked at you like, if you were a bird he'd rip your wings off and stuff 'em down your throat. Maybe that's extreme, but I've always had a bad feeling about him. Gotta go, I'll call you later."

That isn't what he would do. This I know for sure. And yet, he would have killed me just to dick me.

I can't believe I'm so stupid. The shakes begin as I watch Blair leave the parking lot. Cursing, stomping, and crying take hold of me, and I hear "Mr. Douglas, Mr. Douglas . . ." Hands clamp onto my arms, and I hear myself shouting, "Take your fucking hands off me." I hear, "Mr. Douglas, it's Mrs. Johnson, your Anatomy & Physiology teacher."

I break free of her. She either collides into me or I knock her sideways. She hits the ground as I take off through the parking lot. I run onto the practice field, a soupy tundra of melting snow. I crash before reaching the street. My face stings from the wet cold, and my glasses are splashed and steamed up. I hide in the hood of my sweatshirt for warmth. The shortest way home is also the most visible—an almost straight line down a long stretch of my street, door to door. I run the miles like I would in a track meet. I lock the front door behind me. I realize then that maybe it's good Blair knows. Maybe I need to tell someone. He's the right person.

There's never enough hoodie to hide from Mom. She shouts for me to come to her. I don't want her waddling after me. I obey and say the usual about my school day. The Twins watch from the playpen. I wonder if I'll be around to see them grow up.

Mom says, "I've been thinking about what you said about Doris Day's husband beating her up. I appreciate that you showed me her book. You're old enough and smart enough that you'll understand what I'm saying. See, a man thinks he can do anything he wants to a woman, cuz that's the way society and the law works, and it don't matter how famous she is. At least Doris Day got the money to get out of her abusive situation. Unlike most of us women. What I'm trying to say is, she probably wrote that book you read for the money and because she's famous, but she probably also wrote it so ladies everywhere gonna know how men get new on you, how suddenly they're beating on you and you ain't done nothing for them to be beating on you, and it don't matter who you are. But you know, most women know that cuz they saw their mom go through it. My daddy never hit my mom like that, but you know what I mean. It takes courage to tell your business like Doris Day did, to put yourself out there for everybody to feel your shame. A lot of us women can relate—at some point, usually when you think the man's gonna kill you, we all have called the cops on our man."

I'm present enough to really hear what she's saying. I snap, "Maybe Doris Day's also saying you don't have to put up with Dad's crap."

"Maybe she is, but most women know that already, they just too scared to do anything about it."

"Why would any woman put up with a man like that?"

"You ain't a woman so you wouldn't understand. When you got kids, you put up with a lot."

"Speaking as one of the kids, I say you didn't do anything for us by hitching up with him. You did it for you. That's why you put up with his stuff."

"Think what you want, but you'll see what'll happen when I reach my limit."

"Oo, you gonna kill him? Huh?"

"I pray it never comes to that. I brought Doris Day up because I think she gotta message for you, too. Some problems are bigger than you. You gotta stop protecting whoever you protecting, sweetie, before it all backfires on you."

"All of y'all keep saying that. I'm not protecting anybody who would beat me up."

"The Detective don't believe you, and your father don't believe you, and I don't believe it either."

For all kinds of reasons, I know I should protest louder. I should even get angry at being set up like this.

The best I can do is an eyeroll and a huffy retreat.

»»»

A relay race I'd remembered perfectly, I now remember differently. Last season we competed against the number one team in our league. I'd been brooding over the coach's last-minute switch-up. Our star runner was home sick, and I now had to run in the first leg of the 200-meter race. First leg is always reserved for the fastest runner, not the third-fastest. In the fifth lane, I lowered myself into the start block, hunched over, head down, butt up. Here's where memory mind-fucks me. In memory, I'm always focusing on my takeoff. But now, out of nowhere, I remember feeling naked and exposed. Nothing else is different. The buzzer, the blastoff, the burn through the turn, my handoff to my teammate. Being mere molecules behind the competition in the next lane. I watched the race finish while shortcutting across the football field. I remember throwing my hands up in disappointment and frustration. I remember thinking we lost because the competition was better. But now I think we lost because of me—though it isn't true. At the beginning of the meet, I think I remember looking up in the bleachers. I remember seeing a man tucked behind a beard, skull cap, and sunglasses. It had to be the motherfucker, jinxing me.

But he was in prison then. So, why do I think—I know—he was there stalking me?

I call Dr. Fang Fang. I'm told she isn't available and to leave a message. I tell her I worry my memory is damaged. I end by saying I'm sick and to please call me back. I'm standing at one of three school payphones, completely convinced the doctor will return my call. Other kids are waiting, but I ignore them. The cold creeps into my bones. I wait for her through fourth and fifth bells. No response. I go home agitated.

"Cliffy," Mom says, "that doctor says it's too soon for you to be back at school."

"I'm not staying home."

"She told you, still you and your father act like y'all know more than the doctor."

"I called her about my memory, that's all."

"She gave you her answer. And she told you already that she can't return your calls because you are a minor and to stop calling."

"I've only called her twice. And what about my memory problems?"

"Talk to your father."

»»»

Chip. A last-minute something always puts the chill on Fuck Sunday. TV news is warning of more record-breaking snow. 1977 epically shatters winter records. Personal ones, too.

Horny as I am, desperate even, I pull the hall phone into my room to wait. When he does call, we hear the ubiquitous crackle and speak in a Morse code of breaths and pauses. I bring up the Arctic cold coming our way, trying to sound like a good sport.

"Looks like another no-fun Sunday for us. Oh well."

"Out here they're saying the worst is coming later today, north of us, and maybe only sideswiping the region. So, the question is, Are you worth the risk? Yes. No. Maybe."

"No, I'm not worth it, and I'm sorry all the driving's always on you."

"Shut up with that! Let's just move up the time. I'm ready to go now, soon as I hang up. See you in an hour, around noon at the latest? Unless you really want to cancel?"

“Let me think about it . . . OK, I’ve thought about it, let’s do it.”

I’m so excited I race to be ready, imagining getting off in broad daylight. His car’s poor heat and our lusty breathing will steam the windows, hiding our humping in the backseat. Bare and bony trees stand between our favorite make out spot and a busy road and snowy hillside. A risk worth the reward.

I’m so excited I tell Mom I’m going with Chip and lie we are hanging out with Kings Island friends. “You and Chip,” she says as if wanting to say more. She then complains about my thin jacket, a proxy for my missing coat, gloves, and hat. “You boys be careful,” she says before letting me go.

I’m so excited. I see his car pull to the curb and run out into the flurries. “Hey,” I say. “Hey,” he says, and we kiss behind the steamy, smeared windows. He turns up the volume, and we sing along with his favorite musical soundtrack spooling on the dashboard’s 8-track cassette player:

Oh, you, pretty Chitty Bang Bang,
Chitty Chitty Bang Bang
We love you.
And in
Chitty Chitty Bang Bang
Chitty Chitty Bang Bang
What we’ll do.
Near, far, in our motor car
Oh! What a happy time we’ll spend
Bang Bang Chitty Chitty Bang Bang
Our fine four fendered friend.
Bang Bang Chitty Chitty Bang Bang
Our fine four-fendered friend

I laugh, he laughs, we laugh together, and suddenly it’s summer love at Kings Island again. Sometimes we break into another chorus. It always feels like Popeye and Olive Oyl are there.

And Snoopy and Toodles are there. And slides and rollercoasters and Ferris wheels are there. What fun it is, what fun we had, our sweet summer that never ends. If only love could stay this way, forever and ever.

The reality is my singing sucks, so I tuck behind Chip's fine voice. We're driving up my street, and I don't care where or what we are singing. Chip's smile of delight turns into a frown of worry. He dials the music down as he swings the car to the curb. A red light ahead dangles above a crossroad. I know Chip knows where we are. Even which street goes where. We don't speak of the psycho motherfucker until he says, "Okay, Cliff, so what's it gonna be, we can have a good time, or we can do what we talked about, I have the bats. Whatever you want to do, it's up to you, it's not like there's an expiration date on getting even. Really, whenever is fine, you decide."

"Well, OK, maybe just to see if he's there. Is that OK?" I ask.

"Yeah, of course, I mean I do want to, but only if you do. I'm ready just in case, but just because I brought them doesn't mean we have to use them."

"No, let's not then, I don't want to, I don't want to fight now. It's Fuck Sunday."

"Sure. Let's not then. We'll deal with him next time, I'll keep the bats in the car. Let's just have fun today."

Surprise! He then tells me his friend Dahlia is having her annual sledding party. There's a ski slope behind her house, he says, "It's epic—steep and long enough that you can get a speed rush if you're stoned, which I was at her party last winter."

I say, "Yes, let's go," and he says, "Cool. Maybe we can find a bathroom for a quickie?" So I say, "Let's do it, I'm like a sex maniac after all these fuckless days and weeks."

He reaches over the seat, squeezes my crotch, and says, "You really doubted we would get together today, didn't you? I think you even wanted me to cancel. But you underestimate how much I want to fuck your brains out."

"I mean, I was a little worried you might be worried about how I look."

"Like I'm that superficial? We're boyfriends, aren't we?"

"Yeah, of course, but honestly, Chip, for me, as long as we're hanging out together, I really don't care what we do. I missed you."

"Except you do care what we do, and what we don't do. Let's be real," he says, petting my leg. Suddenly his mood, bearing sharp teeth, is a third, snippy passenger in the car. I say, "You're right, I do care. As much as you care." He says, "I care a lot."

I feel like he's been stewing over the psycho motherfucker all along. Anything I say short of attack will make it worse. But then he starts venting about his dad's new woman. His new nickname for her is Uncola, for her Pepsi addiction. He says, "I knew the second I laid eyes on her that she—Wanda Purple, that's her name . . . what kind of name is that?—would move in like an infestation. First it was scrambled eggs—she puts in so much milk, you need a straw to slurp the slop up. Then came the Pop Tarts, and now she's telling me to clean up the bathroom. Who does this emaciated hairball think she is?"

I'm just happy not to be critiqued. I giggle, though I worry about his anger. That between him and his father are swinging fists. That's what I know, living in a domestic war zone since my Dad's return. Prescription medications are the only reason the ceasefire holds. Not love, apologies, promises, or the turning over of a new leaf. I don't know Chip's dad at all. But what I suspect about Chip is that he's unforgiving once betrayed.

I don't like conflict. I can't see a reason for him to blow his life up. Better to ease than escalate the tension. I remind him we're just a few months from graduation. Then summer work and fun and the freedom of college. He says, "Cliffy, tell me something I don't know. The number of months and seasons aren't the point. The point is my mom is being erased, and he's rubbing it in my face, which may be his point in the first fuckin' place."

»»»

I don't want to become the dartboard to his frustration. I decide just to listen, like the good boyfriend I am. I squeeze his arm at the right moments; I sigh at the right moments, too. We're speeding eastward along I-71 amid light flurries. The traffic enters into a pretzel of interstate and expressway. Surprise traffic congestion stretches out and slows us down. I'm distracted by his maneuvering the stick shift and clutch; the car is his puppet. He will teach me to drive when I have my learner's permit.

Clouds pile like couch cushions. Snowflakes switch between rushing and floating. The congestion clears and the car winds up to fourth gear. Chip's mood stays down-shifted, and I am glad.

He says, "I know you're right. I just need to be patient, then get the fuck out. It's better to focus on the countdown. Drawing X's through the days on my calendar. Isn't that what you do?"

"Yes. Well, not literally, but yes. Deep breaths and a lot of counting the days."

"I feel a little better already, just you being here for me. I'm so glad we're together. Thanks, babe."

Love is suddenly gentle and kind.

His wandering hand lands on my crotch again. What we need is the full, naked get-down. Honestly, I can't remember life before fucking. Its takeover of my soul is complete. Even phone sex, which I don't love, turns me on. He loves it enough for both of us.

Now he wants my face in his crotch. A blowjob while speeding on the Norwood Lateral would be a first. Chip's carnal grammar is vivid and vulgar, mostly with primate oohs and aahs. He reaches for my head and says, "Come on and warm me up for the big sled ride." I say, "In case you haven't noticed we're in a snow globe. I can barely see beyond the windshield." He says, "Just keep your eyes on the big prize."

Together, we have looked at *BlueBoy*, the gay version of *Playboy*. The main headline is always dick size, so I joke about ending up impaled on Chip's nine-inch stick shift. He finds this funny; we laugh, we always have fun together. Which is why what the psycho motherfucker did is so difficult. He stole from us. We can't joke, we can't laugh. We cry. I feel we are angry with each other in a way we don't understand. I'm going crazy. And so is he, my true love.

»»»

Ahead, another interstate pretzels in new directions. Suddenly the couch clouds expel all their stuffing in a heavy snowfall. The windshield wipers struggle to keep up. I swipe the fogged window with my sleeve and a sign for Winton Hills appears; we exit into farmland. Through the snow I see large stylish houses and pretty horses. Chip is sure we are nearly there. The curling road plunges into a valley then vaults to a hilltop. He points to our destination, a house barely visible in the snowy fog. Cars like bracelet charms along the road's narrow shoulders.

Chip says that last year's snowy party ended with cars sliding and crashing downhill in a pile-up. We park where we are on the road's shoulder, in the valley. We agree to hang out for an hour or two. We are excited by a pair of sledders toppling downhill; the wind marbles their shrieks and laughter. We hold hands, then swing our hands back and forth. It's like stick-shifting as we climb the steep road. Chip says sledding makes him feel like a kid again. I only remember sledding as cold.

He's so freely queer at times that I've become more freely queer. I'm not afraid of holding hands now because I know the kind of people we'll be among. The kind of people who Kings

Island anoints as stewards of joy and fun. We hear their chatter and laughter some fifty yards away, and then at the hilltop where they're louder and even happier. The party is inside a rich man's car garage. It's big enough for many more guests than the thirty or so we see. We are winded, sweaty, and dusting snow off each other when we hear Dahlia calling for us—her favorite boy lovebirds, she says.

We kiss her hello, beautiful Dahlia. Her eyes are like looking at the earth from the moon. We love her pink ski-bunny getup, her rabbit ears and whiskers. We laugh when she tells us she's hopping mad at her cunt sister for bailing on her—it's hard to see anger on such bright, shiny red lips. She leads us to the new batch of hot chocolate and confides that her secret recipe kicks with vodka, Kahlua liqueur. There's a dash of the fieriest jalapeño pepper she could find this far north of Tijuana. Chip claims what she served last year had been spiked with a narcotic. She doesn't deny it, her bunny tail sashaying.

We queue for the last of the current batch. A wood-burning stove beams warmth throughout the space, even with the garage door open. A couple of guests wear sweaters, shirts, and shorts. Most in the small crowd wear hoodies or ski jackets. For some reason I picture my coat. I see it piled on the floor of the gas station.

For every person I know, Chip knows at least five. His Kings Island job had been to roam the park as Huckleberry Hound; he first met Dahlia as Cindy Bear. Chip says they—plus some of the other Hanna-Barbera cartoon characters—were, occasionally, stoned. Chip is super friendly when he's buzzed, but who isn't? Right now, we aren't stoned as much as overstimulated. Neither of us had more than cereal early this morning. Chip waves, hugs, and introduces me to his friends. Three are gay, and two are coupled off like us. I feel safe.

A half hour passes, and the crowd nearly doubles. We gobble

chips, guacamole, carrot spears, french fries, and hot dogs. We have downed our second hot chocolate and dragged off a circulating joint. KC and the Sunshine Band's "Get Down Tonight" plays. We now dance together in place, like many people around us. We work the room, bumping and boogalooing into all kinds of conversation. We hear about upcoming summer concerts by Michael Jackson and the Jackson Five. Peter Frampton, Fleetwood Mac, the Supremes, and Abba. We hear who got an audition at Juilliard, Curtis, Manhattan School of Music, the Cincinnati Conservatory. We hear who was chosen for a summer job as a singer in a musical on a Carnival cruise ship. We hear who will understudy for the new Broadway musical *Annie*. We hear who got tickets for Liza Minelli's upcoming concert in Vegas. I tell Chip I'm so glad we came and that I needed a sprinkle of Kings Island magic dust. And he says, "Honestly, I get a little bored with all the show business talk, like they're all on the inside track to the big time. Every last one of them will get a reality check in the mail. I mean, since I was like seven, I was sure I'd be playing for the Cincinnati Reds. Then, around fifteen, I realize I was like a lousy fuckin' six on a scale of one to ten."

Shut up, I want to say

The Bee Gees sing "How Deep Is Your Love." Chip, an engine of warmth, is overheated. I watch him pull his sweater off, exposing bare arms to the cold. I twirl closer to him, but he seems far away. Now I'm overheated. I pull off my wool cap, forgetting about my scar and not noticing the pinch of resistance. Disco Donna Summer is singing "I Feel Love" when a guy we just met tells me my head is bleeding. I touch the scar and there's a bloody ooze on my finger. Chip freaks out, I can see it in his eyes.

I make my way to the bathroom above the garage and press a wad of tissue soaked in cold water to the wound. I can see the broken-off scab snagged in the knit's weave. I worry about blood, an unlikely bleed-out. It's all so upsetting, so gross. So telling.

Several windows show the snow has picked up scarily. It's after 3:00 p.m., and we've been here almost two hours. That's all the time we agreed to spend. Chip and the guy who noticed the bleeding, plus a few other guys, are all talking. My return from the bathroom stops them cold. Now they are staring at me. Before I can explain the blood, Chip cuts me off, says loudly, "Look at his face? You can still see the injuries that gaybashing psycho motherfucker caused—and Cliff was hospitalized for five days. I'm so fucking pissed, you have no idea how fucking pissed. More pissed than Cliff is, even."

I'm embarrassed by their *Oh my Gods*. I'm ashamed when the guys lock on me. One guy tells of a friend murdered in the parking lot of a downtown gay bar. Another describes being harassed and chased on Miami University's campus. For some minutes I listen to comments about bottles thrown from moving cars. About guys being outed on chalkboards or bathroom graffiti. About guys who medicate themselves just to step outside. One of the guys in this group asks me what the cops are doing about what happened. I can see they all want to know. Chip cuts me off: "It's complicated, unbe-fuckin-lievably complicated. But we all know who the psycho motherfucker is, and he'll get his. He will get his."

"Stay tuned," I say. Then to Chip: "The driving's gonna be bad, we have to leave." And Chip looks at me angrily, as if I were the psycho motherfucker. It scares me and then angers me, before I swallow it. "You're right. We'd better go," he says.

He tussles with his sweater. I throw my arm around him. He throws his around me. We wave goodbye. We are outside the garage when he starts.

"I'm sorry, I just freaked out over the blood. I know it's your story to tell but technically I was stating facts, not telling a story —but I am sorry, I don't want to fight, I'm just so pissed, not at you

—though I don't understand your calm about this, and sometimes I feel like if it weren't the injuries that put you in the hospital, you wouldn't have even told anybody what happened to you. At the same time, I know it's your story to tell or not to tell. I'm just pissed at the situation, I'm pissed at everything, sweet Jesus, I could just kill this dude."

"Must be something in the hot chocolate, huh?"

My comic relief works. We laugh a little, pretending again. A wind gust pushes us toward the downhill slope. I feel its power like I do his anger and resent it at the same time.

"I get how you feel, Chip, and I think I'd feel the same if it happened to you instead of me. But it didn't, and I feel like you've got to let me figure it all out. I don't need you to figure anything out for me And I don't need you to tell me how I should feel, and I definitely don't need you telling my business."

"Cliff, I know I blew it. I'm really sorry. Forgive me?"

I try to figure out what to say, how to say it in the right way. I don't want to make him feel worse.

"I just love you so much, and I feel responsible, Cliff, I'm the one that left you there."

We've been through this a thousand times. I accept his apology with an *It's okay, don't worry about it*. But I'm stuck on how selfish he is, how everything is always about him.

"Do you forgive me?"

I don't forgive him, and now I know what to say. "What I need you to do is back off!"

"I promise."

"Then I do forgive you. I love you so much, too. I want us to be boyfriends forever."

We kiss and makeup. "Thank you, I don't want to blow it with you," he says, and I smile. I suddenly think of Mom pretending just to keep the peace with Dad, when what she really wants is to smash him in a way that hurts like hell.

I say, "There's a limit with me."

He promises, his lashes sponging tears, and we hold hands. The driveway is diagonal to the hill. We follow it to the street. I hear the shouts of the sledders, too. Chip says, "Let's sled downhill, it'll be fun. We came to have fun, didn't we?"

He's right, fun is better than stewing. We take the hill on a mat meant for one, Chip at the front and me at the back. My arms lock around his waist to never let him go. I stare at the people dots at the hill's bottom, my anger, disappointment, and betrayal sidelined. It's that roller coaster feeling of love on replay. I kiss the little nutsack of his earlobes. We speed and bump downhill into the whiteness. We bob and teeter to hold on until the fortune-telling best part: will we land together, or will gravity, physics, and fate separate us? We careen sideways at the slope's bottom before toppling in the snow. Turning, tumbling, sliding, we are a tangle of arms and legs at full stop. We laugh and we kiss, and we are in love again.

I love you so much, we say. But love isn't like it was, easy, breezy, logistical. We leave our mat at the bottom of the hill. Soon the tension of weather treachery plays out everywhere. Cars sliding, colliding, and jackknifing into snowdrifts on the main roads. On I-71, the ride home is smooth except for slick stretches and pileups along overpasses. Fuck Sunday gets the last word. We are kisses, fast hands, and more apologies. Too soon, and maybe not soon enough, I'm watching the fastback's rear snow tires spin up the hill and tread him homeward.

»»»

The ground should feel solid again, and yet I wait for the word that it's over. No calls come later. No word is coming at all. He still loves me. And loves me for me. I feel the same.

»»»

I had a feeling about the night's high winds. My dreams became colder the longer I slept. And I awoke shivering, seeing windows wide open. The psycho motherfucker lurks in the glass. He's been waiting for me all along. I scramble into the *right now*, knowing my mind has tricked me again. The cold wasn't part of the plot. The truth is just a gale that detoured from the Arctic with bright white deepening snow. The mercury strip outside the window bleeds into the negatives. My dream was cold because our house is cold. Our poor insulation, poor windows, poor furnace, and poor LACK are outmatched. I find Dudley in his bunk cursing the timing. Mom waddles in with news that schools, banks, daycares, government buildings, cultural centers, and churches are all closed. Planes have skidded off runways, planes are grounded, buses have crashed, all public transportation is halted. All travel on the roads is inadvisable except for emergencies. "Nothing you can do about lost wages, it's in God's hands," she says. She loves putting things in God's hands. God has deep pockets to cover the losses of the faithful. TV news calls the weather upheaval a polar vortex, which Mom says has nothing to do with God, though it was God that warned her to be ready. She heeded the forecasts, stocking up on canned food and snacks. She had Corey fill the water bottles in case the pipes freeze over. She doesn't trust God to watch over the pipes. She does trust God to keep the house from exploding. She bought manmade logs in case the furnace fails. Dad says we'll all be blown to Kingdom Come; Mom argues the gas line is permanently sealed. Mom says we'd all freeze to death if left up to him. It seems she does trust Dad not to murder us in a mad rage, but she doesn't trust him to keep us warm, any more than she trusts God to keep the pipes from freezing—though God will keep the house from exploding.

The polar vortex comes with the threat of fire. This makes me think of "Fire and Ice," the Robert Frost poem about our destructive world. Personally, I've tasted enough desire to favor fire. There's something calming about the frozen world outside. I side with Mom and her God faith. Only Mom has a plan to not let us all freeze to death should her faith in the fireplace turn out to be misplaced. She has Dudley seal off the poorly insulated den. Corey and I carry the television, playpen, and TV tables to the living room. Mom has thrown bed sheets over the good furniture. The babies are there, Dad is there, Corey and me and Mom are there, too. The TV chatters about the polar vortex, and ice floes jamming the Ohio River. We watch fools frolicking in the deadly cold. Dad points out that the fools ain't Black. Dad says, "Ain't no Black people gonna be out there throwing no damn snowballs and building some damn snowmen on the damn frozen Ohio River." Mom says, "Yesterday Cliffy was sledding in the blizzard," and Dad says, "It's cause he be hanging out with all them white people." I ignore them, and they ignore each other. Dad brings his V8 player and installs it on the TV. Even Dudley comes down when Richard Pryor is on with his nigger this, nigger that. His standup routine turns Mom's bladder against her. She scuds to the bathroom, a hand shoring up the breach between her legs, a wrecked urethra after so many childbirths. Later, we watch *Blacula*, *Superfly*, and *Shaft*, with Dad on the couch, Mom spooning against him, the babies in the playpen, Corey and me in the mister and misses chairs. I notice Dudley putting aside his LACK anger. Lured by happiness, the distance he normally keeps shrinks. He parks in a dining room chair, then moves the chair a little closer to the TV. Dad himself is a spectacle, glowing like a sun meant to heal, not kill. He squeezes Mom to him, an arm akimbo on her hip, a hand resting on number six. LACK rubbing ankles that light up the happiness. Mom will say this day of togetherness was God's plan. I think it's Dad's plan, for he is the conqueror. Though it's hard to give him credit for anything, his popcorn is better than hers.

I've always thought his Kool-Aid was just right. Now I can make it exactly the way I want, better than either LACK. At dinnertime, Mom includes the dining room table, used mostly for homework and piling stuff to be put away. The good dishes stay in the hutch now; there's never holiday turkey and dressing, only hamburgers and french fries prepared by LACK. My heart says this is the togetherness the holidays never deliver. This is what family must feel like. This is what I've never experienced before. The evening begins a slide to -20°F with deepening snow and more fitful wind. The telephone rings, and at least one of us teens races to answer. The call I've been waiting for changes everything. I forget about them, for I love Chip more now than ever. We are bashful, we are tender, and we are daring. How lucky we would be trapped in a storm together. Sledding, snowballs, cuddling, stripping before the fireplace, fucking, fucking, fucking—such fun we'd have, even on the last night on Earth.

»»»

I'm alone in the storm again. There's light above me, but it's like I'm buried under snow. The harder I try to break free, the dimmer the light grows. Then a hand cinches my wrist, pulling me down down down. I scream and am shook. My eyes open onto Dudley. "Cliffy, wake up! You're making a lot of noise. You need better mouth tape or just stuff a sock in it. I have bad dreams sometimes, but you are going mental, every time I spend the night you're a nut job. It's the beatdown that's fucking with you."

"Leave me alone. Is it five in the morning?"

"Like I said before, you gotta protect yourself. Might help you dream better. Don't be a victim, be in charge."

Fuck, it's cold. On my way to the bathroom for a piss, I notice two open boxes and two duffel bags. Where is there to go in twenty-two inches of snow? And in -11°F? Before the crack of daylight?

What's going on?

I flush the toilet, and on my way back to bed he says, "You can make all the noise you want once I'm gone. Soon as I get all my stuff, I'm leaving for Army boot camp in Fort Dix, New Jersey. You're the only person here that knows I'm leaving, and I want to keep it that way. I'll tell LACK myself. I can't wait to see Big Man's reaction."

"Dud, I don't want to ruin it for you, but Big Man can't wait for you to be gone, forme and Corey to be gone, too. That way it'll be just him, and Mom, and the babies. No reminders of what an asshole he's been. He's got a lot of guilt."

"You think?! Fuck that nig, he should have a lot of guilt. He isn't even worth talking about. I was gonna wake you up anyway. I have something for you."

He unlocks a toolbox and removes a blue pouch. We haven't given each other anything since the forced swaps of Christmas and birthday gifts when we were kids. I can't imagine what he would have that I would want. Including his collection of football cards and stash of dirty magazines.

But it's none of these things that boys collect. It's a pistol, so small it looks like a scary toy, or a killer cigarette lighter.

"Yeah, it's real alright, something for Big Man, if he ever gets in your face. Or anybody else that gets in your face. I was planning to sell this little bad boy but I'm giving it to you. You remember that trip to Dayton when Big Man pulled a gun on Mom? I got it right after that, to take care of him. Lucky he got his pills now, else the nig would be dead."

Wow. Wow.

"This is a Saturday Night Special. Use it in an emergency situation, to save yourself or somebody else. If you had the gun when you got jumped, you might have gotten away without getting hurt. You still might need it. You ain't out of Evanston yet."

I close my eyes but still see the toylike weapon, a mouse compared to a rat. He wants to show me how to use it, in the spirit of saving our mom. I follow him to the bathroom.

"What you got here is junk that can kill. Basically, you point and shoot. Point and shoot. With this kind of gun, you definitely don't want to be too far from your target, you only get one shot before you have to reload. You aim for the chest, it's the biggest target and your best bet to get away. You might kill the person, but . . . I don't believe in senseless killing, but I also don't want to be senselessly killed. So, you do what you gotta do."

"Wow. 'Senseless killing?' Is there any other kind of killing? Considering you're going to war."

"The US is a war monger, so maybe. But I don't understand what you mean?"

"I don't understand what I mean." And I don't.

"Well, I guess I'll find out pretty soon. I'll let you know if I'm in a war where it's kill or be killed."

The cold is death, dense, enveloping, as if we are buried beneath a snowy avalanche. My hand goes clammy at the touch of the icy metal. Even the idea of it scares me. That the answer to a problem could be a pull of the trigger. I don't want it, but Mom's rule for gifts means I can't reject it.

"Now hold it. It's not loaded." He wants me to pretend to shoot him. I've given him the finger over the years, but I've never imagined hurting him. "Go ahead, we're just acting," he says.

What I know about guns I absorbed from TV. I extend my arm and find his face bobbing at the end of the pistol. When I pull the trigger he says, "Wrong." He pushes my hand down to aim at his chest. I pull the trigger again. "Better," he says. I'm embarrassed when he compliments my posture, like posing with the gun makes me more coordinated. He removes a stash of bullets from the toolbox. He demonstrates the trigger safety, loading and unloading. I repeat the steps like I've done it all before. I hand the gun back and watch him return it to its berth under the bed. He says, "Keep the toolbox locked and hidden. Don't ever let Corey know you've got this. I can see him shooting out windows and at whitey, birds, cats, dogs for fun." I promise I'll find a better hiding place, and he says, "It's gotta be someplace where you can get to it easily in case shit goes down with Big Man."

The duffel bag is slung across his body. He stacks his two boxes and sneaks them downstairs. From the solarium I watch him trudge with his stuff through the morning dark. Sometime in the night, snowplows made a first pass, channelling through and shoving snow into high piles that now barricade cars parked on the street. I probably should help him dig out his car, but I just watch him hurl the snow one shovel at a time, pondering the shoot-to-kill gift he just gave me. Weird to think that Dad is an authority on killing.

Parking on the downhill side of our street works in Dudley's favor. It takes ten minutes or so before he drives away, glad to be rid of us, I guess. Especially LACK. But Mom will feel the pain. He hasn't even left her a note. She learns he has gone when I tell her, reluctantly. She is teary. I tell her I didn't know anything until just before he left. She doesn't ask me why I didn't come to her immediately. I guess she knows I admire his cruelty. It's what she deserves for putting Big Man over us.

"The military will be good for him," she says, resigned. "It will make a better man out of him."

»»»

Dad was supposed to make men of Dudley and of us. Mom told us that when we pleaded with her not to let him live with us.

Dad cares even less that Dudley is gone. "Cliffy-boy, I hear you got the room to yourself. Congratulations."

I awake lying on the floor, face to face with the tacklebox.

I climb into bed and go back to sleep.

I dream I'm outside in the cold, but I'm dressed for running.

I am outside in the cold in my running clothes. I don't know the time, but our street is asleep. The lamplights are dim, and everything glows under fading moonbeams. The snow piles deck the street like mini ski slopes. The snowmelt streams in open places and pools where corners meet. I jump for the splash, not caring about my feet or what lurks beneath. I'm waterlogged and weighted when I reach the track.

Some other runner has carved a first trail through the new snow. Maybe they were bored on this restless night.

I follow the sloshy trail they left behind. Around I go until the track splits open, and I fall through a fissure wide and deep. Through the strange portals of dreams, I hear myself screaming and waken to this strange state. I feel my body falling through the air. The drop is brief and confusing. My bones meet the carpeted floor with a loud thunk. I look up, seeing the cliff of my top bunk.

Now I am lying face to face with the tacklebox. I reach under the bed for the one thing that explains nothing but changes everything.

With the gun in my hand, I hoist myself into the bottom bunk. And I sleep.

»»»

Finishing my run, I notice the hole burrowed through the sky where the sun beams down cones of light. I think of paintings of heaven and angels. I wonder if the ground is just reflecting back what the sun gives. Like the way lightning discharges from the ground to crackle in the sky. I'm not having heavenly or scientific thoughts now. I'm waiting for Mom to finish her call. Mom says *Poor man* into the phone, and that she will let him know—and she eases the handset into the cradle so there's no sound when she hangs up. She looks at me with soaked eyelashes.

That poor man is Granddaddy Douglas. Dad's dad died from a stroke in his bed an hour ago. I know his stroke was the finale of injuries from a fall, but I don't remember anybody mentioning a skull fracture until now. "He never woke up," Mom says, with trembling lips and tear-streaked cheeks. In church, there's a painting of faithful souls ascending to heaven on an escalator of light. Granddaddy was a religious man and believed in such things. Like Mom does. She glides her hand over my head. I squirm free as she thanks God I'm okay. Sparing me, or maybe swapping Granddaddy for me. Then she says, "You tracked water all through the house yesterday, but you're not getting away with it today. Take those shoes off now and mop every drop up, everywhere you've been since you came in."

Maybe because of Granddaddy, I'm cool. Nothing in Mom's pantry of aggravation bothers me now. I've had sleep. Like I curled up in some kind of warrior-sorcery that Dudley left in his bed. I awake feeling calm with thoughts clearer than ever. I fetch the mop from the basement. I drag it across the linoleum floor from the kitchen to the front door. All the while the phone rings. Grandaddy is the first person I know to die. Blood relations I've never met or don't remember have died. They meant nothing to me. Granddaddy means nothing to me, except I know him. That's if you call sitting on his lap and getting five dollars for Christmas every year from age six to age eleven is knowing someone.

Soon as Mom hangs up, the phone rings. I feel sorry she has to say the same thing over and over. Most of the callers want Dad. She says several times that he won't be home until the afternoon. Panicky, she sends me upstairs to disconnect the hall phone. I eavesdrop on the line, hearing her say, "Your brother was out all night playing cards and losing money. He needs to sleep it off before dealing with his dad being gone, God only knows what he'll do."

"He'll be fine." I recognize the voice of Dad's phlegmy, pack-of-Kools-a-day older brother. "I think everybody's just glad it's over." Mom's whispery yes is equal parts mad, sad, and afraid.

I stand under the shower, imagining learning of Dad's death. I think I'd be somewhere between Dudley and Corey's feelings. Neither of them has budged on Dad since day one. The Twins will grow up with diaper-pin-Dad. I'll have witnessed brief flashes of that Dad, too. I'm pretty sure I'll feel sad for Mom. How he dies would factor in. A sudden heart attack or a car crash would shock me into feeling sad. If he was murdered by some woman's husband, I'd probably feel he was served just desserts.

I put on fresh clothes for Granddaddy and show my face in the kitchen. Mom is scraping dregs from the baby bowls when the phone rings yet again. Before answering she hisses to me, "All these calls are for your father and yet and still I got to spend my morning picking up the line pretending he ain't here." And I say, "No, you don't, Mom. Don't answer." She waves me off like it's the dumbest thing she's ever heard.

The Twins slurp the last orange juice in their cups and then I set them free. The snowy backyard is their favorite playground, but Mom mouths no. The Twins yell they want to go out. I notice the boy twin wheezes to the den. Neither protest once they're in the playpen. They stagger around its perimeter before curling up and napping. I grab a banana and sit in the recliner, feeling nappy, too.

I wake hearing LACK. Dad's on the kitchen phone and Mom seems to be shouting from the basement. I tiptoe through the dining room and notice his fingers drumming the kitchen table. He says to the person on the line, "Right, yes, right, I don't know how much, but I feel like we might be lucky and hit the jackpot. Then, returning the phone to its cradle, he says to Mom, who's now in the kitchen, "I can't believe the old bastard's dead." She says, "Clifford, at least act like you care." And he says, "Oh, I care, all right. The old stingy bastard's rich, and we will get a share to pay for all the bullshit we've taken from him!"

Dad isn't immune to mourning rituals, so neither are we. Nothing I can say would let me out of this family show. We pile into Dad's Marquis, offspring in the back. I have the window seat behind Mom, with the Twins between Corey and me. The sky is overcompensating, so bright my eyes hurt. Dad grinds on about a recent rate hike in car insurance. This animates him until Corey wants to know how much money Dad will inherit. Dad says we'll be living high on the hog. Corey says, "I hope that don't mean chitlins. I hate chitlins." I realize I might be sadder for a dead Dad if an inheritance is involved, whatever the cause of death.

Granddaddy lived in Avondale. That's catty-corner to where we are in Evanston. Green lights are on our side door to door. Parking takes longer than the drive over. We end up wedged between snowbanks. The sidewalk is buried, and we stray into the street to reach the stairs to the house. I stare at the driveway that cost Granddaddy his life. Dad says to us, "The old fool ain't got nowhere to go that he even needed to be sweeping the damn driveway in the first damn place. Damn stupid if you ask me."

The family all seem angry at Granddaddy for sweeping the drive and at Grandma for letting him do it. One thing about the Douglasses, nobody's afraid to make themselves clear in liquored-up back-and-forths. The family is divided about the money. Dad's oldest sister says, "Daddy ain't got nowhere near $100,000, making a janitor's wage all his life, unless he was a heroin kingpin and we didn't know about it. If it's $10,000 I'd be surprised. It's probably more like seven." This sets off a rowdy discussion about inheritance and debt. Nobody has anything loving to say, or tears to shed for their newly dead and gone father.

Many cousins show up. We crowd in the kitchen with a bottle of Jamaican rum. We see each other only at holiday gatherings and funerals—though all of us are topics of the family grapevine. Including my beatdown. A Rum & Coke in hand, I give my script and one cousin says, "I don't even go to Evanston, OTR, or Coryville anymore." Another cousin says, "I love my people but when you put too many welfare niggas in one place, somebody's bound to get hurt." Another cousin says, "What about the cops?" I mention Moneymaker and this same cousin says, "Those pigs'll turn you around so bad, you think you're guilty for beating yourself up. CPD don't got no love for black people."

Voices grow louder and the doorbell rings and the screen door yawns and bangs. The kitchen soon overcrowds and overheats. We cousins are hemmed tighter in the corner as the gathering swells. I follow cousin Elijah outside to the porch and then to Granddaddy's old LeSabre sedan. Somebody warns about smoking in the car, then somebody else laughs that the dead won't know. We climb in the backseat for a hit off a joint that's so strong I can't stop coughing. Cousin Cecil is Dad's brother's equivalent of Corey. Cecil sits behind the wheel and dangles car keys. He switches on the ignition, and now everybody's cheering for a joyride. I climb out before the car backs out of the garage. I watch it roll down the drive through a canyon of snow.

Corey calls out and says Mom is pissed at me. I find her upstairs in Grandaddy's bedroom. She's not there to commune with his spirit, she's hiding out with a few other mothers. She complains that we were only supposed to be here an hour and already two hours are wasted. She has chores, shopping, and more on her to-do list. Then, turning up her nose at me, she snaps, "You been smoking that funny stuff? I got a ride and you're coming with me."

Just then I realize how buzzed I am. Now that I'm here I don't want to leave. But I don't fight her. It's one of those times I feel for her. She worries I'm too high to be trusted carrying the babies, so we walk them out instead. Our ride is with Miss Veronica, mother of three kids with Dad's youngest brother, Cecil. She left her kids with a sitter because she's disgusted by what she calls the Douglas Drinkhole. Her potato figure waddles ahead of us. In the car Miss Veronica says, "You know Daddy-Douglas never even touched the stuff. Six out of seven of his kids are dirty drunks, and yet and still he is as sober as a saint. How could he stand it?"

"Girl, tell me about!" Mom says.

"Maybe Granddaddy was shoveling on a suicide mission," I say, half joking, half serious.

"That's heathen nonsense, Granddaddy was God-fearing," Miss Veronica says. "The Lord protects his own. You ever think about why you got beat up. You need to start going to church, ask the Lord to protect you."

I'm sensitive to her evil eye. Mom is strangely silent. I shut up after that.

Miss Veronica drives slow as molasses. The Twins are asleep when we pull up between snow piles on either side of our driveway. Mom fears the newly slickened sidewalks. We guide the Twins into the garage. She waits until the babies are in their playpen and we're in the kitchen before lighting into me.

"Never mind you being so rude to Miss Veronica. What the hell's wrong with you? Smoking weed, drinking, acting like the rest of them, like you ain't got a bit of sense. It's ain't alright, Cliffy. It ain't. You are not like them! I'm not gonna let you grow up to be like any of them!"

It's the diabolical person inside me that laughs and says, "Who am I gonna grow to be like then? You?"

"I'm not a perfect role model. But I'm the best you got in this house, remember that."

"Like that Billy Preston song says, *Nothing from nothing leaves nothing.*"

I see the slap coming but am too buzzed to react. It lands mostly on my jaw and lower ear. She seems as shocked as I am and looks like she's about to cry. I run to my room, locking my door to piss her off even more. When I hear the garage door close, though, I run back downstairs. I watch her car heading toward the parkway. I hear the babies in the playpen. Somehow this erases the pot and rum and sobers me up. I have a right to be pissed at her, but I am soft. I am a Momma's boy, like Chip. I love her more because I hate her now. All this love and hate, I can't stand it.

I bring my things to the den. I climb in the playpen with the Twins, which they love. I'll never leave them if Mom doesn't come back, whatever the reason.

Mom does come back, an hour or so later. She looks frightened, like she just realized I might have left the Twins in the house alone. I apologize for my mean words. She doesn't apologize for slapping me. She says, "I only want you to be your best. Always remember you are my heart, and I'm counting on you. Always remember that."

»»»

Dad hasn't nagged me about Detective Moneymaker lately. Seems the Detective and I both have been pushed aside for his own dramas. Not that I mind. My own craziness is hotwired to him, I think. I listen to him go on about enrolling at Cincinnati Technical College—can he handle a full year of working all night and school all morning? The Twins to daycare problem is his to solve. Should he buy me a new bike with a bar on the back for the Twins to ride on? Or get me a fake driver's license for a hundred bucks to ferry them back and forth in a used car?

Driving us to daycare he says, "You know, I shoulda told your

Granddaddy when he was breathing about me going to Cincy Tech, and maybe he woulda left me some bonus money on top of my share. He was always pushing me to go to college, and you know, funny thing is, all these years later, I have come to see that I resisted it just because it's what his old, mean ass wanted. I spent the high school years you're living right now doing the opposite of what he wanted. Ain't that something? You know what I'm gonna say to him in that coffin? I'mma tell him I'm gonna be taking a CTC course, just like he woulda wanted."

He laughs maniacally, though nothing's funny. I notice he flicks a finger at his eyes to thump a tear. We pull up to Lilliputian Daycare and he says, "I understand he meant good, because, you know, it's all the shit Black people got to deal with in those days–well, in these days, too, so I didn't see the point of high school, never mind college. And then it was him, I hated him telling me what to do. He never liked me. When I turned thirteen, every summer he shipped me and my oldest brother off to be sharecroppers in the middle of nowhere in Georgia. His brother would beat the hell out of us if we didn't work. Your Granddaddy was always against me. I mean, me and him ain't nothing like you and me."

I hide my shock. I'm already exhausted by him. He's talking even as I scoot the Twins through the back seat passage and close the door on him mid-sentence. I'm mumbling to myself as we three gaggle up to the entrance. The Twins seem confused when I don't reach down to kiss them goodbye. I watch them run inside before turning back to deal with Dad. I wish we could go back to a time when he paid no attention to me, except I don't want the fists and raging and worrying. Back in the car I lie and say, "Dad, I've got to join a math study group that meets mornings before school and, well, that means you'll be on your own getting the babies to daycare. Sorry it conflicts with your school plans, but I didn't know anything about your school plans until now. And you know, I won't get into UCLA if I don't ace calculus."

I'm thinking he'll be angry over the crash of his CTC fantasy. Or demand that I figure out something else. But he says, "OK, Boy, you do your thang, don't let me stand in the way." And I say, "I know you've been riding me to school for my sake, and I appreciate it, and I'm fine now. I really am. So don't worry about me." And then he says, "Boy, I'm glad you're better and dealing with shit better, and me and the Twins gonna miss you but it ain't like we ain't done it before without you. And you know, the CTC thing is wannabe thinking, I don't know if it's worth the time anyway cuz I ain't got the time, not now anyway . . . and boy, timing is everything, right? I need to see if there's a summer slot. That would be easier."

I'm staring into my lap. A weird feeling hits me as the gas station mushrooms over the windshield. We bounce onto the curb and Dad flashes two bucks in front of me. "Get me a pack of Kools Regular, get two if they've got a special like last time," he says.

I see the psycho motherfucker as still as a cardboard display. I feel the fate of this encounter. We are like planets locked in a death spiral. There's nothing I can do to change the vaporized finish. I don't freak out. Somehow, I focus on Dad's familiar ask. I can picture Dudley's pistol in the tacklebox, waiting. I push myself from the car with a burst of brazen will. I step up to the store entrance, aware that the psycho motherfucker sees me. We watch each other through the glass door, as we have watched each other through tricks in glass windows and two-way glass. Glass and a counter junked with candy, gum, and antacids stand between us.

I hesitate before going in but not out of fear. I notice someone else in the glass, a person in the coffee area of the store. I push through the door. Now the psycho motherfucker is a few feet away. I can see the muscles in his jaw grinding down on teeth. I see the steep ridge of knuckles in the span of his hand. I hear a bronchitis wheeze in his breathing.

"A pack of Kools Regular, two if you've got a special."

"We don't got a special now. Ended yesterday."

I want to correct his grammar. I want to insist the special should be extended to improve our customer relations. The absurdity makes me laugh. He probably thinks I'm fucked up or cracking up. No different from the other boys he's demolished. I'll show him.

He pulls a pack from the overhead dispenser and places it on the counter. I set the buck beside it and he cashiers, coins rolling out from the butthole of the cash register. I'm still giggly as I scoop up my change. I do look at him now. I watch his disgusting lips mouth the words *my bitch boy*—his words as he'd dragged me across the floor that night. I watch as his tongue glides across first the thick top lip and then the fat bottom lip. "Come back again soon, babyboy, I got something I'm still waiting to give you," he says.

I will shoot him. Nothing has ever been so clear.

Somehow, I walk like normal to the car, though my legs are pegs. I'm climbing in as Dad says, "Cliffy-boy, I see that's Buster at the counter, go back in there and tell him you're my son and to give you an extra pack."

But I'm climbing into the seat as he's talking, not understanding what he's saying. He grabs my arm and repeats himself. There's a grip in my throat and this force rising in my gut. I push the door open and vomit.

"Ah shit, not in my car. Boy, you need to go back home?"

"No, take me to school."

"OK, I'll get myself an extra damn pack of cigarettes. I'll get some ginger ale for you, that's good for the stomach," he says. He runs into the store and comes back with an extra pack of Kools and a cold, harsh ginger ale for me. "Looks like you missed my car," he says.

He asks again if he should take me home. I tell him I feel better. I tell him this because I know that if I go home, something will happen with the gun. It's like it's calling for me. I can hear Dudley saying to aim for the chest.

Now Dad's talking talking talking, and finally he says, in a scolding tone, "Boy, you hear what I said about the Pennysaver?" I tell him I heard him and agree to check the Pennysaver for a used bike.

Though I know I won't.

»»»

I could be wrong now. This could be some other brown, bony dude, with his same long black braid biking through a spastic intersection. I yell to him, but he disappears behind a bus passing in front of me. I can just make him out through the plume of exhaust.

The light changes and I run through the intersection shouting his name. I track him as far as the next block and stop. The L.L. sign is in that same block. I see him hop the curb in front of the dime store. He parks the bike against the wall. Old, beat up, and dirty-looking, it's the kind of bike nobody would steal, even in an area of bars, winos, druggies, and prostitutes.

It's some time before he comes out. He seems excited to see me, even claims he was thinking about me on his way here. I mention that I called his name several times since he crossed Montgomery Road. I want to bring up his death-defying dogfight with a speeding sports car, and how I tried to warn him by flailing in my window, but he cuts me off instead. Pointing to the L.L. on the corner, he says, "Don't let me stop you?"

"Huh?"

"Isn't the L.L. where you were going? Trying to get up the nerve to knife the sonofabitch. But you can't because you feel like a fucking coward. But are you? Really?"

"*What*?"

"Sorry, I'm projecting, I used to play those head games with myself. For all I know, you really could be on your way there now to shoot the sonabitch. You're not his bitch boy. Right?"

"I'm on my way home from school. Then I saw you."

"Anybody would understand why you'd want to shoot him. I've seen and talked to him. Buster, right? He's definitely a fucking monster."

"*What*? *You've talked to him*?"

"Yeah, I didn't make the connection when we met at the hospital. I told him I'm an artist and he posed for me. Butt naked."

"Butt naked."

"I paid him ten dollars. You want a copy."

"Why would I want a picture of him?"

"Dart board? Give it to the police. Keep it long enough and it might be worth something. Up to you."

"I don't want his fuckin' picture. And the cops know who he is."

"Maybe ask your boyfriend. Chip, right?"

"Wait a minute . . . I didn't tell you his name. And I don't remember telling you the name of the gas station or where it is. You some kind of mind reader?"

"Nope. I have perfect recall is all . . . a photographic memory, or so they tell me. I can remember every second of every day in technicolor detail. What I ate, who I was with, how the room smelled, what I read in the paper—pick any day. The good days and the bad and the worst, they're all the same. My kind of memory is actually a medical condition."

"That's why you were in the psych ward?"

"Something like that."

I'm totally weirded out by him. I tell him I need to go home and am so glad I didn't say where I live. He wants my number, but

I ignore him and run off. I look over my shoulder every few yards to make sure he isn't following me.

At home, I pull the tacklebox out from under the bed. The gun looks bigger, even heavier. I flip the safety on and off, finger the trigger some.

I tuck the gun under my pillow.

»»»

It's 5:15 a.m. now. I listen for Mom's readying for work. Her heavy feet pad past my door, sending vibrations through the carpeted floor. I can hear her mumbling to herself. Probably to remember something she'll leave behind or something she forgot to tell Dad. The heavy back and forth finally passes. Now the sound of the marshmallow soles of her work shoes descending the stairs. Normally she leaves through the garage via the kitchen, but this time she goes through the front door. She does this only when Dad's parked her car on the street. He's too lazy to re-park hers behind his in the driveway when he comes home late at night. No matter how many months pregnant she is, and even knowing she's scared of these mornings in the dark. She imagines creeps prowling in the shadows. They're there year-round, even in the freaky bitter winter we've been having this year. She's afraid she'll be seen and refuses to turn on the porchlight, relying on the handrail to lead her off the porch. I run to the solarium and watch her go down the remaining stairs. She moves in a sideways motion, then quickly gets across the street to her car. The brightness radiates when the interior lights come on. Now the headlights peer into the dark. She makes a quick U-turn before vanishing up the street.

I'm already dressed in sweats. Sleeping in Dudley's old bed has primed me to do what he all along knew I was capable of. I now think nothing of tucking the gun between my underwear elastic and lower back, like it's part of my running gear. The metal discharges a current of cold up my spine that jolts me into action. I'm scared to look at myself in the mirror. I'm scared I'll see I'm not in my right mind, what being out of my mind looks like. I'm scared I might see where I could be an hour from now. On the run. Run down. Dead in hail of bullets. In police custody.

I leave through the front door. The good athlete I am habitually warms up with knee bends, calf and heel-to-butt stretches, and windmilling arms. All the motion slides the cold, hard gun from my underwear's waistband to between my butt cheeks. A weird foreplay that fuzzies my reasons for whatever is about to happen. I force the gun back to my hip and then take the hill slowly, speeding onto Woodburn. My skullcap tweezes my eyebrows, and I slide the fabric out of the way. I run in a faster gear, passing the Coca-Cola plant entrance, then over the bright gash of I-71. I switch to the street to avoid the mini lagoons from melting snow piles along the curb lawns. Dogs stir and howl, and I hope I won't have to fire the gun to scare off a hunting pack. Now I run past the Twins' daycare, it's dark and childless at this hour. I detour to the Doris Day House and the one next to it, hoping my bike is on the porch. Stealing what was stolen from me—my coat, hat, gloves, confidence, nerve, love, self-respect—is half of the reason for this run. I stop between cars, breathing hard, and staring at the house through the foggy morning. It's somehow creepier at this hour of sun-up than on the darkest night. No sign of my bike, or any bike. I take off, fearing being seen.

I sprint the full block but then slowly pass the L.L. gas station. Only the store part of the building is lit.

»»»

The garage is as dark as it was that night. I still don't remember being worried about being seen kissing Chip goodbye. Maybe I don't remember because I wasn't worried. What I remember most is lust and love. But it seems now that maybe I did notice someone peeping through the glass panes of the garage door, and at the time I just didn't care. So, I told Chip he could go, I would be fine. I got out of the car, walked to the store entrance, and it seemed the psycho motherfucker did, too, but from within the store, arriving at the same time I did. He opened the door, staring at me as if I had just exited a spaceship, and I stepped inside, smiling like I was happy to see him, and the lights suddenly went off. The psycho motherfucker was in a rush, saying he needed to close down because of the weather. I waited while he switched off the signs, locked the air hose outside, the gas pumps. It was completely dark except for the light coming from Montgomery Road. I remember the snow howling and flowing sideways like a river. And then he announced he was done. I remember he smiled at me. He seemed almost bashful. I wasn't afraid. At all.

»»»

Finding the right lookout spot is impossible because there isn't one. Where I was before on Montgomery Road didn't give enough cover. Where I am now hides who's manning the gas station store. The cold tamps down Montgomery's usual devilment, as Mom would say. A bar murmurs with music. DayGlo prostitutes and filigreed pimps are probably inside. A pair of winos hover close by. One squats on the cold curb and the other leans against the liquor store entrance. Neither notices me.

I decide it's better, and warmer, to keep moving. I retrace my run to my first position in the middle of the block. This time I circle back on the sidewalk at a slower pace. Now I see the lights of a cop car on the lot switch on. I didn't notice the car before. Two cops emerge, walk toward the store. I can see the person behind the counter, it's the psycho motherfucker. Maybe the cops were surveilling him, too. They seem to be talking, they seem to be friendly. I've seen enough police shows to guess they're getting free coffee and donuts. Whatever. If things go my way, if this gun and I collaborate, it won't be long—tomorrow, the next day, or the one after that—before this gas station is crisscrossed in crime scene tape.

I wait some minutes where I am, pacing back and forth, probably looking suspicious, too. The cold and my paranoia win, and I quit. I wish I could run to school for a super early start. I can't carry a gun to school. Plus, the building opens at seven.

»»»

I want to set my alarm and take off before Mom's up. Unlucky me, she'll probably discover my absence, wake the whole house and freak out the baby she's carrying. Last night Corey joked that she looks like she's about to pop, even with another month to go. I remember the violent howls that announced the Twins' coming into the world. I remember the ambulance rushing a delirious Mom to the hospital and wondering if I'd ever see her again. Last night I dreamed her water broke, and she gave birth racing herself down I-71.

I stick with what works and track her morning from my room. I'm relieved when the front door finally closes. I run downstairs and wait in the solarium to see her totter through the dark to the car. Only I don't see her, and I panic that something's wrong. I'm about to check the porch when the front door suddenly opens. I tuck myself behind the drapes, knowing I'm busted. Pulling them back she says, "What are you doing?" I say, "Making sure you get to the car." She says, "In your running outfit? Where are you going at this hour?" I say, "Out for a run, obviously. Track season starts soon, and you know I'm not in shape."

I try to act normal, knowing she's onto me. I imagine her shaking me and the gun falling through my underwear and sweatpants.

She grills me about the time, she insists it's too dangerous to be running outside in the dark. I listen, knowing time is on my side, that the more she talks, the more likely she'll be late for work. "Mom, let me walk you to the car," I say. We leave together, and she holds my arm the whole way, almost short of breath. I say, "Mom, you can hardly walk, should you still be working at all?" She says, "Can't afford not to, we gotta eat." I'm scared, thinking of her in my dream giving birth driving down I-71. She says, "Cliffy, promise me you won't do anything stupid?" I say, "Mom, I promise. I'm just going running. Don't worry!"

Oncoming headlights show her sad eyes kissing me goodbye. I wait until she's out of sight before beginning my mission. But I'll be damned if my focus hasn't been thrown off. Back in my stakeout position, I stall between two parked cars on the L.L corner. The whole time I'm thinking how stupid this is. I see the psycho motherfucker behind the counter and two cars gassing at the pumps. In my fantasy I run inside to pop a bullet into his face. Or I recreate the inferno scene in Alfred Hitchcock's *The Birds* firing a bullet into the gas pump. Neither fantasy lights up my will, and I stall. The cold sends chills through my body. I pace back and forth waiting until he's alone. For some reason, I notice that the car in front of me has California license plates—633 EBXS. The ocean blue background and sunshine-colored typeface fills me with hope. A license plate is the symbol of the SOCAL life I'll never see if I do something this stupid. Mom's right.

Finally, the psycho motherfucker's alone. Now he's standing at the door, daring anybody in the dark to take a shot. I wonder if he sees me on the street watching him. Other eyes can see me though, the cars passing in both directions. All around us the windows of apartments, houses, and businesses are lit.

I run home. I'm not thinking of Mom or of being seen. And I am not thinking of UCLA and the Santa Monica Boardwalk, with its hot guys on roller skates—all the things the ocean-blue license plate stands for.

I'm thinking the cold has a lock on me. My teeth chatter and body shakes just thinking about the warmth of home that's accessible to me right now.

Mom has won.

»»»

Chip calls to say he's on his way. I hang up wondering if I really want him to. I feel stuck between a hard-on and wariness I can't explain. And I don't want to try to explain. I pass through the shower with lusty thoughts. They give way to a bad feeling that has me reaching for the tacklebox. I wait for a counter-feeling about this Fuck Sunday before taking out the gun. Don't do it, I tell myself, sliding the box back under the bed.

But I rush out the door, taking the steps two at a time. I'm happy he's here. So happy.

"Hey, babe," Chip says, and I *Hey, babe* him back. Our gestures kiss since our lips can't just now. Chip U-turns with zero traffic in both directions. "As you can see, I'm excited for Fuck Sunday," he says. He juts his hips forward to show off the outline of a blunt hard-on. I harden instantly, and we touch each other there. The clutch in play, the car heaves, and we climb the hill to a red light ahead. If we could tumble into the backseat now, we would. I'm dick-matized by this crazy passion between us. I slide my hand between his legs and search for the zipper. "Down, boy," he says with a wink of control. I am controlled.

The glowing red light stops us from going further. I'm looking from my love to the traffic ahead, and the dread I've felt all morning comes to life. Suddenly the psycho motherfucker passes in front of us like a poltergeist on a bike, the wicked witch in *The Wizard of Oz*. The fastback sits low, and he sits high on the bike—my bike, the bike Dad gave me for being a good boy. I cower in the seat, his shadowy presence sweeps over the windshield and blocks the light. Chip shouts and hits the horn, and now we are seen. The psycho motherfucker is reaching for the passenger side when I say, "Chip, just go, Chip, just go!" I search for the door handle and the motherfucker rolls out of the way. We lurch forward and speed through the intersection. We're up the hill now when Chip swings to the curb and says, "That's him, isn't it, isn't it, isn't it," and I tell Chip to just go.

He ignores me and launches from the seat. The trunk is at the front, and he pops it open for what I know will be the bats. He shows me he has grabbed two, one for him, one for me. "Game on," he says, jumping into the car. The fastback lunges to the left and the tires squeal in a rubber-burning spin. We speed downhill to the same traffic light we've just bolted through. It's red again, only this time we've glimpsed the future and lunge to grab it, to seize the light's split-second change to green. Horns scream as we hook a left into oncoming traffic. We charge forward in a way that seems to buck the car off the road. The stretch ahead is straight, but parked cars distort the view in places. Chips says, "There's that motherfucker!" And I say, "Yeah, that's him, that's him."

Now the real chase, and the roaring, lunging, shifting. And now the distance between him and us narrows and closes fast. I hold onto the dashboard to sturdy myself against all forces in play. We're just behind the motherfucker now, so close I can see the ridge of his ankle as the bike pedals rise and fall. Our speed slows enough that we almost sneak up alongside him. Except now he's looking dead at me like he welcomes what's coming. With just a jerk of the wheel, how easy it would be to crush him against a parked car. But we dart left like we're going around him, and then swing back to cut him off. Chip shouts, "Aim for the body, not the head, break his fucking knees, hurt that motherfucker, bad."

Warrior Chip catapults through the door, braced for battle. In the seconds I'm alone I'm scared shitless. I have never hurt anyone before with more than words, and now I don't have words. I don't want to get out, but I have to get out, Chip will never forgive me if I don't. I tell myself the psycho motherfucker deserves crushed knees and cracked elbows, even a death blow—his head bashed in by gay boys like us. I push myself outside and break free of the loser voices inside my head. I want to be a winner; Chip expects me to be a winner. Now there's the whacking sound of the bat pounding flesh and the crashing sound of the bike hitting a parked car. I see the psycho motherfucker crumple to the street and then pull himself up to his feet as if by will. Gripping the bat, I follow Chip's voice into the battle. All I hear is a ping-pong of shouting: *Fuck you, Fuck you, You wanna kill me, I'll kill your ass, You dick-sucking punk, Fuck you, You motherfucking motherfucker, Fuck you, Motherfuckerfuckyou. Nigga!*

Now I fly toward the shit as the motherfucker growls like the psycho he is. His eyes glow at me, I am the spoils of this battle to the death. "Fuck him up, break his knees, bust his fucking head," Chip shouts at me, his bat twirling like a samurai sword. I freeze long enough to see my bike flying in the air and nicking Chip before crashing in the street. I tighten my grip on the bat until I can't feel the bones in my hands. Now I fly toward the shit wailing, "Fuck you!" My bat hits his shoulder—*whack!*—to stop him from punching Chip to the ground. I swing at his back, and he whirls his legs to trip me to the ground. In the seconds it takes to roll to my feet, he wields the bike like a battering ram, and Chip swings the bat but never gets past the metal and tires and somehow ends up slammed flat on his back. Now I surge forward to save my love, this time with both hands gripping the bat. The motherfucker lifts the bike into the air for a death blow. I swing and meet his knees with a *thwack*! The bike free falls before crashing down on Chip.

The motherfucker reels sideways and hits the ground raging that he will kill us, that *Y'all ain't shit*. I bring the bat down on his body again and again, until it cracks and splits into two. For seconds nothing moves, it's as if time has stopped everything but the noise around us. The car horns and the yowls of a growing crowd on the sidewalk. These are the psycho motherfucker's people urging him to get up. I lift the bike from Chip's body. He is dazed and bleeding but insists he's OK. We stagger to the car, and now Chip's behind the wheel. The psycho motherfucker uncrumples to his feet and lurches like Frankenstein toward us. The crowd is behind him, and I'm scared we won't get away, that we will be caught, bashed, and flattened into the street. But the engine roars like a dragon to whisk us free. We hear the *whomp!* of his fist punching the back of the car as we speed to get away. We hear him shouting *Bitch-ass punks*.

"THE BITCH-ASS PUNKS THAT KICKED YOUR PSYCHO BLACK ASS, NIGGA!!" Chip shouts out the window.

He reaches across the seat to lift my hand in triumph. We have done what he's been wanting us to do. We have won by his definition. Blood splashes down the side of his face and sponges into his sweatshirt. A gory reminder of what it took to stand up to the psycho motherfucker. Now I can see the geyser above his ear where the bike gouged skin. I see the swelling where punches landed around his eyes and jawbone. Blood leaks down his forehead and he insists he's fine until he's seeing red and feeling dizzy and has to pull over. "Babe, looks like you're going to learn how to drive a stick, like, right now," he says. "I'm ready if you are," I say. I feel ready for anything.

But his lightheadedness worsens. Switching seats is way harder for him than it should be. He thinks we should drive to my house. I insist he needs professional attention, saying nothing about us freaking out Mom. We are a traffic light away from a right turn in the direction of the hospital, about five miles away. We lurch along until I've mastered the gears and stopped worrying about crashing. Chips tells me I'm doing great, weaving like a drunk before slumping sideways against the door.

Don't freak out, I tell myself. The ER is near, and we will get there in time.

»»»

He is confused and disoriented. I see a wheelchair between the double-door hospital entrance. Just getting him from the car to the chair leaves him groaning. We are screened immediately when I mention a bike crash and concussion. Now waiting is the easy part, but I'm not good at it. Forty-five minutes pass, and then who should appear but Dr. Fang Fang. I tell her my friend is the one hurt, not me. She says, "You're not as hurt. And, considering you were a recent patient here, let's have a quick look, just to be sure."

I agree. She has me stand up. She shines a light in my eyes and probes around my head. "Good, you're all healed up, looks like there are no new head injuries," she says, with her hands feeling around my arms, shoulders, and back, before letting me go.

"I'm not on drugs, I wasn't before either . . . if that's what you were looking for," I say.

"The eyes have a lot to say not just about drug use, but concussion, brain functioning, whether you're alive or dead. Bruises are also revealing. For instance, the knuckles of a fist make very distinctive marks on the skin," she says. "Your friend is banged up but no concussion. We're stitching him up now. He's sedated and will be out another hour or so, then he can leave. But no driving for the next twenty-four hours."

I plead with her not to call my parents. She says, "Mr. Douglas, you're still a minor and your parents would have to be notified only if you were a patient here today, which you're not. But I'm sure they'd want to know that you're OK, and maybe help you to not have more accidents. From my experience, dealing with boys here, with accidents like yours, I worry about the condition you or your friend will be in the next time you end up here. The police exist for a reason. Use them."

"There won't be a next time. I'm going away for college in the fall. He is, too," I say.

"I remember you said UCLA?" she says, smiling.

"I won't know until early May. But we're not like the boys you see around here. Nothing like them."

"I'm glad. Now have a seat. You should be able to visit your friend soon."

"He's my boyfriend, and I was fagbashed when I came here before."

She smiles. I thank her for everything. Especially about the cops. Chip will wake up, then what? Crash at my house? We'll need a hell of a story to explain to LACK. That's assuming Chip would agree to stay over, which he wouldn't. Dazed or not, he'll insist on driving home for school in the morning and work in the evening. I'll be left to deal with the fallout from our beatdown. I'll be the one most likely to end up here again.

The only person I can think of calling is Blair. I catch him on the first try. Just mentioning the psycho motherfucker does the trick. He shows up exactly as we are leaving the ER. Chip predictably insists he can drive himself home, screw the blurry vision and an ankle sprain that makes walking painful. His attempt to press the clutch and brake with that same foot fails. We agree that I'll take him in his car and Blair will follow us on the hour's drive.

Now we cruise along interstates and through snowed-over farmland. We finally arrive in a rural subdivision of split-levels and ranch styles and towering snowbanks. Chip's vision is still blurry enough that I have to call out street names at every intersection. We stop in front of a nicely paneled split-level house with two cars parked in the driveway. Chip says, "So, as you can see, Uncola is here."

We are expected. The front door opens and out comes an older, white, bald version of Chip. They share a squarish face and body type, with Chip being the taller. And maybe they share a temper. His dad says, "I got the call from the hospital but you were already gone. What happened?" Chip says, "Bike crash. Just a few stitches and an ankle sprain. They'll send the bill."

Chip introduces me and points to Blair, he's still in the car. His dad says to me, "Thanks for not crashing the car since you're not insured to drive it." Then Chip says, "You should also thank him for not getting pulled over since he doesn't have a driver's license or a permit either. And, you really have to thank him for learning to drive a stick on the spot. I wouldn't be here if it weren't for him, which you'd probably prefer but, because it's the right thing to do, you should thank him for that, too . . ."

Our already awkward hand-off is even more so. Chip blows me a kiss for anybody to see. A brave, crazy, reckless gesture that will only backfire. I can imagine the tense words passing between father and son the moment we are gone.

"Chip is cool, but boy, he's a live wire," Blair says. I tell Blair about our bat-beatdown revenge, and he says, "That crazy mofo deserved a beating, but you and your hot guy just whacked the hornets' nest. I know you know his cousin or uncle or whatever, that dude named King—I've heard him called Kingpin—is to him. If I were you, I'd tell the cops what went down and tell your folks what's going on in case those savage assholes burn your house down . . . yeah, Cliffy, it's like that with these niggas."

"*Nigga* this, *nigga* that! I hate that word!"

"I'm talking about you saving y'all's ass, and you want to crusade against a word. A word that's ours to do use however the f-u-c-k we want!"

"Sorry! I'm just freaked out. We're in deep shit!

"Yeah, you are."

I know he's right about everything, the blowback could be lethal.

But Chip was right, too, we could not not deal with what the psycho motherfucker did to me, and to us. "We got him good," I say, feeling I won a race knowing a team of just him and me will lose.

»»»

Corey claims some of his friends recognized me in the melee. He tells me that his boys thought the psycho motherfucker—or Lurch, as they call him—was fighting only one dude with a bat, and that it looked like he was coming in for the kill when a second dude jumped in swinging a bat. He tells me that none of his friends had a gun handy and that everybody was a little afraid of Lurch after he told them to *step the fuck back*, so they were all waiting for him to finish them off when the bat-swingers took off in some "weird-ass foreign ride."

What I feared would happen has. I deny knowing what he's talking about. Corey then shares a vague description of Chip—vague because distance blurred out Chip's three standout features: golden eyes, freckled skin, red-brown hair. Corey has never seen Chip up close to match him to a description. I deny everything, I tell him Chip and I were touring the UC campus. Then Corey says that Lurch, according to these same friends, isn't giving up much about what happened either, except claiming the dudes that got him were from Northside. "Lurch's gotta be lying. I mean, why do all my friends that was there think they saw you? It don't make no sense. I ain't never even said nothing about you, and the ones that have seen you before ain't the ones that were at Lurch's beatdown. To them that was there, I've never even pointed to you and said, that's my brother. You've never even come up in a conversation before. I told them you ain't a brawler, you a bookworm kind of dude, and one of them said he heard you was a cocksucker. I told them you ain't because they might really come after you then, some of them with their dicks out . . . huhhuhhuh! And, hey, you never know what Lurch's gonna do. He might send them fools swarming after you. I don't know if they said anything about you to him, though, cuz like I said, he's kinda nuts. Honestly, I wish it was you, though. Not just because I can't stand that crazy motherfucker either. I wish it was you because, whatever he did to you to make you get back at him like that, y'all got that asshole good. Just cuz you're smart doesn't mean you gotta take shit from a beast like him. Cocksucker or not, the homies respect a dude that stands up for hisself."

I can't believe how he glows just thinking it was me. I know I'm giving myself away, but I can't help feeling proud that he's proud of me. Twisted as it is, I even feel proud to have earned the respect of people I don't respect. I'm proud of what I did for myself. I'm proud of what Chip and me did together. I will never not be proud. Even if we can't stop the psycho motherfucker in the end. Even if we only sicced a swarm on ourselves. Even if what we did was just damn dumb.

»»»

Chip is laid up and has to stay off his foot for a week. It's after 9:00 p.m. and the calling rate is cheaper. We speak freely—he's alone and Mom and the babies are asleep. I cheer him up with my brother's gossip. What gets the most reaction from him is the psycho motherfucker's not calling us out, telling the hornets to *step the fuck back*. From Chip's point of view, it's no surprise that the psycho motherfucker would claim some other dudes jumped him. He doesn't want everybody to know that a couple of queers kicked his ass. Then Chip says, "I called the gas station at three strategic times just to see if he's there, and he wasn't. Get this, I was told he's on vacation. *Vacation*! Ha! We must have really jacked him up."

I admit to running by the gas station once during what I think are his usual hours. But just because the psycho motherfucker wasn't there doesn't mean we didn't fuck up badly. I bring up Blair's comment about the hornets' nest, but Chip isn't impressed. I realize then that Blair's right, my live wire boyfriend doesn't get Black Evanston like me and Blair do—or how Corey does, for that matter. He in his white, middle-of nowhere world can't understand survival in a Black Evanston that makes people turn on each other. I've told him that the only time I look up from the sidewalk in Black Evanston is when I'm running. I've told him that looking these dudes in the eye is like a challenge to a pit bull or German shepherd.

What's my next move? I have only one plan. To keep Chip's hands out of whatever I do next.

It's all on me.

»»»

I stare at a doll-like Granddaddy in the casket right in front me. I feel shy, like the little boy I once was sitting in his lap. I touch his shiny, brushed-back white hair and cold, dark skin. The minister has asked that we reflect on the dearly departed's life. I don't know about Granddaddy's life to reflect upon it. It's easier to reflect on being in that casket instead. How did I die? Was I murdered? Who would care? Mom. Chip. Blair.

I realize Granddaddy's pipe is missing. A fixture of his face, like the mole above his lip, or the gold trim framing several teeth. That tall chimney severed from him now, seems cruel. I can almost hear it clicking between his low teeth, like an angry Morse Code, that anybody could be so callous to overlook something so essentially him. I realize I'm holding up the line when those who are paying their respects detour around me. Some squeeze my shoulder in a caring way, like I'm grieving his loss. But all I can think is, *Where's his fucking pipe?*

"Mom, the undertakers forgot Granddaddy's pipe. Can you believe it?"

"Good, that ole tacky, nasty thing—what he gonna do with that pipe in heaven?"

"What does he need with a tacky Lincoln Continental casket?"

"It costs $4,000."

"And who says he's going to heaven?"

"He's a God-fearing man, went to church every Sunday. Of course he's going to heaven."

"Wherever he's going, Granddaddy wouldn't be Granddaddy without his pipe."

"Well, as far as the pipe is concerned, it ain't up to him. You know what they say about funerals—they ain't for the dead, they're for the living. The family probably didn't give the undertakers his pipe."

The Douglas assholes.

I don't know why I would rush to tell Corey, of all people. I shouldn't have been surprised he would think the pipe great for smoking pot. Of course he wants to steal it.

»»»

First the church, where the service of preaching, mourning, and the whiny organ is long. Then the cemetery, which isn't far but the weather sucks. We are near the front of a beauty pageant of cars showing license plates from Michigan, Tennessee, North Carolina, Georgia, Alabama, Mississippi, New York, Illinois. While folks pile into cars Dad is chattering about cousin This from Atlanta and aunt That from Montgomery, whose kid What's-his-name goes to college in Southern California. He says, "You know, I ain't seen them in like thirty years, since I was like Corey's age. Ain't nothing like a funeral to bring everybody together, even for a mean ass nobody liked." "Ooh, Clifford," Mom says.

Dad abandons us to ride in the limousine with his siblings and mother; he can't stand her, either. Mom has to drive the Marquis, a car she fears. Corey rides shotgun while I calm the Twins in the back seat. They are cranky for lack of sleep, restless for lack of play. We are in the middle of the long procession that snakes through Avondale on the way to the cemetery. After passing through the Spring Grove pearly gates, the road narrows and zigzags along snow-covered hillsides like pastry shells. Mom is terrified we will slide into tombstones, and relieved when we don't.

Dad finds us. He says to me the oldest grandsons have the honor of carrying the casket to the gravesite. After fussing about Mom's parking, he growls at me, "Whatcha waiting for, Cliffy-boy? You gotta represent. You're the oldest here. You got to carry your Granddaddy."

The clamminess of my armpits has oozed down below my belt now. I'm not the only sweaty grandson who doesn't feel honored. There are plenty of us but not enough available or willing for the job, based on the "eldest" criteria. We wait until a cousin or two volunteers.

One of Dad's sisters has us playing musical chairs around the coffin. We lift the heavy chariot by its railings, and then are eliminated based on our size. The process seems to shift Grandaddy. There's a thump from within the coffin, as if he weren't seat-belted in. In the end, eight of us, all ages, haul Grandaddy graveside. Zesty lime Astroturf covers the slippery, frosty path we walk along. I hear Dad say, "Now don't y'all drop your Granddaddy." We are terrified we will, but we park the heavy casket on a sling that will lower him into the ground. The preacher says holy things about the dearly departed and the dust he must return to. Am I the only one who thinks it's silly to stick a body into an expensive box to be in the ground?

The gathering at Granddaddy's house is just as awful. I find Granddaddy's pipe, but not beside his favorite chair. It stands in a pipe caddy on the fireplace mantel, among the family photos and the grandfather clock. I wait until the guests arrive before making my move. They pack in, a gathering of black flamingoes moving through the kitchen, front and back porches, sitting on the steps climbing to the second floor. The music is loud, the booze sloshing, and smoke billows through the living room. First, I pretend to be interested in the photos, then steal the pipe I remember wedged between Granddaddy's lips. I find his tobacco pouch and lighter in the end table drawer. Our coats are piled up in the upstairs bedroom. I get mine and leave without telling Mom, or caring if I've been noticed. The cemetery isn't that far. Outside isn't as cold as it's been these many weeks. My dress shoes aren't meant for the forty-minute-plus walk, and my feet are hurt and numb, but I'm on a mission. The sun hides in clouds and the snowy hillside looks spackled like our plaster ceiling. I retrace the delivery route to Grandaddy's new neighborhood. The lime Astroturf remains in place, but the grave workers are gone. The dirt is cold but loosely packed. I dig with my hands down a foot so Granddaddy can grab a smoke anytime he likes.

»»»

Chip thinks I'm still making lugubrious rounds to my family. I wonder what he is doing with our Fuck Sunday, absent me. Maybe he's picked up a work shift, or he's doing homework, or he's shaping up on the track, or at the gym—the new baseball season starts in March. Or maybe he's just laying around fingering the worn-out pages of *BlueBoy*, or his one and only *PlayGuy*? Sometimes I worry he's getting off with somebody else behind my back. Maybe one of the guys at his gym, or maybe he's at the truck stop again, getting or giving service. After he blew a kiss to me in front of his dad, I know I shouldn't, but I call his house, and can't seem to make myself hang up. What happens if I don't hang up and nobody picks up? Can a line be rung to death? After what must be fifty rings, the line goes from a dial tone to a recorded message, "Please hang up and try again."

Worried, I leave a note telling Dad I'm back on Twins to Daycare duty starting tomorrow.

»»»

After dropping the Twins off at Lilliputian, I say to Dad, "I hope you're stopping by the gas station, I need a ginger ale."

"Cliffy-boy, you got a lot of stomach problems, between the shitting on yourself and the gagging."

"It's stress. I have a lot of stress. My stress is like PTSD, except without the crazy dreams."

"Stress? Boy, you don't know the half of it."

He complains about all the things he's got to worry about. He says the only thing I should be worried about is graduating high school, getting into college, and fingering the guys that jumped me. "That's all, what other worries you got?" he says. I say, "That's it. I can handle it."

We are pulling into the gas station. The psycho motherfucker is at the pumps. Just like I want him to be. He's hardly cowering in worry, but at work like everything's normal.

"Dad, not to change the subject, but how do you know that dude there . . .?"

"You talking about Buster? . . . He's the nephew of a cat I went to school with. See, before me and your momma got together, I was seeing this cat's sister. Why you wanna know?"

Fuck! What if the psycho motherfucker is one of Dad's bastards? Me and my brothers have already met two Cincinnati half-siblings.

"He ain't like my stepbrother, right?"

"Hahahaha, well, I thought he might be one of mine once upon a time, but he looks dead on like the drughead his bitch momma was running around with behind my back. Why you wanna know?"

"Just curious. I remember him from junior high. I don't think he remembers me. Seems like something's wrong with him."

"Yeah, the poor motherfucker got dropped on his head or something when he was a baby. His momma had a drug problem, ain't no telling what happened to him with that crazy bitch, she's dead now. See, his daddy got her hooked on heroin, he's dead, too. Buster was raised by that fool's momma, and now he stays with his uncle, King—the cat I grew up with."

Dad glides over to the pumps. The old fear supercharges me to make a run for it, but then I see the psycho motherfucker's on crutches—and it's like, *I did that*.

Dad lets his window down and greets him saying he wants ten dollars of regular. I hear the nozzle jiggering into the mouth of the gas tank when Dad says, "Hey Buster. What happened to you?"

I hear him lying about a bike crash.

I know he knows it's me in the car, so I say, "See, Dad, I told you he doesn't remember me. Introduce me."

Dad says, "This here is my son Cliffy, he says you don't remember him from Sawyer?"

I lean toward Dad so the motherfucker has a clear view of me. He nods and I say, "You clocked a bully problem I was having but you probably don't remember that?"

"Naw, can't say I do."

"Dad, he's the only reason I got through Sawyer."

“I got to thank you, Buster. My boy here is going to UCLA in the fall, that’s in SoCali, that’s Southern California.”

“I know where it is,” he says. “It’s a busy morning here. I best get to it.”

He pulls the nozzle from the gas tank and collects the money from Dad as another car pulls onto the lot. And that’s when I shout, “Hey, Buster, we need the windows cleaned. Dad, don’t we need the windows cleaned?”

Dad gives me two dollars for cigarettes. I spring from the car as Buster dips his cleaner wand into the window wash. I get Dad’s cigarettes and chewing gum and my ginger ale. I’m crowing to myself like I’m some Beowulf slaying my own Grendel. It’s all an act, and I know the motherfucker now lethally staring at me knows it, too. Still, I can’t help giving him the finger as I jump into the car.

We are pulling away when Dad says, “Cliffy, you know, what you said about Buster helping you with some bullies back at Sawyer—that made me remember his uncle telling me that Buster got some anger problems. He went apeshit, beating on folks, over stupid stuff. A couple years back, somebody accused him of rape. No charges came out it of but . . . I think you should steer clear of him, he’s bad news.”

I’m too busy admiring my own mind-fucking skills to think that Dad just might be connecting the dots. At my usual drop-off, I open the car door, and also one into Dad’s thinking. He says, “Buster raped some boy, don’t know if that’s true because, like I said, no charge was filed. He did a couple years of time a year or so ago, but that was because of an accessory to a burglary, I think.”

I’m outside the car before he can say more or question me. I take off running, I feel even more supercharged than after the bat attack. I forget to thank him, and I feel bad about it. Maybe for the second time, he’s done something important for me.

Something like what a dad should do for his good boy.

»»»

I scribbled a note to Dad last night saying that I have a field trip this morning. Just to make sure, I knock and then open LACK's door just wide enough to poke my head in. He's naked and sprawled on the bed playing with himself, teasing his dick-boy to one side before tonging it to the other. The alarm clock rings, and he rolls to the end of the bed for the snooze button with his high rump roast of a butt out. I say, "Dad, I'm leaving now for a field trip, like I told you in the note I left you last night. The babies are in the playpen ready to go"—and he says, "Yeah, GE Day."

OK, see you later, I say and run downstairs and outside with only a few minutes to spare. Mr. Woodley is a stickler for timeliness, and I don't want to start off the day disappointing him. He and his wife live in the biggest house on the White Evanston side of our street. Dudley and I used to mow lawns and rake leaves our first two years in Evanston. Mr. Woodley still dangles small jobs at me. He always leaves a message informing LACK first—"Mr. and Mrs. Douglas," he says—and I promptly call him back ready and eager, wanting to correct him, a good Catholic, about my divorced but still-together parents. Not that he's judging us. Though he did once ask about the police showing up at our house. I'm not surprised he made a way to get me a spot at GE Day. A couple of weeks before, he had asked me what I wanted to study in college, and I told him I didn't know yet. He said, "Ever thought about designing airplanes?" He then told me he wanted to include me on a list of students competing for a summer internship in General Electric's aeronautical engineering division, where he works as a product director. "How's that?"

It had been Thanksgiving weekend, one holiday before all the psycho motherfucker shit. I had said yes , only to change my mind. I guess I never canceled, though. He called last night to tell me to meet at his house at 7:15. I didn't have the nerve to cancel at this late hour; he's been decent to me.

That his car is backing out of the long driveway without me, makes me think he's changed his mind. He stops to let me climb in and says, "I'd thought I'd meet you halfway."

His sagging eyes and sickle eyebrows mark him as mean and unfriendly, but the opposite is true. He asks all the questions a former high school math teacher turned aeronautical engineer might ask of a favorite graduating senior. I lie with all the versatility of a son still distracted by the hot image of his dad playing with himself. We drive to pick up three other student candidates, all attendees of Cincinnati's best high school. All are probably more suitable than me for an engineering internship. We hopscotch between three neighborhoods, the farthest being downtown. Two of the three students—a Chinese girl and an Ecuadorian boy—impress Mr. Woodley with their speedy minds and almost-unaccented English. I'm too busy feeling like a dime slipping between seat cushions to listen. I'm looking out the window and suddenly see Detective Moneymaker. He's exiting a parked car and stops just as we drive by. I look the other way, but it's hard to believe he didn't see me, because that's my luck.

I notice the precinct's on the corner. So are kids, including one waiting to join our little engineering party. He is handed off by a Black woman with a small child poking out of yellow fabric slung across her body. This kid, who is Nigerian, knows the other two brainiacs. That's probably why Mr. Woodley wants me to tell the others a little about myself. All I can think of is the detective, and after stumbling some, I give up searching for the impressive response and say, "Well, for starters, I go to Withrow, and I live across the street from Mr. Woodley, I used to mow his lawn. As for college, I'm not sure what I want to study. Aeronautical engineering, sure, but I haven't ruled out the law or maybe being a TV reporter. I've never been anywhere, and it just seems like it would be cool to have a job that sends you all over the world, like Max Robinson for ABC News."

Mr. Woodley simply says "Well," but in a way that could mean anything, including disappointment. He's a good man and really does stand for minorities; he even says things like "fighting colonialist tendencies" and "social justice." I realize I'm his Black American cause, and that he probably expects less of a kid who is more handyman than math whiz.

On the bright side, I'm just glad to not have to do my *I was jumped routine*.

But I feel unworthy of this gesture. I almost ask Mr. Woodley to take me home when the Asian girl says, "I know what you mean. I like architecture a lot—actually, I love it." The Nigerian kid says, "My country needs engineers and I'm going back home after college. But I do have other interests." The other boy, the Ecuadorian, says his only interest is making airplanes, or flying them. Mr. Woodley says, "Cliff's got the right approach. It's important to discover your passion and pursue it with all your heart. Whatever it is. On a personal note, I wanted to sing opera, and I did until I realized I wasn't as good at it as I was at math and science. But I'm glad I had a chance to pursue it. That's why this GE summer internship, or a professional summer internship, is a great opportunity for the right kid."

All I can think of is the weird, wobbly singing that opera is, but thanks to Mr. Woodley, all the distractions and worry fade away. Soon we're passing through a series of linked buildings where jet engines are designed and made. The gray Mr. Woodley is now pastels of charm, teasing us with talk about corporate espionage and high-level secrecy in a hostile world. The James Bond images are outdone by the main building, a colossus as long as two football fields. We tour it and climb into jet engines that are wider, longer, and taller than Dad's Marquis. I'm wowed by the physics of air being sucked in at one end, ignited, and accelerated out the other end. Mr. Woodley asks us to imagine a 220 ton 747 taking off from the ground and hurtling through the atmosphere at 600 miles per hour. I'm sure I'm the only one in our little group who doesn't already know that a 747 crossing oceans isn't some magical feat but the skill and passion of aeronautical engineers. But who cares. This is the best field trip I've been on.

I'm surprised when Chip calls later that evening. He wants to know how my day was, and I tell him about forgetting to cancel GE Day and Mr. Woodley calling last night.

"So, how was it?"

I hesitate, and then say, "Boring. I like airplanes, that part was cool, but spending the summer working with a bunch of old, dusty engineers doesn't sound like fun. Besides, I'd rather work at Kings Island with you, like we planned."

"But that internship pays more than what we'd earn together working all summer at Kings Island."

"So, if you got the invitation instead of me, you'd take the internship if they offered it to you?"

"I think the point is, I didn't get the internship."

"Chip, that's like a 180° about-face from when I got invited. You're the reason I canceled . . . I would have canceled if I had remembered ."

"I was just jealous you got invited and I didn't. And well, let's be real, your prospects are better than mine."

"Even if I wanted it, the three geniuses that rode up with us are way more qualified than I am."

"But your neighbor chose you."

"He also chose them."

"Well, I'd choose you any day."

All is cool between us. We hang up and I'm thinking how nice it is to have a conversation that's not about cops or psychos or

Uncolas or any of the shit we usually end up talking about. It isn't until I'm in bed that I wonder if the real reason he called was to see if I would lie about GE Day.

I'm glad I didn't.

»»»

I know I will never feel normal again. I wake up cold like I slept on the porch. My lips burn and taste of blood. A gory blob of Scotch tape is stuck to my fingers. I remember dreaming of running coatless and hatless along dark, howling, snowy streets. Now all I hear is Dad shouting that I've overslept. "Boy, get up! You're having a PTSD fit."

I jump into sweats and scrape through our Lilliputian routine. We skip breakfast in highchairs for a banana and dry Sugar Bears on the go. The Twins chew and warble as I buckle them in the backseat. Dad doesn't seem more annoyed than usual. In my mind, though, we're setting off for the apocalypse. He's about to shift to reverse when I insist I forgot something important. I race for the tacklebox like life depends on it. I feel nothing but relief with the gun in my hand. I wrap it lovingly in gym shorts and a T-shirt. As we drive, I shove it to the bottom of my backpack, wedging it between my legs as we rush to daycare. Dad talks and talks, but I can't understand him. Mainly because I'm not listening, I'm just staring out the window at a blur of drab color. I run the Twins into the Lilliputian ladies, then run myself back to the car. Dad still talks and talks about whatever he's talking about, and suddenly we're at my drop-off. I don't say goodbye, I bolt from the car. I run toward first bell, dragged by my backpack's added weight. I'm the last Black boy at school anyone would suspect of being armed.

I'm some minutes late and running down the hall, but I feel a drag that's never slowed me down before. Suddenly I couldn't care less about class or school. I hang out in a shiny bathroom stall, like I have nowhere else to be. I overhear certain pussy-crazed loudmouths. I don't plan to leave the school grounds, but I do anyway. I end up wasting second period outside in the cold. I'm a zombie by third period but make myself return to classes. After my last period I show up at the gym during rush hour. I ignore the chatty guys and shove my stuff into a locker, including my hoodie and shirt and the pistol. I roll up the legs of my sweatpants and then head to the indoor running track, a flattened donut suspended over the basketball court. I think of all the times the dribbling, prancing teams never picked me to play. I think of the crazed kid who broke his neck in a kamikaze dive onto the court during a game, the score tied. Rumors say he was aiming at a basketball player who'd harassed him brutally. He missed but made his point.

I circle thirty times before grabbing my things from the locker. On the homeward run I don't even try talking myself out of passing by the gas station. He's the one injured, not me; I can't think of a better advantage over him. But I know I need to be smarter about this mission than the kamikaze kid. Two payphones are near the entrance. The one closest to the street is my best chance of getting away if it came to that. Except I can't see the psycho motherfucker clearly—a play of light, a plane of light, shadow and reflections blur him. I rake the bottom of my backpack and dig through its pockets. I find a stash of dimes, each an opportunity to drive the motherfucker crazy. I punch in the number on the payphone. The store clerk transfers my call to the garage. Now I see the motherfucker leaning on a crutch—"Yeah, this Buster," he says. And I shout, "Fuck you, faggot!"

»»»

He wanted a blowjob from me. He wanted to fuck me. If I'm a faggot, he's a faggot. F-A-G-G-O-T!

»»»

The dimes ping in my pocket like a kamikaze pinball designed to shell him one after the other. Each detonates a more destructive blast than the bats ever could. Each gets closer to driving him into a frenzy, tripping him up. He's not a calm, cool, collected type. A guy like him has probably been to the psych ward a few times already.

After four tries, I decide to continue my mission from home. It's hard to focus on anything other than tormenting him, but I do. I wait until Mom's in bed before starting up again. I redial the gas station, imagining him hobbling to lock up the garage. He answers and we both float in the silence of the line.

"You're a faggot," I say in boldface into the phone like his secret's out. "All your friends are gonna know you're a faggot."

Just before hanging up, he says, "Bitch boy, I'mma fuck you up!"

I sleep in the lower bunk, but in the crawlspace between fear and fury. I'm excited. I have a gun. *Pow*.

»»»

My lips are still a tortured hemoglobin red with the icky residue of Scotch tape. I try wiping it off, pushing the gunk into a dot of accumulated lip skin, sleep crud, spit, and glue gunk. I push the gathering slimeball past the lip border where I pluck it off. My upper lip seems to have been spared the glue, but then I wonder if hot drinks haven't simply dissolved it. I'm probably slowly poisoning myself. This scares me before its Inspector Clouseau-ishness—*Death by Scotch Tape!*—becomes a joke.

What's better than tape? A gag? Sock in mouth?

Fire power.

»»»

On the way to Lilliputian, Dad is talking, talking. I'm not listening, I am thinking. I want him to talk about what he wants to talk about.

"Dad, Dad, I have a question? It's about PTSD?"

"Shoot."

"Ah, that's the word. So, I was wondering about when you were a soldier. Did you have to psych yourself up to kill?"

"You mean when we was on patrol?"

"Yeah, I guess."

"Psych myself? No, I wouldn't say that. More like, I was nervous and wound up. I wasn't alone, I was with a group of guys, and we were trained to do this thing, and to do it together, and to do it having each other's back. I was damned good at it, better than most of them. First time in my life I was good at something. I wanted to be the best at it. So, no, I didn't have to psych myself up. I'd say I was charged up. I couldn't stand it when we didn't have shit to do. That's when my mind started running loose. Some of the guys were scairt shitless. Not me."

"Did you think about the man, woman, or child you just killed?"

"Naw, not at the time, I just did my job. But, you know, all that stuff comes back. That's the PTSD."

Then he says, "You might be shocked hearing me say it. But doing that job was easier and more satisfying than doing the boring, stupid shit job I got now. So there you go. Figure that out."

»»»

My mind is one-track, in war mode, hunkered down, in the dirt, face grease blackened, meditating on driving the psycho motherfucker crazy.

Mom knows what to do to snap me out of it. A McDonald's dinner of my choice! All I have to do is go with her on a quick trip to the Twin Fair. We both know a trip to Twin Fair's never quick. But she has an appointment to get baby pictures for a steal. Imagining the worst, I want the goodies first, but a finger's swipe of peanut butter is all we have time for.

Babies are so raw, all feelings, all the time. They're always a frown or peekaboo away from giggles or a meltdown. I make a mobile playpen out of the shopping cart. The boy stands at the front of the basket like he's leading a charge as I zigzag the cart across the parking lot. Mom wobbles behind us, which doubles their fun. My own mood sours entering the store, though. We're at the end of a long line for this last day of the Baby Portrait Fifty Percent Off promotion. I count ten families ahead of us. Seems like everybody on the line has an appointment. They all gripe that there's only one photographer to do everything. That if it was white people on the line, they would have had more photographers. I watch a woman place a whiny toddler on a table-size stage with a blue screen behind it. I see a black curtain and a person moving under it. Then I notice the long black braid slipping by the curtain, and the skinny body it's attached to. It all adds up to Punch, just stepping out from under the curtain. His toolbox of bunny ears and gag bag of sounds and funny faces seem to confuse and then calm the toddler just enough for a good shot—all costing about ten minutes. I don't know which freaks me out more—the wasted time or having to deal with him. I complain to Mom that we'll be here until closing time.

Mom's all in on getting what she came for. She wants me to hold our place while she grabs a few lady things. I take a position at the side of the cart. It's impossible not to be seen out here in the open. The Twins stand up and holler for me to jostle the cart. Other kids on the line seem jealous, crankier, more restless. The exhausted mothers slingshot the evil eye at us. It's clear nobody wants to be here. Ten minutes go by before Mom returns. I wonder how she can even stand up when just sitting isn't comfortable . Now she wants fruit punch and pretzels for the Twins. The one thing that moves fast in this slow store is the snack bar. The line is near the store entrance and, at the moment,, short enough that

I can step outside. I bet I could run home for my backpack and be back before it's our turn. Mom would be furious if I did, but knocking off homework might be worth it. I'm looking out over the parking lot when I think I see the psycho motherfucker, hobbling against the rusty sunset. The grizzled, cane-carrying old woman at his side looks familiar. I turtle into my hoodie, worried I've been seen. I fidget on the snack bar line debating what to do. On my turn, I buy three pretzels, salivating for the salty soft dough. I turn leave just in time to see them entering the store. I wait some seconds until they're out of sight. They must be shopping for her—why else walk an old lady through the cold and giant store? I note their general direction and deliver the goodies. Mom complains she wanted pretzels for the Twins and popcorn for herself. She tears a pretzel into pieces for the gaping mouths of our baby birds. The queue hasn't moved at all. A mutiny starts with two of the five families ahead of us. The mothers complain about wasting time and being late for work. They have choice words for the "hippie behind the camera," as they call him. Now a third family abandons the line, leaving just two ahead of us. I tell Mom I'm going to the bathroom. She says I've got five minutes.

I last saw the oppressive pair in the women's clothes aisles. After a quick pass-by, I head toward housewares. Now I'm on the other side of the photo studio when Punch calls my name. He grins and waves, but I ignore him. I find my targets in men's winter outerwear, where coats are fifty percent off. I watch the psycho motherfucker hold open a jacket for her to slide her arms through the sleeves. They're positioned at a mirror, and both seemed pleased with the look and fit. It's almost too weird to think about, this same scene that happens every winter with me and Mom. How does a monster like him get to be normal, too? I inch closer toward them, just an aisle away. I don't care if he sees me. He's the one on a crutch, hitched to an old lady, in the biggest, whitest store in

Norwood, aka KKK land. A cops' precinct and the fire department are behind the mall.

And he's a faggot! I love licking those two syllables before spitting them out.

My five minutes of freedom are up. I see Punch setting the Twins up in the little studio area. I introduce myself before he has a chance to say the wrong thing. We shake hands with Mom watching. The bubbly babies are primed for fun. They grin at me as I move toward the humming camera. My usual slapstick gets the desired laugh. A few minutes pass, and we are gathering our things to leave, when Punch says, "You're hired as my chief baby entertainer! That was the easiest session I've had all weekend. Can you do cats?" I laugh and say, "Sure, I need a job." He says, "Too bad it's the last day of the promotion. Maybe next time. Seriously."

Looking over the registration info Mom provided, he says, "Hmm, Mrs. Douglas, I just noticed we almost have the same telephone number. Switch the last two around, and you'd be calling my house." Mom acts surprised, though she couldn't care less. Looking at me, he says, "I'll put a rush on your order. Two or three days, tops, not the usual week. I'll call when they're ready. Or you can call me if you have questions."

As we're walking away, Mom says, "I don't like that freak."

All I can think is he knows where I live.

»»»

I'm feeding the Twins breakfast when the phone rings. It's Mom reminding me today is Dad's first day of school. She says, "He's a little nervous. Maybe you can pump him up a little. Encourage him, tell him that you appreciate him taking on school to earn more for his family's sake. Coming from you will help because I know he cares what you think."

Really! The thought makes me uneasy, queasy. I doubt he cares what I think about anything, saying he does is just Mom's way of manipulating me. I tell the babies what I really want to say about suddenly-sugary LACK—"Like I give a flying fuck about his stupid class!"

I clean faces and fingers and free the Twins from highchairs. I notice they tense up hearing Dad clunking downstairs, too. Like they're bracing for the worst of his many moods—"Hey Twins," he says, "y'all ready?" I can smell the whiskey on him now, a stench greater than his Pierre Cardin aftershave. He staggers a little, his speech slurs a little, but he's smiling and not the fire-breathing drunk I've faced many times. "Y'all ready?" he says again. I don't know what to say or do, so I do what we usually do. I say we're all ready to go. He follows the usual path through the basement and garage, but he forgets to take a baby. I scoop them up, one in each arm, and lurch step by step into the basement. I hear the engine turn over, wondering if he'll drive off without us. Surprise of surprises, he's sitting in the passenger seat. "Cliffy-boy, you're driving," he says. "it'll be just like a driver's test. Show me what you got!" I complain I don't got a temporary permit and haven't even taken Driver's Ed. He says, "Since you so damn smart, let's see what you can do!"

I buckle up the Twins in the backseat. I want to remind him what this car means to him. But he's right, because I've studied his driving like I have Chip's. If I can maneuver a VW stick-shift through city traffic and forty-plus miles on the highway with a bleeding boyfriend riding shotgun and do all that after a beatdown and escape from a relentless psycho motherfucker, I can manage a bloated Marquis. I back the car from the driveway with a lurching start. I get us up the hill and make a near telephone pole-swiping right turn. The car is so wide I feel I'm over the median, but in the side-view mirror I see that I'm not. Dad's too busy mumbling about

Detective Moneymaker to care. "Moneymaker," he says loudly—"Moneymaker thinks you're just pretending you don't remember what happened. And I'm pissed off, because, you know, I'm your old man and you wouldn't lie to me. He thinks you're a homo."

"Dad, I'm trying to drive, remember—"

"Oh, right, don't you crash my car, boy!"

"Dad! I really need you to help me. I've got to take the Twins inside, okay."

"Yeah, right. Sorry. But you gotta wonder how many Black people get locked up because the cops need to pin a crime on somebody."

"That's right, Dad. Good point."

I see a parking space close to the daycare. Too tight to squeeze an oversized car into. I double-park instead and then free the babies. I deliver the girl first and then return for the boy. "It's my dad," I say to Lilliputian ladies, as if that explains everything wrong with the world.

A tailgate of angry drivers glares at me. A station wagon darts across the median and speeds by hurling curses. Dad's eyes are closed and his head rests in the crook between the seat and window. If I have a plan, it's to not let Dad fuck up my day completely. I head for the nearest McDonald's Drive Thru, hoping coffee and an Egg McMuffin work on him. We aren't far from the CTC building, which I remember from bus rides downtown. I park in a lot close to the school, and I say, "Dad, do you have your diaper pin?" He nods, and I can see that breakfast and coffee have soaked up some of the drunkenness. I rip some paper from my notebook and a pen from my stash. We cross the street near the building entrance with the sun eyeballing us. I witness his struggle and cheer for him to stick it out. I lock my arm through his, and we enter the CTC building. We take an elevator to the third floor and then walk down a long gray hall. We enter a large industrial room that seems to double as classroom and workshop. A supersized mixing bowl shaped like a baseball stadium. I hand him the car keys, pen and paper.

"Good luck, not that you'll need it, you'll be fine. Isn't that what you always say to me?"

"Cliffy-boy, I need something."

"You want me to stick you with the diaper pin? Or you want your daddy to come get you?"

He finds this funny, and says, "No I'm all right, and my daddy never did shit for me!" Then he says, "Don't tell your mom."

I pat his shoulder the way he pats mine when I've been a good boy. I just hope today's slide is a one-off and not a new thing. I wait some minutes to see if he goes truant.

Then I grind my way to school.

»»»

Mom never found her missing fifty dollars. Now everybody's trying to pull a fast one on her, she thinks.

Three days have passed without news about the baby pictures. Mom says to me, "Why that hippie tell us he'll get a rush then?"

She is anxious enough to call the Twin Fair. She learns photos usually come in around 4:00 p.m. Unsatisfied, she leaves a message at Punch's home, then says to me, "Whoever that was that answered is just as weird as the hippie is."

Her paranoia spreads. Each time the phone rings I wonder if it's Punch calling. But not about the photos, about the psycho motherfucker.

Mostly to avoid her, I walk the twenty minutes to the Twin Fair at about 6:00 p.m. Daylight is leaving, and starlets draw inky sci-fi blobs over the treetops behind the college.

The photography stand is dismantled, replaced by a clerk, a table, a basket for pickups, and a counter holding a display of photo albums and picture frames. Our photos aren't among the pickups, and I'm told they're probably still being processed. And what of the Native American dude? The clerk says, "You mean the Indian?"—and I say, "Technically, no, but yeah, that dude." She tells me he works at different locations around the city but today could be his day off.

L.L. isn't far from here, just in the opposite direction. I pursue my mindfuck plans, my motivation all along. A ten-minute sprint, and I'm in position. I see other workers but not the psycho motherfucker, not at the pumps, not in the store. I wait some minutes in case he's in the bathroom, and then wander in. I'm told he's off today. I head outside to the telephone. I'm psyched to escalate, why not go to the Doris Day House? Take the fight to him.

But I forgot the gun.

»»»

I run home to find Punch standing in the dining room talking to Mom. She says, "Looky here, Cliffy, he brought the pictures by out of the goodness of his heart, ain't that nice?"

"Like, our addresses are close, you're not far from where I live. So, I figured, what the heck," he says.

"I just came from the Twin Fair," I say.

"I tried calling here first but the line was busy," he says.

"That's because his brother's been hogging the phone," Mom says.

"I gotta go," he says. "Enjoy the photos Mrs. Douglas."

Mom's faith in the motivation of others is restored. I walk Punch outside. I thank him again.

"Now I know where you live," he says, and I wonder if this is a good thing. "I'll see you later."

His bike is propped against the driveway door and hidden by Mom's car. I watch him roll to the curb. I hear someone, a black guy, calling his name, and watch him dart across the street. The two seem happy to run into each other and stand close as they talk. Both smile a lot, and the other guy is taller by an inch or more. Punch always seems to be running into somebody he knows. I'm surprised, he's so weird and not at all like a homecoming king, or like super-friendly, funny Blair.

Punch and the guy cross the street and walk up the hill. I make it just in time to see them separate at the traffic light. Punch in the direction of Twin Fair. The other guy straight up my street.

Some hours later, I answer the phone and it's Punch. He wants to know if we're enjoying the photographs. I go on about how happy Mom is and that she's planning to give a copy to her siblings, parents, and in-laws, and we'll probably need more. He says to just let him know, and I tell him I will, soon as I talk with my mom. Then he says: "I have a gig in Norwood on Saturday, you wanna come with me?"

"Why? You paying me?"

"No, it's not the cute baby or cats kind of picture taking."

"What kind is it then?"

"It's sports shit, but you should find it interesting."

"So naked dudes, baby pictures, cats, and now sports."

"It's all art. Gotta make a living. You interested or not? I know you don't have a bike. My roommate has one. I'll ride it over with me. I'll be there around two."

"Can it be earlier?"

"No, we need to get there by 2:30. Cool?"

"Okay, sure."

If only I could be sure of anything.

»»»

"Fuck Fuck Sunday," I say. Emphasizing fuck, as in *Fuck* you, *Fuck* Sunday. All I meant was let's not make a big deal out of missing our fuck day.

We're on the phone. I'm calm enough to sense he's about to go nuclear over something.

"Because, Cliff, I look forward to Fuck Sundays, it's important to me, so what if shit happens and we have to postpone."

"I mean this Fuck Sunday, not all Fuck Sundays."

"It's not like something's come between us, is there?"

"What do you mean?"

"Like another guy. Is there another guy?"

"Of course not."

"I feel like you're drifting away from me."

"I'm not."

"What's going on with the psycho motherfucker?"

"Nothing."

"He's back at work. Nothing?"

"Nothing. Maybe he learned his lesson."

"Any word on the internship?"

"No, and I'm not even thinking about it. They'll never give it to me."

"You know, stop it with the negative. It's boring."

Before now, I wasn't in my own meltdown state. But I've had it and can't listen to him any more. . Still, I'm startled by the handset punching into the cradle when I hang up on him. I can't believe what I've done and feel bad about it. If he calls back, I'll make up some lie. As if there were any other explanation for that cradle-punching sound.

I'm outside in the cold at a payphone near the Xavier campus. He's on break and at a payphone in the mall where he works. And so what if it's a regular call for him, a dime for ten minutes, the benefit of being within the city limits—he's not going to call, and it's probably over between us. I'm about to leave when the phone rings again. I lunge for the receiver but something in me just can't.

I take off down the parkway, never imagining I'd be running away from him feeling like this.

I don't remember making a decision to go to the track. That's where I end up, running in circles, mimicking the loop of my thoughts, a dog circling its tail. I drag home twenty laps later, shower, and hide in my top bunk bed beneath the stars. I'm mad at myself for fucking everything up. So stupid and childish, and what excuse can I make? I'm not ready to break up. I love him.

I made a mistake.

I hear the catch of my door opening as I push my face deeper into the pillow. I'm prepared to howl at Mom to leave me alone, and then I hear, "Thank God, you're all right, I thought something happened to you."

Chip? I can't believe he's still there, even after I blink. "I'm sorry . . . shhh!" I say. "Before you speak anything, let me lock the door. My Dad's on the other side of that wall, and my brother is on the other side of that one."

In the few seconds it takes me to lock the door, tears flowing faster than I can swipe them away, he is standing close, so close our foreheads meet.

"I'm so sorry I worried you and that you came all the way here. And climbing all our steps—your poor sprain."

"No, it's better, no more crutches, see. It's still uncomfortable driving the stick so I took my Mom's car. My Dad's gonna flip out, but I had to see if you were alright. After everything that's happened, I guess I'm paranoid about everything and easily freaked out."

"But you were at work."

"Yeah, I told them I had a family emergency."

"So you lost hours and money because of me . . ."

"Can we go so we can have some privacy?"

"Yeah, let's get out of here."

I wedge my feet into sneakers. We step outside my room, but Dad's coming from his room. He looks from me to Chip like we're hiding something under our sweatshirts. I feel I'm seconds away from being found out. I can't not introduce him. Chip smiles and they shake hands. I tell him we're prepping for the upcoming calculus midterm. Dad's heard this before and seems to want to fact check what I've said about this particular Kings Island friend. But Chip has kept track of the college lies and mentions our weekend trip to Ohio State. Our recent tour of the University of Cincinnati campus. And then does me one better, saying we might drive to LA to hang out before UCLA starts. Dad is a sucker for SoCali and Chip easily sets him up for the win: "Cliff tells me you're taking a course at Cincinnati Tech, I hope it goes well for you." Dad laughs, seems surprised, then says, "You know I don't think I've ever heard anyone call Cliffy Cliff. I'm Cliff, he's named after me, and damn, I guess, boy, you've outgrown a kid's name, huh?" We all laugh.

Outside, we snicker on the way to the car and once inside let our laughter loose. "Chip, wow, you know you can do no wrong after that performance. I mean, the bit about driving to LA was a masterstroke. You're like a secret weapon I didn't know I had."

We go on a little more. I wonder if he thinks I'm greasing him the way he greased Dad, which I'm not. At the top of the hill, we turn toward our make out spot, where our feelings are like lightning bugs in the darkness.

"So, you hung up on me, didn't you?"

"Yeah, I'm sorry, I overreacted. Just don't call me negative. I don't want to be criticized."

"I know I was being a jerk, I'm sorry. We've both got a lot of shit going on, and the last few weeks have been tough for me, missing my mom, feeling betrayed and desperate and just really awful. But, Cliffy, hanging up on each other . . . nothing deserves that."

"I know. Like you said we've both got a lot of shit going on. But the thing is, you think you're trying to help but you always end up criticizing me. And I hate it. I realize you're just frustrated, but you're not here, and you don't know what it feels like to be here in the middle of it. I listen to the way my dad talks down to my mom, and it feels like that to me. I don't need that from you, and I don't criticize you."

"And I don't hang up on you, do I?"

I think of LACK when I say, "I know it was the wrong thing to do . . . stupid, really stupid, and I'm sorry. I don't know why I didn't just say I had to go or something."

"Yeah, that woulda been cool."

"Sometimes I feel like we want to break up but just don't know how to say it." I'm looking away from him and yet feel like we're standing on a cliff. He says, "I don't feel that way, at all, ever"—and looks so sad and scared when he asks if I want to break up with him that I feel no choice but to say no.

"It's just it's so hard sometimes. The driving, the long distance, our schedules. I feel like we're on a tightrope right now, and I know we're only trying to help each other not go crazy, but all we're doing is driving each other crazy."

"I don't feel that way."

"Well, I do, sometimes. Not all the time, just sometimes."

"Why?"

"We're so different. I mean we're alike but we're very different. When we first started going out, I wondered if the only reason you were with me was because I'm black, and that that was just another part of your queer experiment."

"Really?" He laughs. "I used to worry I wasn't black enough for you. And now, I think I'm too black for you."

"If you mean the n-word, it'll always be nails scratching the chalkboard, no matter who says it. I just thought we were on the same side."

"We are. We're boyfriends. I'd do anything for you. Anything."

"Yes, we are boyfriends. And correction, Richard Pryor cracks me up."

Now is the time to list the things I haven't told him because I don't want him telling me what I should do. That the motherfucker knows my brother and my dad and where we live. That I'm mind-fucking the psycho motherfucker by harassing him on the phone. That I keep a gun in my backpack. But I keep the list to myself. He doesn't ask about the psycho motherfucker either.

But we do agree he'll stop criticizing me, and I will speak up when I'm upset with him instead of overreacting, like hanging up on him.

Our pledge is signed in cuddles, kisses, and lovebird eyes. He leaves me at my house, and I watch him drive away.

»»»

Chip's mom comes to me in a dream. As if I'd known her for years and we were friends. Though we never met and spoke only once on the phone. I remember Chip was in the basement or something. During the wait, she started a conversation with me. I guess to get to know me, but maybe also to let me know her. She asked where I'm from. I told her Evanston, emphasizing our closeness to the university. And I didn't mention the Findlater Gardens projects where we had lived before Evanston. She told me she grew up near the University of Cincinnati, and she earned her BS there. She told me she misses living in the city, she misses the mix of people and cultures that were a fixture of her growing up. I told her that my high school is very mixed. She said it bothered her that Chip doesn't have any Black friends where they live. She explained that as a mixed-race family, it's been hard for him and his sisters. She said it had also been difficult for her to adjust in the first few years. What she said next stays with me. Just before Chip got on the line, she said: "I'm so glad Chip has you, I know my son, and he's different since he met you." She said it like our relationship was some kind of blessing. In all, we spoke for maybe five minutes. I'm sort of haunted by it now. Like I was a dying wish come true for her son. I've also wondered if she wasn't saying she understands about us. Before she died, he did tell her about himself and us. She whispered he should always be honest and true to himself. She said nothing more, as far as I know.

»»»

I'm waiting in the window for Punch the daredevil. I already know to expect him to be riding one bike,steering another uphill in busy Saturday afternoon traffic. The kid in me thinks his trick is cool, but the guy with UCLA dreams can only see the street's sharp curves where I've nearly been run over twice and where cars smash in totaling collisions. That UCLA dreaming guy also notices the unoccupied sidewalks on both sides of the street that Punch would have all to himself. It makes me wonder what I've gotten myself into.

I rush outside through the garage and wait for him beside Mom's car. The chuffing from his breathing creates tiny clouds in a cold, cloudless morning. The cold must be nothing to him. His leather jacket's unzipped. A black scarf loops around his neck. His blue jeans look summery thin. I'm about to go back in for another sweater when I see him waving and look up toward the solarium windows. There's Dad, shirtless and maybe naked, staring down at Punch. Punch seems dazed and I go, "Hey."

"Wow, is that your old man?"

"Yeah."

"Hot Pop! You've probably heard that before."

"Yeah, I have." The image of Punch blowing some guy in a parking lot, and now him salivating over my dad, and at my house, is too much! I must be nuts to go anywhere with him. I try to joke about it. "Don't ask him to pose butt naked for you."

Punch laughs. "Okay, no problem, not that you control me or him."

"Who said anything about controlling anybody?" I laugh.

He is as whacky as the spare bike he brought. An old, rusty, cobwebby five-speed Sears model that's probably older than I am and abandoned. Punch's fancier, battle-scarred bike doesn't inspire confidence, either. He still won't say where we're going, though I follow him and the sorry bike anyway. I ride on the sidewalk until we're out of Dad's sight, then jump the curb into the street. We pump side by side uphill to Montgomery before a swerve into Norwood. Keeping up is a workout, but the cold has a lock on me. We've been riding for like a half hour and I'm sweating ice. Punch's jacket is fully open and the scarf's flying loose like streamers. He yanks it off and tosses it to me, shouting that where he's from it's probably -20.° I wrap my neck and face in the soft cotton fabric and feel better, my teeth chattering less. I notice the sign for Norwood Bowling Lanes, never guessing it's our stop. We lean our bikes against the building near the entrance. I say, "Far as I know, bowling is a hobby, not a sport." And he says, "Tell that to the *Wide World of Sports* people, not that I give a fuck. It's money in my pocket. That's all I care about."

He pulls out a canteen and takes a swig of what he calls antifreeze. He offers me some, and I gulp what feels like liquid flames. But the flames spread from my throat to stomach and instantly warm me up. I resist a repeat, and he stashes the canteen in the camera bag's pocket, warning we'll get thrown out if we're busted with booze: "The antifreeze is tequila and chili peppers, in case you want to know."

I shake my head like I don't care because I don't care. My innards are toasty by the time we go inside. A sign welcomes the

Soul Brothers League, and we're greeted by the crash and clatter of bowling pins. Punch says, "It's also my rocket fuel. When I ain't taking dumbass portraits at stupid department stores, I'm running around the city to sporting events, civic events, parades, concerts, protests. I sell my pictures to the *Cincinnati Enquirer* and *The Post*. Anything about Black people that's not crime-related sells."

"What am I supposed to do while you take pictures?"

"Act like you're my assistant."

"You're trying to get free labor out of me?"

"Just trying to give you something to do. Bowl, if you know how. Or you can cock-watch, that's always fun. Whatever you wanna do, do it."

I didn't know what to expect. Still, I can't believe I came for this. Knowing him, there's more to it.

"This is the final day of the two-week tournament. It's starting in about ten minutes. It'll be over in two to three hours. I gotta stay to get shots of the winners."

My booze buzz is exaggerated on an empty stomach. Punch tosses me a bag of peanuts, saying they're two dollars a pop at the bar. We walk along what's like a red and beige highway connecting the bar, restaurant, and bowling lanes. Suddenly afros are everywhere, like a field of dyed cotton balls. The soul brothers are all herded together, decked out in primary color team smocks and gold chain necklaces and earrings. The tournament creates a color line, black on one side of the alleys, white on the other, otherwise it's mostly Saturday afternoon regulars from my age up. The beer's flowing and the bowling balls are rolling. The cheers are loud and the cussing too.

"Okay, I'll be your flunky," I say.

"This ain't a buncha kiddies we're trying to trick into a smile."

"I get it."

"Act like you know what you're doing. Stay close by for when I need more film and batteries, but not too close."

"I get it, OK? And I know how to bowl."

"Cool. Let's get some pictures."

The leaderboard shows the teams' standing so far. I can see the match is close, with the top six teams within fifty points of the highest score. Most of the pack aren't far behind. Scores are projected, giving us a look at each bowler. I follow Punch as he picks the three most likely to take home trophies. "I ain't horse racing, but I'm usually right."

Maybe it's just the antifreeze, but I've got the giggles. We approach today's leader, the Kunta Kinte Warriors, as in the TV series *Roots*, which totally cracks me up. Punch talks up the team captain, Amadullah, and gets his picture on the shiny tarmac. He's clumsily tall and takes ballerina steps to the default line before pitching the ball into a gleaming spin. Pins fly up and crash down. He shouts, "The Lord is talking to me today! Thank you, Jesus!"

Punch says to me, "Hallelujah Amadullah there is packing about twelve inches, I'd say." It takes me a minute to get the joke and another to stop the giggles.

Next, we go for today's likely second or third place winner, The Crew. Punch says, "I guess you recognize that dude, the thick one?"

I can't see who he's talking about through all the dudes and puffy afros crowded around their lane. Then I do recognize him, and Punch says, "That's King, and those that aren't his teammates are his bodyguards. He's the uncle of Buster—or psycho MF, as you call him."

"I know who he is," I say. "Some of the others, too. My brother Corey's best friend is his son, and on top of that, he and my dad went to high school together."

"Ain't that quaint," Punch says. "You told me that you got away because Buster got into it with somebody that turned up at the gas station while he was trying to dick you. It's probably Uncle King there."

"Why you say that?"

"Because the two of them were arguing one time I stopped by—again, this is before I met you—and King was saying he was tired of saving his ass because of sick urges. He meant Buster's boy cravings."

"Did you know he was going to be here?"

"Yes and no. Yes, because I took their picture last year, they won second place, and no, because they could've bailed, shit happens. It ain't like we keep in touch."

"You wanted me to tag along because of him?"

"Yeah, I figured you should know it's a conspiracy. That nigga's as guilty as Buster."

The longer I stare at The Crew, the stronger the feeling the psycho motherfucker's around. Then I see him, in a brief clearing between the men. I say to Punch, "And there's that motherfucker, sitting in the booth. I guess he bowled on the team last week, too?"

"No, I guess because you and your batboy Chip busted up his knee."

"You said you worked at the tournament last year, too. Did he bowl in that?"

"Probably he was in prison. Look, dude, I met him after he came out of prison, but I don't know these people or keep track of them. This is how I make money, and how I make art. I'm not anybody's friend. Now, if you're gonna freak out seeing them, you can either wait for me at McDonald's or you can bike home. Up to you."

"Sorry, it's just that it feels like that motherfucker's everywhere I go. He was even at the Twin Fair when you were taking pictures of my brother and sister. Did you see him?"

"Yeah, I did, with some old lady. And so what? You think pedophiles and killers don't live their lives cuz you can't? You're lucky, though. I looked it up once, and Cincinnati's got a population of over 300,000 people. Imagine what it was like for me growing up in a place with a population of, like, ninety fuckin' nosy people. You deal with it, it's how it is. Now, if you don't mind, I'm at work."

Punch grabs the camera bag hanging on my shoulder and hustles toward The Crew. Something big's happening, it's like James Brown, the ultimate soul brother himself, has just stepped out onto a tarmac so shiny he can almost see himself bowl. If only it were the King of Soul and not the psycho motherfucker and his crutch hobbling to the foul line. I'm pulled toward what I'm seeing. I move closer, risk being recognized by the armed Crew, or somebody else in the posse who Corey said saw me. All eyes are on the psycho motherfucker, though. The ball rides on his hip to the foul line and then lifts onto his fingers and palm. He plants the crutch at an angle just beyond his foot. He swings his arm backward and pitches the ball down the lane. The spinning sphere arcs toward the gutter, riding the edge like a wave and then breaks to the center for a shattering takedown. His team high-fives and cheers while the competition shakes their head. I look at his scoreboard and see only strikes. I'm impressed. I'm disgusted that I'm impressed. I run to bathroom with tequila oozing out of my mouth and through my fingers. Most of it lands in the toilet in time. I soap up the stain on my shirt. I wipe off the foulness and swish soapy water around my mouth.

Punch ignores me, has moved on to the next team on his hit list. I stop close to where The Crew's friends are hanging out. I notice the psycho motherfucker is surrounded. Maybe they're hiding him between turns in case the police wander through. Any of these dudes might claim to have seen me at the bat beatdown. Nobody seems to notice me, though. I leave, and Punch says, "Oh, my assistant finally returns!" I say, "Sorry. So fire me." We eyeroll each other. I guess that means truce.

What did Punch know, and when did he know it? I see Punch for what he is, a devious, treacherous, slut—that's what a brutal life has done to him. I should abandon him now and go home. I keep my eyes on The Crew. They're racking up strikes and spares with each roll. When the psycho motherfucker's up, a pin explosion follows. It's disgusting to me that he could end up being MVP, a hero.

We work our way through photographing the competition. Everything in me hopes my enemy will fail. I come to my senses and stand back as the inevitable happens. The team places second, but the psycho motherfucker wins the day. He fist-bumps the air as the league cheers him. I can't take it.

»»»

Outside, the cold is hard to face. Punch takes a swig of the fiery cocktail in the canteen. I should but don't decline seconds. We backtrack to a McDonald's on Montgomery Road, and gobble Big Macs. I drink a hot chocolate, and he spikes his Coke, saying he wants to shoot me with his remaining film. I feel shot already, but in the wounded sense.

The sun is a floodlight shining in our eyes. I feel like screaming but let out a whimper. Punch slides sunglasses on and off we go. He wants to bike to the other side of the highway bridge we're on. I notice a small fancy mall beyond the road, but I doubt we're riding there. We hop off at a break along a chain link fence and walk some before laying the bikes on their sides on the frozen ground. We climb down a hill until we're just clear of the bridge girders, then scale a steep, cement-covered slope until we're sitting in a crawl space beneath the bridge. Cars speeding along I-71 just above our heads.

It feels even colder here to me. To him it's nothing, and he uses his jacket to prop up the camera and set the timer for self-portraits of me and him. I'm so cold I ignore my rumbling stomach and take another swig of fire from the canteen. I feel the flames rising in my throat as the camera snaps our pictures, the spine of the expressway inches above my afro.

Without thinking I say, "That boyfriend you told me about—is he still alive?"

"How would I know?. Why you asking about him? I don't wanna talk about him. He's scum. Scum don't matter. Nobody gives a shit about scum. Nobody misses scum like him. He's the type that ends up in prison or dead."

"Aren't you even curious to know what happened to him?"

"News flash: I'm done with him. He fucked me up, I fucked him up back. Case closed. You're a kid, so maybe this is a little advanced for you, but I live for the moment. I'm, like, so fucking present, and I avoid the past like the plague. You want to waste your time in the past, then poor you. You might as well kill yourself now. Find yourself a therapist to write prescriptions to make you numb. Or find yourself one of those groups where they all sit around talking about the misery shit that's happened to them. But I'm not that guy, you understand?"

His fierceness surprises me. I can't help but wonder what really happened. It's just a feeling, maybe the fire tequila talking, but I realize Punch could turn on me, even hurt me. I could tumble down the embankment onto the highway shoulder with a wrong move, or a light push. But then, so could he, if it came down to a struggle. I watch him drain the canteen like it's water. We take a last picture together, cheek to cheek, arms looped over shoulders.

He says, "Don't worry, you ain't my type at all"—and I think of the guy I saw him with on the street.

He says, "Yeah, my type is like the guy you saw me talking to, I saw you watching us from the window. I saw you there. Did you like him? He's got a horse dick you can ride, if you want. Take it from me, yeehaw. I'll hook you up. He'd love a little stuck-up prissy jailbait like you."

I tell myself to play along. That warning feeling gets louder, though. I tell him I've got to get home to help my mom with the babies. I say, "But you stay here if you want."

"Thanks for your permission. Leave the bike at your garage door. I'll pick it up on my way home."

"This was a lot of fun. Thanks for bringing me."

He says nothing. Though I'm anxious he will kick me or trip me into tumbling down, I keep my eyes on the slope. I look up and wave as I walk away.

I've already climbed up to Montgomery when I realize his scarf is wrapped around my neck.

»»»

Dad walks into my room, without knocking. "Hey, boy, didn't you hear me calling?"

I feel drunk, but immediately stiffen and go on guard, just in case the madman is back.

I say, "No, I only heard the TV when I came in. Sorry."

"Some boy called for you. Punch or something like that. He said for you to call him."

"Thanks for telling me."

"That boy that just come by here . . . he a Indian?"

"Yes, he's a Native American."

"Our people got Indian blood, too. My daddy's mother was a Indian. I don't remember the tribe, though."

"Chickasaw, that's what you told me."

"Yeah, that's right. Good memory. The Chickasaws were down in Georgia and Florida, though. I ain't never seen no full-fledged Indian like him. He from around here?"

"No, from someplace in Wyoming?'

"Figures. How you know him?"

"School."

"Hmm, he seems a little old for you to be hanging around."

"Oh, I'm not hanging around with him. I'm working for him." I tell him about the Twins' baby pictures, and that Mom was there when I met him, and that I acted as his assistant while he photographed the bowling tournament last Sunday.

"That's smart, alright then." He sort of smiles. "You got your Chinese and Africans, a little bit of everybody in Cincinnati these days. Ain't seen no Vietnamese though. A whole lot of brokedown vets at the VA might be wanting to kill them."

I truly don't know what to say. "Thanks, Dad"—just comes out.

He nods and he's off again.

»»»

The Twins are snoring in the playpen when I touch them awake. I lift them out one at a time and watch them stagger forward in their slapstick way. Mom takes the boy by the hand. I follow holding the girl's hand. We are the last of a little train rounding the living room. Now their little feet begin climbing the stairs. The girl wants to sleep, not be lead around, and tries to slip my hold. I tighten my hold. We cross the landing and reach the third step when she snatches her hand out from mine. Before I react, before I can stop her, her little body twists and tumbles downstairs. Her head collides with the railing's hard edge. I leap down to the landing too late to spare her. Her open-eyed shock turns into terrified shrieks. I gather her up fast. My ears ring from the piercing cry. Mom's panicky "Oh shit" merges with my "Oh, sweetie, I'm sorry." I press her to me, kissing her little forehead. Mom coos from the top of the stairs. Now the boy twin cries for the hurt state of his other half. I place her in her crib, suddenly scared she will close her eyes and never wake up again. Death is stealthy like that, I think. Mom checks her over. No broken bones, just a little cut that just missed her eye. "Thank God," Mom says. I get ointment and make a cold compress. Mom tends to her while I undress the boy, now fitfully sucking his pacifier. Mom thanks God for the carpeted steps. She reminds me that my brothers and I have given her worse scares. There's the time Dudley swallowed an open safety pin that he miraculously pooped out, damage-free. The time Corey fell from a second-story window into a hedge with only scratches. I've heard of these feats before, but I don't love my siblings equally. I cannot believe she will be OK. I'm convinced we should go to the ER to be sure. But Mom's magic calms her, and now she's sleeping. I lay in bed, wishing I had carried her. I tried to remember what I was thinking about that so distracted me. How could she slip away from me so easily? Mom pokes her head in my room to say it's not my fault. She says, "This is how it is with children, shit happens, and you worry, and somehow, they grow up. Just like you have grown up, Cliffy. I don't know what I'd do without you." I hear Mom's bedroom door closing. I wait some minutes just to be sure. I switch the lamp on in the Twins' room. I see bruising and a scab in the making. Her arms are suddenly twitchy and reaching out for something to hold. I wonder if she's dreaming of herself falling or flailing. Then her eyes open and she lifts her arms out to me. I cry as she nuzzles in my arms.

»»»

Corey comes into my room; he wants to talk, he has an update. I place my sister in her crib. He says, "Your friend from Kings Island drives a VW Bug, right?" And I say, "Yeah, but it's not a Bug, it's a Type 3 Fastback." And he says, "A what?" I say, "It's a little bigger than a Bug, it's got a fastback." And we go back and forth on the anatomy of VWs. Then he says, "But now Lurch-the-psycho's saying he knows it was some niggas from OTR driving a Pontiac

Ventura. He's saying he don't even know who you are. We need Columbo to straighten this shit out."

I wait some minutes after Corey leaves before returning to the Twins' room. I lay down on the bed to watch the babies. I listen as their breathing syncs. I hear a dreamlike whimper. It turns into a cry. Mom's cry. "Please don't." Then, "Bitch, if I told you once I told you a thousand times . . ."

A hand goes up and comes down on flesh. The sound is brutal, not a bat against bone, but a whack sucked into fat, flab, and muscle.

I have my sister in my arms. I carry her with me to check on Mom. Our sleeping mom.

In another dream, I hear them fucking. Real or not, it's how she can stand him.

»»»

I wake up hearing Dudley telling me to do it now. I lean over the mattress to ask him why. That's when I see the gun lying on the floor. But Dudley is in New Jersey's Fort Dix. Logically I must have put the gun there sometime last night. Or maybe this is a dream? Am I sleepwalking when I peek into the hall from my door? When I hear snores and the TV's murmur coming from LACK's room? And Corey mumbling in his room? When I douse my face with cold water?

It's 5:00 a.m. and I'm tingly awake. I take the hall phone to call the gas station. After a dozen rings, it's his voice that answers. I quickly hang up this time. I throw on my running gear with an extra T-shirt against the cold. The thin elastic of my underwear isn't tight enough to holster the pistol, but the broad band of my jockstrap holds it in place. I slip into the hall again, then downstairs. The yodel of the furnace covers my escape out the backdoor.

Outside a cold, chalky fog glows from streetlights and the lit end-table lamps of sleeping houses. I burrow deeper in my sweatshirt's hood for warmth. Somehow my mission lets me see better, noticing the cracks in the sidewalk as clearly as I can my fingers. The crossroad ahead glows red and bleeds out on the wet tar road. Cars grind by in either direction, with cameo faces in the rush of headlights. On Woodburn I speed up to a slow jog. For seconds, I'm blinded by the bright Coca-Cola entrance, the racket of industry spookier in the fog. I cross railroad tracks onto a barrier island of Black Evanston houses, a remnant of the neighborhood that was razed by the I-71 expressway. I dodge the headlights of a passing car with music shouting into the morning void. I hide in the midriff of a curbside tree, then I see taillights pulsing red in the dark. Everything seems distorted now, and the closer I get, the further the Doris Day House appears.

I must be dreaming while being awake at the same time.

And now the trees, cars, and lights line up as they should in the world as I know it. The block looks the same, yet the house is marked so that it's not like any other. The downstairs is blackened out, but the upstairs flickers in glowing TV light. The shadow of someone moves past the window shade. I wait a few seconds before searching the porch for my bike. Before I can approach, a dog barks from inside. I sprint away with the strange feeling I'm coming and going at the same time.

The gas station store is see-through clear with fluorescent brightness. The garage glows in blotches of red and green partial lighting. I see him now, only he isn't alone. I cross the street for a closer look. He's with King, head of The Crew bowling team, the person arguing with the psycho motherfucker the night I was attacked. I have wondered about this mystery man, the single reason I got away. As I laid dazed and facedown on the icy floor, I remember what he said: *What the fuck are you doing . . . Buster, are you fucking crazy . . . You just got out . . . You wanna get locked up again over this sick shit? I'm not covering for your ass no fuckin' more. Man, when are you gonna learn?*

If that was King, maybe he wouldn't mind his nephew dead. I picture myself walking in for a Coke and then firing a surprise bullet. King stands there shaking his head at his dead nephew—*What'd you think was gonna happen fool?* I wait some more minutes and then he leaves through the front door. I watch him heading back toward the Doris Day House. He vanishes into the silvery fog like a vampire.

I've been idle for too long and the cold creeps in. It controls the switchboard of my brain now, and I'm overcome by shivering. But I aim myself toward the door, because the reason I'm here now stands on the other side of it. First, I take the gun from its jockstrap holster and grip it in my sweatshirt pocket as I'm crossing the lot. The door trips off the buzzer, and I hesitate just outside of it. Then I push in and fling my arm out to find his face at the end of the pistol. He isn't startled and doesn't look worried. Just the opposite. He stares at me with eagerness, like he's been expecting me all along.

Now we are standing face to face, just a few feet, a counter, and a pistol apart.

»»»

I hear Dudley's voice: *Point and shoot, just point and shoot.* Dudley saying, *You can look the other way and be a fraidy cat for the rest of your life.*

»»»

Pop! A single, ear-tingling shot with a wimpy wisp of smoke from the gun's mouth. I want to see it rocket from the weapon, but it vanishes quickly, with only the reaction, the impression on the target, the wound.

But there is no wound, he isn't shot. I missed. He hasn't even moved, I haven't lowered my arm, I haven't looked away. There's no pleading for me not to shoot, no begging, no sorrys, no anything, just a dead stare. Suddenly he puffs his chest out, jabbing the area where the bullet should have landed. I pull the trigger again, but nothing.

"UCLA, huh?" he says, clicking his tongue, "You know, you only get one shot with a Saturday Night Special. Bitch boy, you blew it."

Then the buzzer goes off, and a car enters the lot. Headlights bounce off the window glass as it maneuvers to the gas pumps. Leaning on the crutch, he says, "You got another bullet? I don't got one for you. Why don't you get it and come back?"

That's when I wake up.

»»»

I am flat-out and can't get up. The alarm clock is furious at me, again. The door to my room flies open with Dad shouting, "Boy, why ain't you up yet?" I tell him I'm sick. He wants to know what kind of sick? Hematoma? Concussion? Bowels? I tell him I don't know. He calls out the PTSD like this is an exorcism and then grabs my arm shouting, "Get your ass dressed so we can get the Twins to daycare."

Asleep, awake, I do as told, don't make waves, keep my head low. In the kitchen he says, "You smell like a clothes hamper. When was the last time you washed that tracksuit? Go put on something clean."

Upstairs I go. Into bell-bottom jeans, a T-shirt under an argyle sweater, plus a Sunday jacket. Following orders like a first-class cadet, I'm probably more suited to the military than Dudley is. I'm easy, he's anything but.

Downstairs I find the babies breakfasting in highchairs. But Dad's in the basement, probably for a shirt. He's done this trick before, him on one floor, them on another. I'm suddenly pissed. Should anything to happen to either Twin, it would be my fault, I would be blamed for his carelessness. Suddenly I'm crying, crying because the babies could be face down in their cereal bowls, crying because I overslept, because it's Tuesday, Wednesday, or Thursday, I don't know, crying because I only got the one shot, and I blew it. Dad arrives and before he says anything, I shout at him through a downpour of tears, "You can't leave the babies eating alone, they could choke on their spoon, choke on the Cheerios, anything could happen, and you wouldn't know because you're downstairs ironing your shirt when you should be here watching them eat. Your stupid fucking diaper pin isn't working, obviously."

He grabs me by the shoulders, shakes me. Then he claps his hands together and says, "Snap out of it! We need to go."

He's right. Dad really does have a way with me. I'm just glad I wasn't slapped or socked in the face—reactions of the madman he is without the meds.

We scoop up the babies. I wonder if I should apologize for cursing and sliming his talisman. Then he says, "Cliffy-boy, I've been there where you talk shit you don't mean and wish you could take back. I won't hold nothing against you. Let me know if you want to get shook again."

Shook me, Daddy! If that is a window to apologize, I don't go through it. I like cursing at him, insulting him. Payback. Motherfucker! We are on Woodburn nearing Lilliputian Daycare. I brace to jettison out the door in case a second shaking is coming. He says, "If my therapy group leader was here, he'd say, 'Think back, maybe you saw somebody or heard something or felt something in your dreams.'"

Right now, it's time to run the Twins to daycare. Holding hands, the twosies outrun me, though I'm never more than a step behind. I hear yelling, but I'm not sure it isn't a voice in my head, the PTSD warning me, saying, *Don't fake left, just keep running from Dad and all this fucked-up shit.* A blaring car horn hits me in the teeth as the Twins disappear through the entrance. I thank the daycare ladies as I always do. "What's wrong?" they say, and I run. I turn in time to see Dad's burgundy Marquis pounce into oncoming traffic. It speeds past the queued cars, then disappears. Along with my backpack and everything I need, including the gun.

I shake with withdrawal symptoms. I'm a gun addict! How fucked I am! What should I do? The clock is speedily counting down to something. I wonder if the ladies would let me hide out. Playtime is my favorite time. I could nap with the kiddies on the Lilliputian alphabet floor. I'm good with kids. Then I wonder, what if the psycho motherfucker finds me there and sets Lilliputian on fire. Roasted children.

I wander down Woodburn. I remember the terror of escaping the psycho motherfucker, terrified he was on my tail. But I don't feel the urgency of escape now. I wander Woodburn until I hear a car horn. It's Dad shouting, "Cliffy, get in the car!!" I notice the bike tires sticking out of the mouth of the trunk like somebody's corpse, an effigy meant for me. I knew he would find my bike! He shouts my name again, with fire and anger. I'm in the street when I hear tires burning and horns screaming and Dad shouting "Cliffy!" I see the snout of a Grand Torino closing in as I'm falling into the street. Everything becomes nothing.

I hear *Cliffy-boy! Boy! Wake up!*—I feel my body being pulled upright and carried away. My face in my father's neck. I remember this carrying from way before.

I'm lying in the spongy backseat, looking up at the satin ceiling, a burgundy version of the upholstery of Granddaddy's coffin. This calm feeling, free of pain or fear, it must be what death feels like, and we are riding to my burial. If I were dead, my eyes wouldn't burn and my throat feel scratchy. Dad's Kool chuffs, and the clouds tumble to the backseat, pulling me back to life. I hear his voice but can't make out what he's saying. It could be he's talking to me, but he could also be talking to himself, steering his thoughts on what to do with me, useless me. And then I realize it's simple, really. We are riding, he is driving, just me and him like a good dad and his good boy. And in a way, like Chip and me rising and falling on the rollercoaster of love. Dad and Chip, I love them, I desire them, I hate them, I'm repulsed.

I feel a sudden change in gravity. I feel my legs being pulled sideways and out of the car. I'm lifted again, and it's a joyful feeling to be in Dad's arms. My lips brush against his neck and I say to myself, *I love you, Dad*, and I hear him say, *You too, boy*. And I know now that the game is up. Everything is out in the open.

A blur of faces, Dad's but not Chip's. And Dad's voice rises above other voices. Bright lights, and then nothing.

Sometime later I wake up again, and everything is clearer. Dr. Fang Fang is here. I say, "I'm not crazy. Please don't put me in the psych ward." She takes my hand. "Mr. Douglas," she says, "We need to look you over. Just relax. I'll get your father."

I hear, "Cliffy-boy, you know you scared the shit out of your old man."

I imagine his spastic diaper pin and giggle to myself. I apologize for causing him problems, and he says, "You're just having an episode, you're not crazy, you didn't do anything crazy, like trying to off yourself or somebody else. I called your name, and you just walked into the street. Thank God that car didn't hit you."

"You mad at me?"

"What? I ain't mad at you. I was excited. I got your bike back. I had to chase down some fool kid. He rode past me, and I saw that yellow lock on the rack and said to myself, that's Cliffy's bike. The fool told me he bought it from Buster. I'm going over there to find out where he got it from."

"Oh," I say. He says, "Look, me and you gotta talk, boy, but right now I gotta get to school, I gotta take a test. Your Mom is on her way."

I feel myself rocketing to the bottom when I say, "Dad, don't! He's the one. He did it. He went to get my bike. He attacked me... he tried to... and I fought him... you know what I mean..."

He backs away from me now, but then comes closer and stands just left of me. He says, "Putting himself on you?"

That quaint way of putting it makes me blow a few brain cells. I watch him turn away, hear him growling *I'mma kill that nigga!*

A chain reaction is coming. I want it though I'm afraid. I picture him driving off with my backpack, all my secrets ready to spill out. Which truths about his namesake will upset him most? Graphic drawings of naked guys? Hearts branded with Cliffy Loves Chip? A loaded gun wrapped in gym shorts? A spare bullet in my chain purse?

»»»

My paranoia peaks. I know the cops are coming. I imagine Detective Moneymaker has told his armed colleagues to expect me. And to call me. I realize I can't stay here. The thought of facing Mom makes me sick. She will be heartbroken. I didn't want this trouble, it came on me. She won't understand my lying. My face throbs with its own heartbeat. In the bathroom, I see raw face bruises and swellings that add up to all the ways I've been uglied by the psycho motherfucker. What kind of person will I be after all this? I don't want to turn into someone I'd be afraid of, someone I'd never trust. I slide into my clothes and walk out of the emergency ward like Chip did. I see Mom crossing the parking lot and nearing the hospital entrance. I run when she calls out to me. I hear my name several times, but I keep running, never looking back. It's the never looking back that will hurt her the most.

The two dollars in my wallet won't cover a cab to school. I have no change for the payphone, not that there's anyone to call. Cops seem to be everywhere in cars, on foot, on corners. A truant target is on my back, same as any underaged kid not in school at this hour. My church jacket is a good cover, showing I'm not the type that would skip school. I feel weightless without my overloaded backpack. I've never bused from this area of Clifton. I arrive at school with one more period left before the end of the day. I am happy now to be in the swarm of kids passing classes. Blair is among them, and we huddle together. I explain just enough to worry him. I try not to let the word *homeless* ping out of my brain. He gets what I'm not saying and offers for me to stay at his house, just in case I'm evicted from mine. His family loves me, he says. "Hang in there, Cliffy. We're so close, just a few months, school will be out, and you'll be going to UCLA."

I figure he's a safe bet, if it all hell breaks loose. He lives closer to the Doris Day House and the L.L. than me, but from the opposite direction, and is about the same distance from school. Plus, I doubt Blair is on anybody's hit list like me.

At home I am braced for a tornado of anger, but it's clear skies with Mom. I don't say anything about what happened today. I stand in the den's doorway after she summons me. The television lights the room but not enough that she can see evidence of my latest trip to the hospital. I tell her I'm tired and going to my room. I watch the clock, and it's eleven-ten when Dad comes home, not through the basement as usual, but the front door, which slams hard enough that I can hear it. His heavy feet don't pound the stairs, and I wonder if he's in the den. I am not brave, and weirdly, I think of the bat beatdown to motivate my next move. Maybe I'll get points if I face him directly. Explain. Shed light. Tell the truth.

The door, always open, is closed. The television must not be on, and I wonder if he's even there. My hand is on the knob, I take deep breaths then head for the deep-end. He is walking toward me with a whiskey in his hand.

"You! Lied!"

"Dad, I can explain everything. It was the PTSD . . ."

"I gave you every opportunity to say what went down, and you lied and lied and lied. Wasting everybody's time. Scaring your mother to death. Disappointing me. And on top of that, running around with a pistol. What the fuck were you gonna do?"

"I don't know."

"The one thing I can't stand is liars."

"But you lie to Mom all the time about your side women."

"Never! And you don't know a goddamn thing about me and your mother."

"That didn't come out right . . . I'm sorry, I didn't mean it . . . Dad, please!"

"I want you outta my sight before I smack the shit outta you!"

The fear of how he was comes back, I do as told, wondering why I said what I said, wishing I could take it all back. All I can think is I need to get out before he makes good on the threat to slap me around. I shove stuff into my suitcase, smarting that he still has my backpack with my tell-all notebook and the pistol. I don't care. I slip out of the house through the front door and run to Blair's as fast as I can.

»»»

It's 5:00 a.m. My face hurts, my chest hurts, even worrying hurts enough that I can't sleep. I'm homeless, but I will not fail school, I will graduate at the top my class. Fuck Dad!

I imagine Chip's also sleepless. We are in a more complicated phone tag than ever, what with me not being home, and him not knowing where I am. Something tells me his situation is worsening, maybe a new Uncola. He's told me he has slept at a school friend's. I know he has slept in his car before, and that his dad neither notices nor cares. Getting our own place has come up before, and we've told each other to just hold on, it's just a few months away from college. Now I'm not even sure where he is. I want to hear from him, I dread hearing from him. I don't dare call his house. I half-worry he'll show up at my house. I'm paranoid not just that the Cincinnati Police will snatch him for sodomy with a minor and homosexuality. I am paranoid that my enraged Dad will hurt him. If I call Mom to let her know I'm OK, she could probably convince Chip to stay away if he called. I can almost hear her teary, frightened little girl's voice promising she won't say anything to Dad.

The two phones in Blair's house have super long stretchy cords. The one in the kitchen reaches the basement stairs. I like the payphone at the end of the block. I'm about to go out when Blair's mom stops me. I volunteer that I'm going out for a run. She says, "Honey, it's still dark, you need to wait till it's light so folks can see you. On the TV they's talking about a robbery and killing at that gas station at Montgomery and Dauner, a few blocks before the expressway ramp. Right over the way. They tune up my car for me all the time. Lord help us." I look up at the news on the TV now, almost giddy. They don't say who the victim is. I picture the psycho motherfucker bleeding out on an icy floor. The same floor that scraped my face as he dragged me from the garage into the store. Just desserts.

Blair's mom's big-boned kindness taunts me with a bacon sandwich. I back away, declining as she tells me it's sunup in a half hour, plenty of time to eat. I know this rambling house somewhat, that the hallways connecting the first-floor rooms are two houses are mashed together. I don't want to be rude and mention having to use the bathroom. I slip outside through one of the front doors. I close it trying not to be heard. I take off in a fast jog down the block.

On Montgomery I slow to a brisk walking pace. Three police car beacons gyrate red on the corners closest to the gas station. An ambulance launches past them wailing into the brightening morning. My heart throbs in my ears as I near the scene. I see a few cops on the perimeter of the gas station. The bystanders are the same nightcrawlers usually around the area, but I also see some of Corey's friends in a car stopped by the police. I hear one of them shout Buster's name. I cross the street and pace the block for some minutes. The sun toes its way through the morning sky. A news truck seems to be packing up at the same time more reporters arrive. One cop car drives off, leaving the spinning red lights of the remaining two.

I have to try Chip's house. I run to the payphone at a White Castle a few blocks down. I feel my breath stop just before the ringing begins. On the first one, I hear "Cliff, thank God." Before he can say anything, I describe the crime scene I've just left. His response is to laugh, which makes me laugh. I laugh because I can't quite believe what's happening. Neither of us know anything, yet we just know it. Even if death missed the motherfucker, I feel set free. Free is what I haven't felt since this shit began. I give Chip Blair's address. He will call tonight.

At school I ask some Black Evanston kids if they know what went down. Seems nobody even remembers the motherfucker from junior high, nobody except me and Blair. But then during lunchtime, one of the guys in this group separates from the others and hisses—"I hope it was Buster, he deserves to die."

His name's Vlad, a slight guy with big dark lips and a girly smile. I know him through Blair as a flutist in the marching band. Blair told me he's gay, but I already guessed. I usually see him on the field, rehearsing for the football season, but rarely in the halls between classes. He's a junior and not on the AP track so there's no overlap in our schedules. We recognize something in each other, something horrible that we have in common. He plans to skip his last class to meet me in studio hall. The five-hour wait drags by.

We both suss each other out. I don't mention what happened to me, just that I know a detective. He says, "Yeah, Detective Moneymaker, he's handling my case." I don't let on that I already know about him from the Detective. That his family wouldn't press charges because they were afraid of retaliation and embarrassment. Then he says, "I had to get stitches down there after what he did to me." He wants to know where and when it happened to me. I let him think we suffered the same sexual violence. I don't tell him that I got away before what happened to him happened to me. I tell him my parents are only just finding out. I say, "My dad went after him, but somebody got there first. He says, "We got threatened by Buster's family. But the real reason wasn't about revenge. My folks didn't press charges because they were worried about our church finding out. We're Jehovah's Witnesses. They don't believe me when I say I'm not gay. I'm not. I'm not."

I can feel his confusion and helplessness and fear. I bet he's felt this way from day one. Something happened to him that he can't understand or explain. And it's like he's never had a say in these things that concern him. I want to tell him about the bats and the phone harassment, but worry it'll make him feel worse. I want to tell him about the lies I've told my parents. Then I realize that his parents really are the kind that disown and dispose of their kids.

He pulls a piece of paper from his notebook and writes down a number. He says, "I was at the library downtown and this nice white guy gave me a card. He told me to call the number on it if I was ever in any trouble. It's something called the Gay Switchboard."

"You memorized the number?"

"Yeah, to keep my folks from finding it. They go through my stuff all the time."

He doesn't explain, but I get that he must be under something like permanent house arrest. He says, "I call sometimes. Just to have someone to talk to. They're really nice people. I know I have to get away from my folks."

I say, "Vlad, I want you to know that I have a boyfriend, and we have sex, and we love each other. And before him I had a boyfriend, and we had sex, and we loved each other, too."

He looks almost frightened as he says, "Really!"

I say, "When you do finally get away from your folks, don't look back. Unless they accept you as you are, because there is nothing wrong with you."

»»»

My performance last season earned me an automatic spot on the track team. I show up for practice a week late. My excuse is the lingering pain from a bike crash. I insist to the coach that I'm ready to run now. "Then get ready," he says. I put on my running clothes in the locker room. I overhear the TV in the custodial office updating the gas station crime. I knock on the door and learn what the janitor knows—that the motherfucker is in critical condition with likely brain damage. The janitor tells me he lives in Evanston near the L.L, and has known Buster most of his life. He says, "Don't know what they mean by brain damage, the boy was never right in the head. In and out of foster care, bouncing around from family member to family member, put away by juvenile authorities when he was eleven. That's the brain damage, you ask me."

News that should boost me drains me. It's too late to back out of practice now. I remind myself that competition is about conquering these kinds of feelings. I know what it's like to be in the running zone, to stay in that zone. I always settle down once the event starts. Practice is outside in the sunny, high-forties ; it feels like snap summertime after weeks of nonstop cold. After each lap my mind wanders toward the bleachers. I know the psycho motherfucker can't be in both the bleachers and the hospital. I feel another sudden rush of emotion now; this time it sends me running back to the locker room bathroom. I'm a pipe-burst of peeing and crying over everything that's happened. My teammates must think I'm nuts. They rap me on the shoulder like good sportsmen.

I get myself together for relay drills. First the mechanics of passing the baton, then the sprinting from our lineup positions. I'm surprised to have a prominent place in two races. I have an untapped boon of energy and go for more laps around the track after practice. It's easier to look away from the bleachers now.

That there are no messages for me at Blair's house is a good sign. I don't doubt Chip will be there. In a way, this whole day seems to be about my life circling back to him. He's the test of my normalcy; him and me together are the test of my trust that we'll get through these last hurdles before we are free.

I'm watching the kitchen clock and TV and doing homework just so I don't fall asleep. It's weird to be in this house without Blair. It takes forever for him to show up, like till 9:30. I tell him I'm meeting Chip and walk the half-hour to our meet-up place at the Norwood Mall, wondering if everything will go back to the way it was. I was really happy before all the psycho shit. I'm sure I was.

Chip's there, leaning against a wall, hands in his pockets, looking too anxious to sit. I see relief come over him, and I feel the same. We fall into each other's arms, neither of us giving a fuck who sees. He's not himself, though. He turns a certain way, and I notice the hickey on his neck. He's been with someone. I say, "You met someone else?" "No," he says, then, "The truck stop. I slept there a couple nights ago. It was nothing. It was a stupid thing to do. It's nothing to do with you. Or how I feel about you. I was lonely and had no place to go. I love you, please don't freak out."

I don't freak out. Maybe I will later, but I don't now. Maybe I don't because he isn't my first boyfriend. And at least he's honest. There are so many things I lied about to him. "I don't care, Chip, I just love you, I really do," I say. Two hours disappear in a snap. There's not enough time to go back to where we were before Christmas, before all this shit happened to us. We're both exhausted after school and practice and worrying and, in his case, work. Even relief over the neutralizing of the psycho motherfucker is exhausting. He wants me to leave with him. He wants us to find a motel between now and college. Then we say goodbye. It feels like the end of the world.

»»»

Every time the phone rings I know it's Chip calling, though it isn't the hour he normally calls. I figure he's been turning over what to do about our relationship like I have. We are stuck with limited options, and I want him to do what's best for himself. I don't want to break up, but it already feels over between us. No matter what happens now, we'll go our separate ways come college in a matter of months.

»»»

It's 5:30 a.m. Mom takes my call, saying she knew it would be me. She tells me she thanks God for taking care of me. She also says she's mad as hell that I don't love *your own momma* enough to call and let her know I'm OK. It's obvious Dudley's brutal goodbye probably will plague her forever. I tell her I didn't call because I didn't want her to have to lie to Dad. She believes me and admits he disappeared over the weekend. She doesn't ask me why I ran away, but I tell her he shouted at me to get out of his face when I tried talking to him. She says he's angry but didn't mean for me to run away, just to give him some space.

"Mom, I'm scared of his monster side. I don't ever want to see him like he was, and I thought he might turn into that crazy man again."

"Have faith. He isn't that man anymore."

"I'm glad you have faith. He must be doubly pissed because he has to manage the babies and school all by himself."

"I've managed all you children and am carrying around number six, plus all the cooking, shopping, cleaning, taking care of you when y'all was sick, loving you all when you all hurt, on top of taking care of him, the biggest baby of all. Juggling work, school, and the babies is good for him."

"I'm sorry for all this. I'm sorry I'm not there to help you."

"None of this is your fault. I pray that this difficulty will pass."

The difficulty will pass?—now I know Mom knows everything.

"Sweetie, you're still my right hand. You come home anytime you want, when you're ready, and let it be soon because I miss you so much. Please thank Blair mother's for keeping you safe." Just before she hangs up, she says, "Oh, and that Indian guy called you last night."

I pretend she hasn't mentioned him.

»»»

Blair's mother says the call's for me. I hear "Hey guy, it's Punch." Mom must've given him Blair's number. Our connection is bad. Loud music in the background, heavy breathing. I ask him to turn the music down, but he keeps talking. I think I hear that he wants the scarf he loaned me for our bike ride. I think he says to bring it to his apartment, he needs it now. I know this guy well enough that there's always more to it. It's probably a stupid thing to do, and I'm about to say I can't when he says, "D'Artagnan."

He lives with a guy named D'Artagnan, an old-school queen, witty, alcoholic, and like Liberace on the piano. "I pay the rent in dick and hole a few times a month," Punch says.

Anybody named after a character from *The Three Musketeers* has to be interesting. And anything is better than sitting around doing nothing but worrying, at times crying, over a breakup that hasn't even happened. Meeting him sounds like the perfect thing to do.

I jump into my running pants and take off. It's a farther run than from my house, a downhill and then uphill trudge. The Belvedere's the tallest, fanciest building around. Anybody would know The Belvedere.

I'm dripping sweat and breathless, walking into a golden lobby of satiny couches and shiny tiled floors and golden and crystal lamps. I feel like I should have dressed up for it, but it's too late to turn back now. I think about leaving the scarf with the doorman, but I'm determined to meet Punch's benefactor. I tell the white doorman I'm here to see D'Artagnan. He looks at me suspiciously but then smiles, phones the apartment, and waves me through.

The elevator's brass doors are shinier than mirrors, showing just how underdressed I am. I arrive to loud music playing along the halls. It's coming from 14R. I ring the doorbell, but no one answers, probably because of the loud music. I ring and wait, ring and wait some more. Then I turn the doorknob and the door opens. I wander into a place of mirrors reflecting gold, dark reds, shiny reds, and black lacquers. The living room is wrecked like a party's just ended, glasses and bottles scattered around.

I follow the music down the hall. Now I hear other sounds, grunts really. I'm led to a bedroom. I find Punch getting screwed. I probably should bolt but it's like I'm too shocked to move. The black dude—D'Artagnan?—fucking him says, "Punch, looks like we've got company."

Punch, down on his elbows like a cat pawing carpet, is hidden in hair. He claws the mane clear so he can see me. "Oh hey, did you bring the money?"

"Huh?"

"The fifty dollars. Ain't that why you're here? Like I told you, my friend—Stacey meet Cliff, Cliff meet Stacy—he got us some blow but we gotta pay for it."

"Yeah," says his friend. "It's good stuff, too. Delicious. Want some?"

"I thought you wanted me to bring your scarf. And I don't have fifty dollars. I wouldn't have said I'd bring you fifty dollars."

I notice on the nightstand a little bag of powder and a doll-size teaspoon and a half-empty bottle of tequila.

"Sorry! I'm pretty sure I called a few people. So, what did you come here for then? Oh, let me guess, to talk. Right? Well, Stacey, he wants to talk. You wanna talk?"

"He said he came to bring you the scarf, stupid!" Then Stacey gives me the once over and stands up. "There's plenty to go round for two, obviously"—and heads to the bathroom, I guess.

"Come on, we'll do a train on your ass, or y'all can train mine," Punch says.

"You know, I'm beginning to think you think I'm gonna wake up and realize I'm just like you. I'm not. I'm not that fucked up."

"Spare me the judgmental attitude and get the fuck out! And don't take anything you didn't come with."

I run down the hall, almost too overheated to wait for the elevator. It creaks and quivers to the lobby, and I rush to the street feeling released. I retrace the trail back to Blair's, then I veer onto a side street and head toward Xavier's gymnasium. Just beyond it is the outdoor track. Three guys are running laps. I make the fourth and am still at it some two hours later.

»»»

I arrive at Blair's house after school, near 6:00 p.m. I can't tell if I'm alone. Blair's house sounds like nobody's home even when everybody's home. His bedroom's in the attic. It's like a big apartment with a couch and chairs and lamps. He calls it his music studio. He even wears headphones to not disturb anyone two floors down. He, his brother, and his mom and dad speak in small, calm voices. Compared to my house it's like a wake for the dead. But I don't miss the shouting matches at my house. I don't miss my radiative dad. And I don't miss the babies' loud crying fits. But you can't have one without the rest of it. It's all or nothing. That's what I know.

I'm in the studio, probably the first to hear a car door slam. I'm probably the only person here to run to the window in time to see Dad walking across the yard— not that they would know who he is. The doorbell rings and I'm hauling ass downstairs to prevent disaster. I feel like a fugitive turning himself in. I can't escape even if there was a way out. I can't put my problems on Blair's family. Dad and Blair's father both are looking at me now. Blair's dad's calm must be contagious. Dad blandly says, "Cliffy-boy, I need you to come with me right now. I'll tell you everything in the car. And I'll bring you back in about forty-five minutes if that's what you want."

I'm all ready to give myself up, turn myself in. He reminds me that I'm barefoot, shaking his head. I run upstairs for my shoes and a sweatshirt. I scribble a note telling Blair I'm with my dad but I'll be back. I'm thinking it's possible we'll never see each other again.

Dad's lighting up a Kool to smoke me out. We're driving, the music is loud, and it's like we're both trying to figure out what to say. I feel like this is my confession time, I just don't know where to start. Before I can say anything, he dials the music down, says, "Cliffy-boy, I know you didn't think I'd let you ruin your life over this sick shit. Hellnaw!"

I guess I must look confused, like I didn't understand what he just said. So, he repeats it, this time big and loud:

"I got a picture in my mind of what happened and what you was going to do about it, so I took the goddamn gun out of your backpack and took care of business. Because I know you didn't think your daddy would let you ruin your life over this sick shit. Hellnaw!"

Bad as this feels, I've been way more afraid of him than I am now. I guess because the guilty part of me knows that I deserve whatever's coming. The weapon plus all the lies alone deserve his worst punishment. In the last four months, I've been smashed, crashed, and trashed. I'm ready for whatever.

But then I'm shocked to see we're pulling up to the curb of the Doris Day House. He says, "Cliffy, you ain't got to be afraid of that nigga now and you had nothing to do with what happened to him, it's all on me. What I need is for you to tell what Buster did to you, that's all. But you don't say shit until I tell you to. Got that?"

A million questions bottleneck. Now I want to run before this turns ugly. Dad's saying, "Like I told you before, me and King go way back, and he knows what's up with his nephew. You just remember what I said, and don't say nothing till I say so."

He rings the doorbell. One of The Crew I saw at the bowling tournament answers. Then King the drug dealer looks at us through the storm door screen. He says, "Clifford Douglas, I'll be damn, what you been up to, my brother?" Dad says, "King, I need a word with you, mano a mano."

Mano a mano? Like out-of-sight guns are already being drawn.

King opens the door. We step inside a hall that's much nicer than the outside of the house. Dad says, "This here is my boy, my namesake, you met him when he was, like, two. Why I'm here is, I want you to know that I'm the man that beat the living shit out of Buster. I did it because he attacked my boy. Man, my boy went to that gas station to get his bike, and Buster beat him up and raped him!"

I feel Dad's grip on me tightening as he tells a story. It's like the blood is blocked and my arm goes numb. I pull away and he lets go.

"I confronted Buster, and he got the nerve to say that my boy came there wanting him, but he's lying his ass off. My boy here is so scared he's been running around with a gun. Anyway, Buster came at me. I hit him with the first thing I could get my hand, a crowbar. Cliffy, tell him about the injuries you had in the hospital. Tell him."

I blow my cue, offering nothing but a face quivering in teary shock. I'm overcome by what Dad says he did, even more than his fierce description of what happened to me. It's all so insane, so unreal, and to think I survived to hear him now defending me!

Dad shouts, "That's my boy! My boy! And yeah, he's a sweet boy, but that ain't got nothing to do with shit and don't make what Buster did right. He's sixteen years old with his whole life in front of him."

King puts his hand up. He says, "Cliff, man, I know all about it. And I'm sorry for what he did. It's some sick shit, and he's a sick ma-fucka. He was in juvie detention for this same shit. And was just in police custody for this same shit."

It's like my mind is in class trying to retrieve the answer to a problem I don't understand. Without thinking, I say, "And Mr. King, you know what he did because you were there that night. It was me in there Buster was beating up, and I heard you yelling at him saying you would call the police. It's because of you that I got away. Thank you."

Dad stands there with a *What the fuck*! look on his face. If he could read my mind, he would see that I'm pleading for him not to fight this man. Then King saves us. "I remember, I sho do. But I didn't know it was your boy in there. Cliff, bro, if I knew it was your boy, I would hit him with a crowbar myself. You know this. But the real deal is, Buster's a grown-ass man and I got no control over him. Don't matter what I say or do. I got no more control over him than I got over you. The nigga's sick in the head."

Then Dad says, "I want you to know I got no issue with you. I mean, you got to live with the fact of giving drugs to somebody that's mental like him. You and me been knowing each other since you was a kid named Courtney King at Avondale Elementary, and so you know me and where I'm coming from. That's why I want your assurance ain't no more harm coming to my boy. He's going off to college in the fall and I want you to tell me and tell my son that you and your boys ain't gonna do nothing to stop that from happening."

"Look Cliff, like I said before, I woulda kilt Buster's ass had it been my own boy, that's your assurance your boy got nothing to worry about." Then, reaching into his wallet and peeling a stack of cash, he says to me, "Sorry that shit happened to you, College. Consider this as my contribution to United Negro College Fund."

Dad takes the money, and they shake hands like soul brothers. In the car, Dad flips through the wad and then hands it to me. He says, "This here looks like a thousand bucks to keep us from not going to the cops, cuz you know a drug dealer like him don't want to end up in a courtroom and spending all his ill-gotten gains on

Lester Gaines, Attorney at Law to keep his black ass out of prison. Especially over some sick, sordid shit like this. And what you said was smart, like a lawyer. You made it sound like he was trying to help you, you made him sound like a hero instead of a fucking coward and a loser."

"Honestly, Dad, I didn't see him, I heard a voice, I just took a wild swing, and he didn't deny it."

"Well, it worked. He admitted he was there because you tripped him up. I mean, shit, I was surprised, too."

"But what if Buster dies, Dad?"

"He'll be dead. They'll bury the nigga. Then King'll be up in front of everybody trying to find some nice things to say about his sorry ass life."

"Aren't you worried?"

"Naw, dead is dead."

"Dad, I mean you might go to prison."

"Nobody was there to prove it wasn't self-defense like I said. This ain't nothing for you or your mom to worry about, either. This is my problem, and I'll deal with it. Your job is to finish high school and go to college and make your momma and daddy proud. You understand?"

We are turning in our driveway before I can say I want to go back to Blair's. He says, "Boy, I'll take you there, but you go in to say hi to your mama who misses you and needs you home. I told her we was clearing the air between us, that's it, so don't you say nothing about our visit."

How can I say no now? I'm grateful, even though I worry now what she would do if he gets caught and ends up in prison. I'd never be able to leave home then. I'd have to get a job just to help her survive. I'd be chained to them forever.

I follow Dad inside. He pounds the stairs straight to LACK's room. Mom stands in the den doorway crying. Her and her overflowing faith in the goodness of everything and everyone. She kisses and hugs me and insists that belief in God always wins.

Then she says, "You got your bike back because your Daddy loves you, Cliffy. You should remember that when you doubt him and the people you come from."

Mom's the only person I know whose uplifting intentions manage to scold and make me feel down.

It's past baby bedtime and I help Mom take the Twins upstairs, just like normal. I return to the den to watch *Sanford & Son*. Corey's home and we crack up over the antics of Redd Foxx fussing with Aunt Esther, calling her a hyena. Corey isn't the type to suffer through a commercial break, filling it with nonsense and gossip. I figure if he knows anything about the gas station he would have said days ago. That's probably a clue that he knows something but is trying not to break a promise.

"So, word is out about you. I ain't confirming or denying, I'm just letting you know. Maybe you heard about my old girlfriend Tasha, she got a new boyfriend, and she told me that after hearing about you, she made him swear on a stack of bibles he ain't sucking on no dude's dick."

He practically creams himself laughing. I ignore him, knowing the difference between general trash talking and something serious. We've been capping on each other since birth with the most outrageous things we could think of. I've never taken it personally until the capdowns felt, well, personal—at which point it's a fast descent into shoves and fuck-yous. To his credit, he lets loose only when we're alone, probably more because of the foul language than out of consideration for me.

I'm just leaving the room when he says, "So, I know you know all about what happened to Lurch. Call it coincidence, but I spoke to that lying fuckface before he got his. He still wouldn't admit it was you."

"What are you talking about?" I follow my eye roll toward the door. He's shaking his head, like *Don't lie, I know what's up.* "What was you doing there with him in the first place? Did you make a faggot move on him and he go crazy on you? Is that what happened?"

I lunge and he swings, and we crash into Mom's old Bike-O-Rama exercise bike, toppling it. We are rolling across the floor, pummeling each other when out of nowhere, Dad roars—"What's going on here?"—and snatches us apart.

"I was just asking Cliffy what he was doing hanging out with Buster and he got a little upset."

"Corey, shut up!"

"I was trying to tell him we took care of it . . ."

"I said shut your goddamn mouth, Corey. Go to bed!"

Then to me: "You brother's an idiot. He played lookout, that's it. He's got nothing to do with shit. Right?"

"Right."

"Good." He leaves, as though that's that. Everything's nice and tidy, put away like the washcloths and towels.

But I'm thinking, Oh my God! How much more fucked up could this situation get? I realize I don't want to know more. I'm overflowing with fears about everything. The truth is a wrecking ball.

»»»

Mom lets me oversleep. I planned to walk out with her after she nearly fell a couple days ago. At this point she is a doublewide, getting bigger by the day. Her scaling the steps with nothing to hold onto terrifies me. It's up to me because installing handrails would cost around $400. Nobody's got that to spare for something she'll need for a few weeks only, Mom is quick to say. She told me

Dad's inheritance comes to $750 and that he's thinking of getting himself some golf clubs.

I climb in bed again, wondering if I shouldn't pay for the handrails. I hear Dad's heavy feet from the bathroom back to bed. I lay there long enough to hear his snores through the wall, then slip downstairs and out the back door, running fast and hard to school. The morning is almost warm, and the run is sweaty. I go straight to the bathroom to throw water on my face. I set up in my first bell classroom to cram for a history midterm. I haven't spent enough time with any of my schoolwork and feel unprepared, a first for me. My anxiousness about failure usually morphs into doom and gloom. Assuming I don't fail outright, I calculate that my overall grade won't suffer too much of a setback. Especially if I do well on the final exam.

Just before the test, I run into Blair at the lockers. We spoke last night, so he knows where things stand—except the parts about Dad, the tire iron, Corey, and King. The parts that might make him a prosecution's witness should Dad end up in court.

He says, "If the doofus doesn't die, it sounds like he's so busted up he'll never remember what hit him. And even if he does remember, he's got a handful of reasons to shut up about it if he wants to stay out of prison."

I agree. But the psycho motherfucker is psycho, so there's no knowing a mind like his, and no telling how this ends. I do know he has been moved from the ICU in serious but stable condition. I wish I had learned that through the grapevine, not from my repeated calls to the hospital for updates. It's not like I care about him, I only care about what happens to Dad. Each day that passes I realize how far he could fall because of me. I try not to picture him wielding the skull-fracturing tire iron. I try to focus on the positive, that Dad saved me. I can see just how close I was to ruining my life, even ending it, but for him. I'm desperate to know how this will turn out.

On my way to lunch I have an idea. I turn up at the principal's office with an upset stomach. The standard procedure is to call the parent before releasing the student. They have no luck reaching LACK, but the official lets me, a senior, go anyway. Soon as I'm clear of school grounds, I run along the bus's winding and twisting route to the hospital, clocking forty-two minutes door to door.

Running is the single reason I miss the cold. I arrive soaked and sweaty. At the patient information desk, I try not to creep myself out saying that I'm the brother of patient Buster King. His room is near where I recovered from the wounds he gave me. Even if I run into someone I know, nobody would think anything of me being in the Black people's hospital of choice, Cincinnati General. I'll say I'm there for a follow-up appointment with Dr. Fang Fang.

His room's 704. I navigate the halls, imagining him lying there. It's like imagining walking in on myself some months ago, wired up to a phalanx of machines, terrified. Except, he isn't me.

He is the reason I was here then, and I'm the reason he's here now.

I follow the long corridors to the elevator bank, and ride to the seventh floor. Too soon, after a hard right turn in the hall, there's only a door between us. All I have are books, funky gym clothes, and a Bic pen, which I grip threateningly as I enter. Then I see him. The hairless skull, the left side of his face blackened and bruised, so swollen it looks separated from the bones. A steady drool cakes around his mouth and chin. His arms look lifelessly pinned at their sides, and I hear the whizzy sound of his breathing on a ventilator. I move close enough to notice his twitchy fingers, as if trying to pull himself out of this state. His pain must be ten times worse than mine was. I've felt pain, and have seen a person in pain, but I've never seen the look of pure pain like this. He got what he deserves—still, I can't help feeling sorry for him. I remind myself why I'm here.

"Too bad it's come to this. All you had to do was leave me alone. My boyfriend says I probably wouldn't have said anything about what you tried to do if I hadn't ended up in the hospital. I think he's right. But I know better now."

He makes a grunting sound and then a slow, horror movie-struggle to turn his head. I think he sees me. He may not recognize me, I could be anybody. He could be responding to any voice, or he could be responding to mine. What, I wonder, is he thinking?

I say, "Your uncle King gave me eleven hundred bucks not to go to the police about you. He told my dad and me that you are sick in the head and that he would have killed you if you did to his son what you tried to do to me. And yeah, he knows all about what you tried to do. He gave me that money because he knows he could go to prison, too, because he was there and knew what was happening and, in the end, just walked away. My dad knows everything. They're friends, and that's the only reason he didn't jack him up, too. Is that what you wanted?"

I wonder if he understands anything I've said. I wonder if he remembers what happened enough to even know what I'm talking about. Somewhere in that thick skull and insane mind he must get it, I tell myself. Whatever he thinks, every move ends in disaster for him. I watch his quivering fingers ball into a weak fist that he tries to jerk at me. Coming here was a waste of time. I realize I'm the one cornered—I've always been the one cornered. How hard would it be to suffocate him with a pillow? If I had the gun I'd aim for his head. I don't call him a faggot. I don't even give him the finger. I just leave.

I wonder what to do. I reach the elevator bank and Detective Moneymaker steps out like the only answer.

"Surprised to see you here," he says.

"I heard he got brain-damaged."

"You care?"

"No, I just . . ."

"Your dad came to see me this morning and told me what happened. That's why I'm here now."

"Don't do anything to my dad. I swear, he was trying to protect me from him."

"I know. I need to hear from you what happened. I need the truth."

"I'll tell you everything, even why I was afraid to tell you anything. I promise. Just don't do anything to my dad."

"Cliffy, we don't prosecute people for being homosexual anymore. It was always a stupid law. I'm sorry I didn't make that clear before."

"OK."

"And just so you know, Buster is on parole. So, he's back to jail for that at the very least. All you had to do was tell your story. But I know that's been hard."

"Yeah, it has been."

"Your dad will bring you down to the precinct and you can give me your statement then."

I nod reluctantly, like I have a choice. I feel beyond freaked out now. It's all become so complicated, about so much more than me and the psycho motherfucker. Weird to say, but I don't believe Dad and Corey even like me. Maybe because I don't like them so much. Corey especially. He'd do anything for Dad's love. I think Dad did what he did out of guilt and for family.

I'm fidgeting in bed for some minutes past the alarm clock. If Dad wants my help with the Twins, he would have said by now. It hasn't gotten any easier between us. I'm avoiding him and he's avoiding me. It's like neither of us knows what to say. But the tension between us is nothing like it was between Dudley and him. They barely spoke in the five years between Dad's return and Dudley's leaving. When they did it was in anger, like dogs in a bitch fight. But I am not Dudley, and there's no chip on my shoulder. And Dad has been good to me going on two years. Of us four, including Mom, I'm probably the only one who knows about his diaper pin talisman. I realize his troubles have brought us closer than we've ever been. I hate to see things go backward with him now. Part of me wants to pretend nothing has happened.

I hang around in my room for some minutes more, waiting to escape. I lace my sneakers to make a run for it. The phone rings just as I reach the bottom stairs. I can hear Dad answering. It could be Chip, he has my schedule and maybe wants to wish me a good race. As much as I want to hear his voice, as much as I miss him, I don't stick around to find out because I'm still anxious about Dad. I rush out the door before it's too late, ignoring Dad shouting for me to get the phone.

The morning isn't as balmy as yesterday. I'm in a hurry to get to school, but limit myself to a brisk walking pace to save my energy. Our first track meet starts at 4:00 p.m. I feel like I'm dragging and have to coax myself the whole forty-minute walk. I cross onto school property, and a familiar car turns into the main driveway. It's the track coach of the team we're competing with today. I remember him, not just because his Falcons ran all over us last year. It's more personal than that. The morning of that race we had words when I found him sprinkling what he called "falcon magic" over the track. He had wished me a good race, and I told him I would be nothing his team needed to worry about, even on my best day. He said, "That's not an attitude worthy of a tiger. Tigers are powerful animals."

I remember acting like I didn't care. I've been on the track team since freshman year; I knew what we were up against, competing against the Falcons. Corny though it sounds, wings will always beat legs in any racing competition. I hadn't imagined they would take every race.

Seems that the Falcons' Coach Ruebin Phelps recognizes me, too. He lets down his window and says, "Hey, Withrow Tiger, remember your spirit animal if you're running today."

"You don't even need to sprinkle your Falcon magic over the track."

"It's called ritual. It focuses the mind. Try it," he says, winking.

He had gotten into my head last year—and my jockstrap fantasies, because I'd never seen a coach so handsome. But that's not going to happen this time. I cross my forearms to block his energy and walk away. I watch his car disappear into the parking lot and see him doing his juju on our track. Whatever! I remind myself this is senior year. Two weeks ago, I was running around with a gun, and track didn't matter at all. Now that I'm here, I want more than just to say I finished my races. I used to care about track. I still care about track.

Still, I struggle and have to coax myself to reach fourth bell study hall. I have plenty of homework, but I sleep instead, with my jacket over my head, to make up for a restless night. Insomnia, nausea, and sometimes vomiting always plague me the night before race day. I usually see this as a curse, but today it's a good sign—and I guess my own ritual. Not exactly an uplifting one.

I head to our stadium for another pre-race ritual. I climb six rows up into the bleachers and focus on the start point. I zero in on my takeoff. That's where my performance could be more consistent, according to our so-so coach. I picture my feet pushing off the start and visualize my body and leg positions lifting me into my stride. The arrival of the Aiken team bus is an easy distraction. I watch as the hottie coach Ruebin Phelps leads his Falcons onto the track. I run to the locker room to huddle in the same bad breath as my teammates. We're switching into running gear while our bland coach tries to rally our spirits. The mood feels like a memorial service for the race we're about to lose. One of the seniors jokes that this is likely the last time we'll have to suffer a humiliation.

Twenty minutes before showtime we make our way onto the track. I watch the charismatic coach's hands-on one-on-ones with his formidable runners. He's the team's real star.. I realize we might have a chance—looks like two of their best athletes graduated last year. These runners look like lesser racehorses than the usual thoroughbreds. Our team is lucky to have gained three superior runners to replace the mediocre ones that graduated out. Maybe the odds against us just got smaller.

The first event, the 100-meter sprint, isn't our strongest; we're off to a mediocre start. The Falcon's three competing runners easily cross the finish line, topping the leaderboard. But a win here doesn't mean a win in the longer races. Watching us place so poorly, though, rattles me. At race time for my first event, the 200-meter sprint, Coach Phelps is downfield at the finish line; he signals his glistening racers two lanes to my right. He might as well be signaling to me. I think about our tiger mascot, my spirit animal. Suddenly this race is about him and me. All eight of us shimmy and flex to find the sweet spot to propel ourselves off the starting block. I imagine myself reaching his open arms first. I push up on my legs, stretching my arms forward. Glancing behind me, then left and right, I inhale deeply, seconds before the buzzer goes off. That carbon-deoxidized exhale helps me to pounce off the starting block. I'm used to seeing Falcons flying by me or leaving me behind, but only one of the thoroughbreds is alongside me now. I don't break form by looking; instead, I keep my eyes on closing the distance between the coach and me. Then the other runner shifts into a higher gear and takes the lead. I fight till the end, barely hanging onto a second-place steal. I'm bent over, heaving and crying. I feel embarrassed. I have never cried over a win or loss.

I feel Coach Phelps clap my shoulders—"Yes, sir, let that tiger lose," he says. I feel good. Excited. Thrilled!

Our team surprises ourselves in the 400-meter relay, my next and last event. I make the leaderboard with a proud second. So does one of my teammates, taking first place. So, it's much more than a personal victory for me. On my way out I cross paths with Coach Phelps again.

"Hey Tiger, y'all really surprised me today, especially in the 200. Good running. Your textbook start and then some."

"I just got lucky today."

"The lesson here is that you exceeded your so-called limitations. Remember your Tiger, take it with you everywhere you go in your life. You going to college, right?"

"Yeah, hopefully UCLA."

"Get outta here! My alma mater! Class of '71."

"Wow, I've never met anybody from there."

"Proud to be your first. The current track coach is a former teammate. I'll give him a call about you. Clifford Douglas, right?"

"That's right. That's me."

"Good grades?"

"3.98 GPA, all AP courses. 1450 SAT score."

"You go, Tiger! I'll be looking out for you."

Wow! If words could be a talisman, his would be mine forever. How can I not tell everybody what just happened?! Jinxing. How can I not at least tell Chip? I call, and he answers. Hours go by before we hang up. What a day!

»»»

I can't believe Chip is sitting across the street from our driveway. I'm sure I said to meet me at the Xavier campus entrance. We've met there a few times before, so he knows.

Fuck Sundays are back, but we haven't seen each other in weeks. Plus, LACK and Corey are scattered around our house. Everything still feels awkward for me. Dad still barely speaks to me, giving one-word responses or pretending not to hear me. He took me down to the precinct to give my statement to Detective Moneymaker. I thought he would be neurotic about it, but he didn't tell me what to say, just not to mention Corey—*that idiot brother of yours*—being there. Even my acceptance letter to UCLA was worth only a bland congratulation. Maybe that's because the letter came the day after he dropped out of technical school. Mom didn't say it, but he probably blames me for that. I blame myself especially after what he did for me. I probably shouldn't care as much as I do. School will be over soon. I'm that much closer to getting out of here for good.

I rush outside and look up in time to see Dad watching from the window. None of my problems are Chip's fault, but I wonder if Dad blames him for me being the way I am.

I decide I don't care.

I'm just happy to see Chip. He's better. No more Uncola problems; the last woman up and left. He told me feels less angry and seeing him is proof. I just hope his dad can hold off on the next Uncola till college starts, when Chip will attend Ohio State in Columbus.

"Hey, sorry, the campus security guards said I couldn't wait there . . . something about a campus mugging . . . and I didn't want us to miss each other. And I wanted to surprise you. I got you a UCLA gift. I got it at a garage sale. It's old-timey but fast and Italian, maybe perfect for getting around LA."

On the sidewalk, a yellow bike with long chrome fenders, a low mount between big shiny wheels and ram handlebars wants my attention.

"You don't have to sell me, I love it."

I take the bike for a test ride up the block to the traffic light and back. Thin wheels and a padless seat make for a hard ride. It feels stiff and awkward, but that's because this is the first time. Chip thinks that lowering the seat and raising the handlebars will solve the problem. I repeat the test drive with better results. I can already picture myself cruising around LA.

Chip says, "Let's go for a ride. The other bike's in the garage, right? I'll ride it."

"I don't think we should."

"Not we, me. I wanna ride it."

"Well."

"Your Dad's already seen us. Let's just act normal, like this is the reason I'm here."

He's right. It's not like Dad doesn't know what's going on. My notebook doesn't chronicle my sex life, but Chip is the inspiration for many of my anatomy drawings. A sexed-up lady's man like Dad wouldn't be naive enough to think we're not in each other's pants. Even Mom would think that. Plus, *Cliffy Loves Chip* randomly floats in page corners.

We cross the street. Chip says he hadn't thought of buying a bike until he saw this one on his way home from practice yesterday. It was being used as the prop for a yard sale sign, leaning against a mailbox at the end of a driveway filled with appliances, furniture, tables, lamps, dishes, clothes, all the unwanted stuff of somebody's life. He says, "All I could see were the tires, but for some reason I stopped. I pulled the sign back and I'm like, this is a decent bike. I asked if the bike was for sale, too, and this lady who lived there said fifteen bucks. I've never even been to a garage sale before."

Much as I like the new bike, it's the old one I'm thinking about now. We lift the garage door. My old favorite, Dad's gift to me—twice now—leans against the wall. It's been there since he brought it home. It's hard for me to even look at it without feeling sick. How do I unsee the psycho motherfucker riding it? I'm not afraid of it. It's more like a rotting rat on display.

Chip says it's in great shape and rolls it out of the garage. I never doubted that. Fixing bikes is one of the psycho motherfucker's skills.

The traffic is light, so we ride side by side in the street toward the I-71 overpass. Because we are athletes, I guess a race is inevitable. The lightweight Italian bike easily edges ahead of the heavier Schwinn, but Chip thinks like a winner and fights. We go another mile, taking turns leading, before stopping because he wants to switch and compare bikes.

"I don't need to, your bike is fine for me, and I know how my old one rides."

"I wanna know for me, not you."

After weeks of clashing schedules, forced abstinence, handjobs, and then pre-breakup status, I agree to switch for Fuck Sunday's sake. I watch him speed away, leaving me and the Schwinn alone to make up. I feel disgusted just being near this reminder of the worst thing that's happened to me. I climb on it, appreciating that Dad gave it to me. Chip's way ahead. I pump hard to catch him, but the distance between us only grows. He's near my street when I reach the overpass. I'm riding close to the curb and notice a bike laying in the tall grass near the embankment. I haven't seen Punch since his cocaine and dick party some weeks ago, and haven't wanted to see him, either. I continue riding until I hear shouting behind me. I know it's him, even before I see him balanced on the guardrail of the overpass like a highwire act. The railing can't be more than a few inches wide, but the drop to the road is about eighty feet.

I circle back. His arms stretch outward, pedaling the air as one slow-motion foot lifts in front of the other. Northbound cars rush below him, while southbound traffic is at a standstill. Drivers rubberneck or stand outside their cars to watch the spectacle. I stop on the sidewalk. The roar of I-71 traffic is at his back; maybe he can't hear the people shouting for him to come down. I shout as loud as I can, too, and then worry my voice will draw him out of his focus-trance, and he'll plummet to the road.

I stand in the street now. He's at least a third of the way across when he seems to notice me. He winks, and as scared as I am for him, I smile back. He once said that he wanted to join the circus to be a tightrope walker, and that he's done this bridge stunt before. I hear sirens, then see officers on the overpass trying to talk him down. He ignores them. Now police cars speed up the parkway. Punch is just shy of halfway across when the cops begin clearing the road of rubbernecking drivers and onlookers. I tell one of the officers I know him. The officer says, "Me too. We've picked him up before on other bridges. He's delusional, he thinks he can walk on air. If he makes it across, we'll bag him and drop him off at the hospital. He'll probably end up at Longview this time."

I ask when a net will be stretched across the road to catch him, and the officer laughs. He forces me out of the road and down toward my street. I can see that Punch has passed halfway across now. A panicked-looking Chip pulls up, relieved nothing happened to me. I tell him Punch is the gay Native American guy who was homeless and hitchhiked from an Indian reservation in northern Wyoming.

Chip says, "I hope you're not worried you're gonna end up like him."

"No, why do you say that?"

"Because I remember you said he was fagbashed."

"He was. He's had a hard life. I feel sad for him."

I don't want to watch how this ends. We bike toward my street and then we hear applause. We turn and see Punch bowing before the cops pull him away, probably to be handcuffed and pushed into the backseat of a squad car. "Wow, at least he made it," Chip says. I say, "I think that was the point," but I'm not sure that was the point. Maybe he really wants to splat in the road.

"Maybe he does dangerous things to stop himself from doing something really crazy."

"Like what? What could be crazier than what he just did?"

But as soon as the question leaves my mouth, I know what.

Killing people. Something about the way Chip says it reminds me of Punch's vanished boyfriend. Maybe murdered boyfriend.

I've already accepted UCLA's offer, and he's accepted Ohio State, but I have the feeling he wants to be boyfriends forever. We stop on a bench near Xavier's campus. I say, "I wish we were driving to UCLA together. I'd do most of the driving. I'll have my license by then."

"Worth it just for that."

"But then I guess I would want you to stay with me."

"I've thought about it, and, you know, as much as I don't want to breakup, I think we should go in different directions. And we should experience other people. Who knows, maybe we'll wind up together in the end."

"That's what I think, too." Still, it hurts hearing him say it.

We ride back to my house. I want Dad to see me on the Schwinn, but the Marquis is gone. We park the bikes in the garage and then head out to our favorite spot to make good on Fuck Sunday.

»»»

It's weird but I miss being part of the morning routine. I've tried to insert myself into it, usually feeding the babies or cleaning them up after breakfast. Dad rejects me every time. I ask Mom point blank if he's still mad at me.

"Naw, I don't think so. You know, you and your dad were getting along just fine before all this. I know it's a lot more complicated than before. But just remember, your dad's head ain't on right sometimes, because of his mental stuff, but his heart's always in the right place. He'd do anything to protect his family. That's why I ain't ever been afraid of him, and never will be."

I would expect Mom to sum Dad up in this way. I don't know if she knows about Dad's crowbar attack. But, no doubt, she stands by her man no matter what.

"Mom, I'm asking you if he's still mad at me."

"Naw, I don't think so. He understands why you were lying. Think about how he found out though. It's not too late for you tell him about yourself."

"Sometimes I feel like I should tell him everything, but at the same time I feel like he doesn't want to know because he hasn't asked me anything about it."

"Maybe he doesn't know what to say."

Mom may be right. It's easy to see how bringing it all up again could go wrong. I stick with my plan and stay out of Dad's way. I bolt into the morning on the Italian bike with nothing but fresh disgust for the Schwinn. I wonder what Dad thinks when he sees it now. Is it a symbol of his disappointment in me? Or is it evidence of how great a dad he is for having nearly committed murder to defend his undeserving, lying son? Or is it just a two-wheeled piece of metal and pleather that he spent money on and now expects me to ride?

I leave the house through the basement as I usually do. I've cycled halfway to school when I imagine hearing Dad's voice calling out to me. I rush home, fearful our house is ablaze, or the Twins are unconscious from carbon monoxide poisoning. I leave my bike on the steps and enter the kitchen through the back porch. But the Twins are having breakfast in their highchairs, and Dad is ironing in the basement. Most mornings I still kiss them in their beds and go. Though I'm no longer part of the routine, they don't seem surprised to see me. It's like they're expecting me.

I lift them from the highchairs, then follow them to the bathroom. I wipe baby hands and faces and hear the phone ringing. It must be Mom calling for Dad. I hear Dad's voice coming from the kitchen. The babies rush to greet him, and I freeze when I hear him say—"So, Chip, I saw in Cliffy's notebook the baseball bat beating. Just curious, I'm guessing that was your idea?" There's more talking and laughing before he hangs up.

"Damn, I was wondering if the babies got out of the highchairs by theyself," he says to me, surprised to see me.

"Nope, just me, I forgot something and came back and then thought I'd try to help you out . . ."

"Sorry . . . That was Chip calling. He wanted to tell you he'll see you at the track meet by four."

"OK. Thanks.

"Cliffy-boy, I just want to say I respect Chip. But if I've said it once I've said it a thousand times, don't let nobody fuck with you. They hurt you, you hurt back twice as hard. And I ain't just talking about fists and bats. Cuz boy, if you ain't hard enough to hurt them back, then be smart enough to kick their ass through the law. Or be somebody with enough money to hire a thug to fuck them up for you. You understand what I'm saying? I won't always be around to fight for you. And your boyfriend won't be either."

I expect Dad's going to tell me all the ways we're going to hell, and then he says, "You know what, I've been thinking back on my relationship with my old man. I realize that I don't want you boys to hate me like I did him. I mean, I know I ain't perfect, but I don't want to die with you hating on me. Well, maybe Dudley—but not the rest of y'all. Maybe Dudley and me will be OK too, someday."

I don't know what to say and fumble around for an unconvincing maybe.

"One last thing I've been meaning to say . . . about your situation. So, I was talking to the therapist who leads my support group. He thinks it would be a good idea if you talk to somebody, like you about what happened, because maybe I'm not what you need right now. Plus, you're gonna be thousands of miles from us soon and we won't be no good to you no how. Anyway, he gave me a card for this therapist who is like you. He can help you and it ain't gonna cost us a cent."

I'm so surprised I don't know what to say. I notice that the card includes that Gay Hotline telephone number, too. I say, "One of the guys Buster attacked goes to my school. He gave me this hotline number, too."

"Sounds like you got a support group."

"Yeah, I guess so." I slide the card into my pocket, still fumbling for the right words.

"Thank you for everything, Dad."

"Cliffy-boy, just doing my job. And like I said many times now, your job is to finish school. When you're grown, you can fuck up all you want."

"I won't fuck up, Dad, I promise."

"Good. Now you should get going, the clock's ticking."

I steer the Schwinn out of the garage knowing this pleases him—which also feels like my job at this moment. I wait in the driveway to watch them take off and wave as they go. He likes my boyfriend, and accepts me as I am, what more could I want? If only it could stay like this until I can leave for good.

I'll never understand his love, but I know that's what it is.

Acknowledgments

This novel would not have happened without my silo of support. A ginormous thank you to Tanya Guré, my dear sister, occasional muse, stalwart superpower, and lifetime bestie. To my rock-solid friends, locally and globally, especially Stephen K. Jones, who has yet to miss those slightly creepy KGB readings I can never say no to, and Elisabeth Nosarios, who has read every version of this novel—and my last book, a short story collection, a novella, and a libretto too!—wielding her red ink with sharp aplomb. Creative, inventive friends Tzu-Wen To and Fiona Ip, thanks for all the thrilling video art that will help promote this project. And to publisher/author/visionary Michelle Tea and her Dopamine Books for saying yes, my eternal gratitude.

Shawn Stewart Ruff is the award-winning author of the novels *GJS II* (2016), *Toss and Whirl and Pass* (2010), and *Finlater* (2008) and the novella *One/10th* (2013). He is also editor of the landmark anthology *Go the Way Your Blood Beats* (1996).